THE COMMUNE

DANNY DAGAN

Copyright © 2026 Danny Dagan

The moral right of Danny Dagan to be identified as the author of this work has been asserted in accordance with the Copyright, Designs and Patents Act of 1988.

First published in 2026 by Guffy Pen Press
Print ISBN: 978-1-9193873-1-4

This book is a work of fiction. Any resemblance to actual persons, living or dead, is purely coincidental. It is copyright material and must not be copied, voiced, reproduced, distributed, transferred, leased, licensed or publicly performed or used in any way except as specifically permitted in writing by the copyright holder, or as strictly permitted by applicable copyright law.

This book, in its entirety, was written by a human.

To the canny folk of Northumberland: a county far too kind for the dark deeds found in these pages.

Synner's Crag Survivor May Hold Key to Commune Tragedy

BBC News, Tuesday, 5 August

Officers from Northumbria Police were alerted by walkers on Friday to human remains found to the west of Synner's Crag Farm in Northumberland. Upon further investigation, they uncovered a gruesome scene in woods nearby: six additional bodies of what are believed to be members of an off-grid commune. One survivor was found a mile from the site and remains gravely ill.

Police sources have said the cause of death for the seven individuals remains under review pending further forensic tests, and that crucial information may lie with the potential witness who is still in a coma at an undisclosed ICU unit.

BBC News has identified the survivor as Luke Bridestone, a thirty-year-old man from New Cross, south-east London. Last month, Mr Bridestone abruptly resigned his job as a crematorium assistant, terminated the lease on his flat and closed his social media accounts. A work colleague revealed that the day before he left his job, Mr Bridestone spoke of his dream to 'go off-grid' and 'leave all the stresses behind'. It would appear that he pursued this dream by joining the commune in North Northumberland.

A police spokesperson would not comment on speculations that this was a case of mass murder-suicide bearing echoes of cults such as The People's Temple in Jonestown, where more than 900 people died in 1978 by drinking cyanide-laced punch at the order of cult leader Jim Jones.

Adrian Kyloe, whose farm neighbours the commune's land, told us, 'They were lovely people, all of them, just looking for a simple life in the woods. It's tragic, what happened. I can't imagine who'd want to harm them. I hope they catch the killer, whoever they are. Such a sad loss.'

PART ONE

WELCOME TO THE COMMUNE

CHAPTER ONE

EIGHT DAYS POST DISCOVERY

Five minutes into his afternoon meeting, private investigator Alex Czerniak already wished for it to be over. Across from him sat the client, clenching and unclenching her fists that were a well-moisturised canvas of age spots. Once or twice, she touched her oversized pearl earrings as if to verify they held firm. Between them, like a safety buffer, was his office desk, which bore a coffee tray, a wire-mesh cup filled with assorted pens and highlighters, a laptop, and a framed picture of Alex's wife and two daughters, kept there to give him strength in difficult moments like this one.

The client was Fenella Cavendish, an elegant, silver-haired woman, expensively dressed in a black tailored suit, looking like she was on her way to sip Bellinis at a shipping mogul's funeral. She stared or glared at him – he wasn't sure which – with a mix of anxiety and tightly coiled fury.

'If it's true,' Fenella said, 'I hope he dies a painful death from a nasty, incurable disease.' She shook her head. 'Sorry, didn't mean that. I just…' Her jaw tensed, and she looked at Alex, bereft, her eyes pleading for a comforting lie. He had none to offer. As an investigator, he only dealt with facts. In any case, they'll know soon enough.

Alex turned his laptop's screen so they could both observe the little red dot as it blinked on a map. Based on his location, Fenella's husband, Thomas 'Tommy' Cavendish, was on a Bakerloo Line train, now stopped at Marylebone.

In the old days, you'd have to follow targets on the street, listen to muffled conversations through windows or doors, always at risk of being discovered, of the operation being blown. Modern technology did away with the need for trench coat missions. Trilbies were replaced by keyboards, used to hack phones or pore through internet histories and bank transactions. Lurid photos were only snapped for clients who wished to make a more dramatic scene before their cheating partner, or a judge, or for the benefit of a hungry press if the client was more than mildly rich and famous.

It was unusual for a spouse to attend in person while a target was being tracked, especially when the methods used weren't exactly legal, or legal at all, but Fenella had been persuasive in terms that Alex couldn't argue with. 'I don't want to hear it. I'm paying the bill, yes? I'll be there as soon as he leaves the house. I take my coffee with cream. It's Wednesday. He usually vanishes on Wednesdays. Couldn't look me in the eye this morning.'

Tommy Cavendish, sixty-five, had been behaving strangely, disappearing for hours, being evasive and defensive when questioned. He and Fenella were thirty years into a fabled marriage.

'I thought I knew him,' she said. 'I really did. But maybe… maybe I'm wrong?'

Alex was losing his taste for cheater cases. He had dealt with his unfair share of aggrieved wealthy partners, married or not, over years of dedicated service to prenups and heartbreaks. What always wrenched his gut was the level of shock and surprise they showed upon learning the truth. After all, they had hired him. They suspected something was wrong. And there were clues. There were always clues. Their partner was behaving out of character, being secretive, hiding screens when they entered the room. Still, when the damning evidence confirmed the existence of a younger woman, a stable hand, the Spanish gay lover with sparkling eyes and designer stubble, worlds came tumbling down, and tempers flared. It was a miserable, unpleasant business. He sighed and focused on the screen.

Alex's tech expert had sent an innocent-looking email to Fenella's husband. Once Tommy Cavendish clicked on the urgent link, a tracking app installed itself on his phone. Not only could they track his movements, but the device's microphone captured his every word.

The dot remained at Marylebone, the sounds coming through in a mix of crowd hubbub and station announcements. 'He might be waiting for a train,' Alex said, to pass the time.

Fenella looked at her nails, which were painted a morbid shade of plum. 'Weren't you employed by the billionaire parents of those kids who got kidnapped?'

Alex nodded. Everyone wanted to know about that infamous case, *everyone*, but he had no wish to discuss it. 'Looks like I'll be working on deaths in a commune next, up north in Northumberland. Got a call last week from a prospective client.'

'Oh, I heard about that. Shocking. I saw the interview with their neighbour farmer. Spoke about it like they lived this idyllic, hippie life. I wonder what went wrong. A cult, you think? *Lord of the Flies?*'

The dot on the screen was on the move again. Judging by its location and speed, Tommy was on a southbound Bakerloo Line train.

'A younger me,' Alex said, 'would have loved the idea of living away from civilisation, growing your own food, a small society, pretty girls with flowers in their hair. It speaks to something primal, like a need to go back to how things were before technology. Sounds like fun, as well.'

'Unwashed pretty girls,' Fenella said. 'Unwashed pretty girls who shit in the woods. I'm sorry, I don't see the appeal.'

'Still...' Alex gave her the kind of smile he used when he didn't wish to contradict his clients. Fenella Cavendish was born to money. Of course, sharing with others and living in a commune didn't entice her, not least, as she put it, shitting in the woods. 'Well, even if I wanted to,' he said, 'I have responsibilities now: a wife, two young girls. Mary loves her Met Police job.'

'Well, marriage...' Fenella said.

Instead of responding, Alex poured coffee into a mug and placed it before her. Fenella was being pre-emptively bitter, and with good reason. Her husband had withdrawn large sums of cash over the previous few weeks, perhaps to fund some kind of sordid arrangement. He had been cagey, distant and uncaring. Tommy's profile wasn't that of someone who'd gamble or get involved in drugs or dodgy deals. He'd been an upstanding member of a set of barristers until his retirement three years earlier. He and Fenella lived a comfortable life, which she described as close and loving. Then, quite abruptly, things changed. Tommy did nothing to reassure Fenella, and she knew in her gut that he had strayed. Women usually did.

Fenella added cream to her coffee and stirred with vigour, the spoon dinging with every half-turn. She grasped the mug and raised it to her lips. Seeming to notice that her hand was shaking, she set the coffee back on the desk.

Alex pointed to the screen. Tommy had left Regent's Park Tube station, walking at pace. He turned onto a side street, walked further, then stopped and seemed to enter a building.

From her pocket, Fenella brought out a white linen handkerchief. She held it to her cheek and whispered, 'The thing is, I can't imagine my life without him. If this... If it's really...'

Alex kept his expression neutral. He turned up the volume on his laptop, from which now came muffled voices. In a gentle, soothing tone, a woman said, 'Come through.' Then Tommy spoke. 'Cash still okay? I don't want my wife to...'

Fenella hunched forward, closer to the laptop's speakers, appearing smaller, a woman who had shrunk into herself.

After a couple of minutes of silences and footsteps, the voices returned, now sounding clearer. Tommy must have removed the phone from his pocket. A chair screeched, and then the woman spoke. 'How are you, Tommy?'

'Been better. Never hid anything from my wife. I just... I didn't want to say anything until you told me where we stand. Please tell me. Please be honest.'

'Of course,' the woman said.

'Is it bad?'

'I'm so sorry, Tommy. Based on your tests, my best diagnosis is ALS, a type of motor neuron disease. It's not definitive, but we've ruled out other causes. Looking at your symptoms... Yes, I'm pretty sure.'

'Oh,' Tommy said with an outbreath. 'Oh.'

'You're welcome to consult another neurologist. I can refer you.'

Fenella looked up at Alex, uncertain, as if she hadn't understood the conversation. *Denial comes first*, Alex thought. *Comprehension will follow, then shock. Poor Fenella.*

Tommy cleared his throat, then cleared it again. 'I've heard of ALS,' he said. 'Tell me, doctor, if you're correct, how long do I... What's the prognosis?'

'You're already experiencing muscle weakness, especially in your left hand, and you reported memory changes. ALS progresses differently for each person. In the later stages, paralysis and—'

'How long?' Tommy said.

'Hard to say. Average life expectancy is three years, but you could live longer, or it can accelerate. I'm so sorry. There's no cure. I keep an eye out for new treatments and clinical trials, but I don't want to give you false hope.' She paused, then softened her tone. 'Tommy, listen. I know you came to us for privacy, but now we have a diagnosis, maybe it's time to tell your wife? You'll need a lot of support.'

Alex clicked to close the spyware app and turned off the screen. The job was done. Listening any longer felt intrusive and uncalled for.

Fenella glared ahead. Her face tightened, and her breathing became laboured. Alex readied himself to offer her a paper bag from the stash he kept in his drawer. Clients sometimes suffered panic attacks.

Without a word, Fenella stood, stiff as a shovel, straightened her skirt with broad strokes, picked up her bag, turned around and marched out of the office. Alex followed.

After he had seen Mrs Cavendish to her taxi, Alex returned to his office and collapsed into his chair. For a long while, he stared at the empty laptop screen. Fenella Cavendish had entered his office with pent-up fury. Now, she'd be struggling to digest, to come to terms with the diagnosis, to make sense of her emotions. Her taxi ride home would be like hell itself.

He felt for her, played in his head the conversations that would follow. Will she tell Tommy she knows or wait until he's confessed his diagnosis? He tried to imagine what he'd do in Tommy's shoes: share such devastating news with Mary, or keep it from her, allowing his wife and the girls a normal life, for at least a little longer?

His assistant, Melanie, knocked on the open door and came in, holding a manila folder. 'How did it go?'

Alex shook his head.

'Well,' she said, 'here's something to take your mind off your parade of cheaters. The commune thing is firming up. Ms Saint-John confirmed she'll see you tomorrow, ten a.m.' She laid the folder before him. 'There's some potential risk with this client, with her ability to pay. You'll see what I mean in my notes.'

Alex felt a knot of tension form in the back of his neck. Two very rich clients were waiting to engage him, and his team's resources were already stretched. He couldn't afford to take on anything risky. 'Did you tell her we charge a premium?'

'I did,' Melanie said, 'but she was adamant. Got a mouth on her as well, that one.'

He took his pen out of his shirt pocket, placed its tip in his mouth, then held it up and stared at it. 'I suppose there's no harm in taking the meeting. Could you let my wife know I'll be leaving early today? She doesn't have to pick up the girls. I'll do it. Tell her…' He thought of Fenella Cavendish, swallowed a mouthful of anguish and looked at his hands. 'Tell her I'll see her at home.'

CHAPTER TWO

EIGHT DAYS BEFORE THE RECKONING

Despite the high winds and relentless torrents of rain, Luke Bridestone smiled and relaxed into the cracked imitation leather of the passenger seat. A moment later, he caught himself, drained his face of any sign of cheer and glanced to check that Dorothy hadn't noticed. Probably not. She was too focused on the road. Luke knew his worry made no sense. His anxious mind decided, against logic, that showing too much contentment might somehow give away the misery that came before it, the all-consuming fear that his escape might be snatched from him.

For the longest time, good luck wasn't something Luke dared hope for, and disaster had been a mere nasty whisper away. But this was different. It had to be. Safety felt closer with every mile of distance between him and London.

The rusty off-white car parted channels through the deluged tarmac while the older woman clutched the steering wheel for dear life, leaning forward in a useless attempt to see through the rain that gushed over the windscreen. Her plastic-rimmed glasses, secured by a red shoestring over the nape of her neck, would be of no use to her against the downpours from the heavens.

Maybe he should say something? Maybe they should stop until the weather improved? *No. Keep going. Get to safety. Travel the distance and disappear.*

'Bugger, bugger, bugger,' Dorothy muttered through tightened lips, her composure seeming to be held together, barely, by the buttons of her threadbare cardigan.

For a moment, the tyres lost their purchase, and the car rose with a shudder, followed by a swerve that Dorothy just about managed to right, though it took them to the opposite lane and back. Luckily, no oncoming traffic was there to meet them, head-on.

'Bugger, bugger, bugger.'

Luke said nothing. He imagined the car as Noah's Ark, the waters beneath it washing away his old life and all its crushing anxieties: the daily grind of the job at the crematorium, utility bills, council tax, twenty-four-hour rolling news, toxic internet trolls, London's public transport and the sounds of helicopters and sirens at night. Best of all, was escaping the horror that had haunted him – a horror whose name was Karla Ruskin-Hughes, daughter of a crime family that prided itself on its double-barrelled name and its double-barrelled guns.

When Karla first sweet-talked her way into his life, she'd seemed perfect and edgy, quintessentially stylish in high heels and silky black dresses. After four months of dating, they were inseparable, other than her occasional disappearances on family business. By the sixth month, he was done for. Luke wasn't impressionable or in the least naive. He was thirty, with some life experience, a level-headed man, but Karla had skilfully subverted his defences and slowly raised the heat. He'd been taken in by her passion, too slow to realise the danger, the entrapment, the dual whips of jealousy and control. *Don't worry, my lovely, we'll always be together.* She had set trackers on his laptop and phone. *We're as good as married, 'til death us do part.*

Not any more. Where Luke was going, Karla couldn't follow: a commune in the midst of wild, remote nature. No social media. No mobiles. No way to stalk him. *Safe*, a foreign word on his tongue. He could almost taste it, and yet... His lips righted themselves to their customary bearing. Not a frown, not a smile: even keel, good enough to hold a spirit-level true.

'I'll always find you, my lovely,' she had told him the last time he tried to escape. 'You're just confused, so confused. Don't worry. Karla's here now, to take care of you.' His plan was to fly out to Thailand and disappear in Chiang Mai. She'd caught up with him at the airport before dawn as he waited for the check-in desks to open. Her brutish brother came along, the family's enforcer. If Luke shouted for help, he'd be discreetly stabbed in just the right place, then lovingly bundled into a waiting car, taken to the family's barn and treated by their trusted vet. What Karla wanted, Karla always got. She was her family's princess, and Luke had become her cherished possession. It was odd, he knew. No one on the outside would understand. The Ruskin-Hugheses shaped reality to suit their every whim. If you fell into their orbit, you would either stay there at their mercy or you'd fall, head first, into a slurry pit.

'Are you all right, dear?' Dorothy said when the rain eased a little, and the river they drove through once again resembled a road. 'You keep looking back. Is the car behind us too close?'

As soon as Dorothy had informed him, then and there at the interview, that he had been accepted to the Synner's Crag commune, that he should be ready to leave the next day – he had quit his job by not coming to work, closed his online accounts, broken the lease on his flat in a one-line email that surrendered his deposit, left instructions for a house-clearance company to empty everything, except the necessities he could fit into a backpack. Then, he cooked his laptop and phone in a pot of boiling water and dumped them in a wheelie bin.

When he did his packing, he'd been so nervous and frenzied that he could not now remember what he had with him. Never mind. What does a person need, really need, for a basic existence in the woods? If it came to it, the clothes on his back and the relief in his heart should be more than enough. On the train to London Bridge, he'd kept a nervous eye out for Karla and her brother, scanning the platform and holding his breath until the carriage doors closed with their customary whoosh-click-click-click.

With the tips of both thumbs, he now touched each finger to count them. Four on each hand, with the two thumbs making ten. Then he counted again. One, two, three, four. Two thumbs plus eight fingers: ten.

The inside of the 2003-plated Peugeot smelled like peanuts and decomposition. When they stopped at a service station in Hexham to fill up on diesel, they both came out for air and stood under the canopy, the rain thumping like drumbeats above them. Luke tightened the scarf around his neck and plugged in the fuel nozzle, breathing in humidity and petrol fumes.

Dorothy apologised with a shake of her head. 'I know how it looks,' she said, 'living off-grid and driving a diesel, but who can afford those expensive electric ones, and where would we even charge it? At least we only drive it when we absolutely have to. It's a bit temperamental, mind. We're lucky Slevin is good with engines. To get from Synner's Crag to civilisation without a car, you have to walk six miles to the actual road and then another two until you hit some houses with a bus stop. And the bus only stops there once a day. Sometimes it doesn't come at all.' She smiled reassurance. 'We live in beautiful isolation, you'll see. You'll love, love, love it. And I have to say...'

Her words trailed off in his mind as he noticed something

that chilled his blood in an instant. Beside the petrol station shop, at the side of the cage where they kept orange and blue gas canisters, stood a lone figure in high heels, skinny jeans and a dark woollen jumper. She held a black umbrella for cover and seemed to stare at him.

He turned to see if Dorothy had noticed his panic. She was still talking to him, unaware. The pump clicked full. He shook the nozzle and plugged it back in its place, doing his best to keep his hands from trembling. When he looked up again, the figure was gone.

He was imagining things. He must be. Or maybe it was just a passenger from one of the other refuelling cars.

While Dorothy went inside to pay, he locked himself in the Peugeot, waiting for her to return. Cold sweat dampened his forehead. He counted and recounted his fingers and thumbs.

When they left the garage, Luke stole a glance to see if anyone would follow. A shiny black Range Rover signalled to turn after them but was left behind, waiting for a gap in the traffic. As the mist cleared from the windscreen, he took a deep breath and refocused. This prolonged silence might give Dorothy the wrong impression, and anyway, he was probably mistaken, looking for danger where there was none. Living on the brink does that to you.

'You were saying... Long way to get out of the commune. No neighbours at all, then? Nothing nearer?'

'There is, but, erm...' Dorothy hesitated and drummed the tips of her fingers on the wheel. 'There's a farm that borders our land. But Adrian, the farmer, he doesn't like us much. You'll see his house on the way. I have to drop off a note in his letterbox, an offer of a peace summit. I'm not hopeful. He's a bit stuck in the mud of his anger.'

'I see, erm...' Luke said, unsure how to react. It was probably best to change the subject. 'You said in my interview, there are no phones at the commune. Not even a mobile, for emergencies?'

Dorothy inhaled a surprised gulp at a road sign she had nearly missed, and then, without indicating, took a sharp left turn onto a country lane. Her shoulders tensed and remained so for a silent minute. 'What were you asking? Ah, yes. When we founded Synner's Crag, we agreed: no phones, no clocks, no solar, no gas. People lived their lives before all this technology. They rose with the sun, grew up in nature, died in nature. Dust to dust. It's not just simpler, it's better. We forget that death is part of the cycle. When our time comes, well, we're all organic. But you know all about that from your job, don't you? At the commune, we're just more organic than most. If you don't have a hospital or doctor to go to, you stop worrying about hospitals and doctors. It's quite freeing, you see.'

Rising with the sun. Simpler. Nature. Luke added words and expressions to his list, so he could use them later, fit in, appear to be one of them. Could he? He was restless for the awkward beginnings to be done with, to belong. He imagined a wheelbarrow laden with wood for fire, sharp axes, a vegetable patch, a blackened teapot over a fire filled with herbs and bark. Did you boil bark for drinks, or was that something he misremembered from a TV documentary?

The rain thinned to drizzle and then stopped altogether. Dorothy's driving style eased, but she still gripped the wheel with steadfast force, as though if she let go, the car would run away from her. Her creased face made her look like an elderly aunt, one who knits and bakes shortbread, but her stone-grey eyes told a different story – like the depths of an ancient lake, hard to fathom from the surface. Or it might have been a false conclusion. Luke had learned not to trust his impressions of people. They never turned out to be who they said they were.

'Well, I don't want to mislead you,' Dorothy said. 'We do make some concessions to necessity. In the beginning, we didn't allow lighters or matches, but now we do. You don't want to stay up all night to keep a fire going, or go through the palaver of lighting one from scratch with a stick spindle thingy. And I'll confess we haven't been too successful growing food. The soil is hard and unforgiving, or maybe farming just isn't as easy as it sounds in the books. Believe me, we tried. We tried everything. We even bought an industrial quantity of compost once.' She shrugged. 'It's not the end of the world. We use my pension to buy essentials: flour, wholesale sacks of beans and rice, potatoes, condensed milk, that sort of thing. Still, you'd be surprised how much you can do without and how much you can share. What I mean is, we're not fanatics and, if I'm honest, hunger doesn't appeal.' Then, unbidden, her hand left the wheel, and she gave his shoulder a gentle squeeze. 'Don't worry, darling.'

His throat tightened.

In his interview, which was held at a Euston station café, Dorothy had sipped water from a refillable bottle while Luke refused a drink, concerned he would make some mistake by ordering one.

'Now tell me, Luke,' she had said, 'what possessed you to want to join a commune?'

His strategy was to show eagerness and interest. He would have said anything, *anything at all*, to win his place at Synner's Crag, to be the one person accepted over the dozens of applicants who must have responded to the tiny ad. Dorothy had taken no notes, and Luke hoped she wouldn't remember the promises, the embellishments, the lies. How difficult could it be, living simply? Wasn't the clue in the name? Maybe he hadn't done as much work as he'd claimed at a friend's allotment, or any at all. He no longer had anyone he could call a friend, not since Karla. He kept details of his role at the crematorium vague, implying he dealt with the mourners. *You have to show compassion. You have to be a people person, get along even when someone is grumpy or angry or sad.* These generic statements were entirely true – about other people. His job was at the business end of things. The dead arrived in coffins and left in jars or urns, transformed from an unseen person in one container to fine dust in another.

He reached into the pocket of his oversized denim jacket, punched out a pill from its blister, placed it on his tongue and swallowed.

Somehow, Dorothy caught the motion. Not a lot got past her, it seemed.

'If you need any prescriptions from the pharmacy, just let me know. We can collect them for you when we do our food runs.'

'Nah. Pills for stress. My last one. Won't need them where we're going.'

This small interaction unnerved him and, as the car turned right onto another narrow lane, he shook his head to free himself of the incessant thoughts. Dorothy had chosen him over all the others. Unless he did something unhinged now, his passage to the commune was assured. He steeled himself, then raised the edges of his lips to form a plastic smile.

The forced joy worked, and, just like that, he was excited again, looking forward to his life in the woods. He could make friends, reinvent himself, be a new Luke: helpful, friendly, dependable. He could become the good person he used to be, kind and caring and interested in people. The waters would drain from the surface of the earth. The Ark would land on cleansed soil, free of transgressions and evil.

'Any tips on fitting in?' he said.

Dorothy braved a darting glance at him before fixing her eyes back on the road. 'People will press you on why you joined us. My advice is, tell them what you told me in the interview.'

'How do you mean?'

'It's fine. No need to pretend.'

He started counting fingers again.

'Relax,' she said. 'We all have our secrets. Everyone tells me they'd like to be closer to nature, blah-blah-blah, what they think I'd like to hear. I'm sure they mean it, but usually, if you check under their fingernails, they're running away from some trauma. It's not a bad thing. It makes them more accepting of quirks and the occasional weirdness, perfect for our kind of life.'

'Can I ask why you chose me?'

'Our commune needs people with a bit of an edge, not coffee-table climate warriors. You're a survivor. I could sense it in you: the pain, the worry. You'll be motivated to do well.'

'I see,' he said, then hugged himself.

'You asked for a tip,' she said. 'Well, this is it: become the best commune member you can be. Don't judge others. Sharing can be tough sometimes. It's not a holiday park. But for our hard work, we get rewarded with something precious, something people out there can only dream of. It disappears when people sacrifice to the gods of modern living.'

Luke liked the words but wasn't focused on their meaning. 'Are there any tensions I should know about? In the commune, I mean.'

'Nothing even worth mentioning. You'll be fine. And you'll pass the vote with flying colours. I'll make sure of it.'

'A vote?' he said, his tone a pitch higher than he intended.

Her hand left the wheel in a dismissive wave to shoo away his fear. 'Just a formality. After a week or so, we all vote to accept you. Nothing to worry about. You'll be tickety-boo. They listen to me, and as far as I'm concerned, you're already perfect for the place.'

He shuddered. She was mistaken. He had plenty to worry about. He readied himself to play the role of the nicest person who'd ever lived, to volunteer for every unpopular job, to never gossip, and always, always smile.

CHAPTER THREE

Dorothy parked the mud-spattered Peugeot where the dirt road ended and the forest began: a wall of trees and ferns, damp and fresh from the recent showers. Luke carried Dorothy's faded blue sports bag in one hand and his newly bought hiking backpack over the shoulder of the other. He followed her along a barely visible path through dense vegetation, their shoes squelching in the sodden undergrowth.

His socks were wet, but he didn't care. He marvelled at the tranquillity of it, the sense of freedom and safety. Oak trees loomed above, their branches like ancient shrugging witches dressed in colonies of moss and decay. He drew in lungfuls of moist air, alive with the scents of leaves and mud and composted layers of death and renewal. A bird cried. A squirrel scurried away at the sight of them. They walked and walked until, at last, the curtains of ferns and nettles parted to reveal an entrance to a wide, level clearing in the woods.

On a wooden sign, a slogan was painted in white, boxy letters:

Synner's Crag Commune
Ye who enters, abandon all soap

'My son's humour,' Dorothy said with an apologetic wince. 'Joel's forty-one. I live in hope some day he'll leave adolescence behind. If I hadn't brought him here, he'd still be in his room, playing on his Xbox.' She closed her eyes, inhaled a deep gulp of air, held it in for a moment and exhaled a contented sigh.

At the centre of the clearing, surrounded by mossy grass, stood the community roundhouse, exactly as Dorothy had described it: a coned structure, thatched like a tribal gathering place in a *National Geographic* feature. Smoke billowed from its chimney, the charred wood smell evoking in Luke nostalgia for times of old he had never experienced: fire and drums and communal cauldrons.

At the far end of the clearing stood a bell tent, alongside a small shed-like structure from whose door a single bed was visible, piled with a jumble of clothes. Encircling the roundhouse were three round log cabins, their roofs covered by a strawed mud-like material laid over a green tarpaulin that was visible around the edges. They looked rough but sturdy. The doors to the cabins were a thick carpet fabric. The nearest one was rolled up to reveal a semi-dark interior. *No electricity*, Luke reminded himself. He wondered what they used for light. Kerosine lamps? Candles? Did the rules allow for them? Which cabin would he sleep in tonight?

Dorothy followed his eyes as he surveyed the commune. 'You like our little encampment?'

He nodded. 'Why is it called Synner's Crag?'

'It's a very old name. Synner's Crag is a cliff about a mile from here. Legend has it they used to test the guilt of criminals by pushing them off the top of the crag. If they survived, they were innocent. Haven't yet had a chance to use it ourselves, but the option's always there if we need it.'

Luke mirrored her smile and repressed a shudder.

A face appeared at the roundhouse's door, beaming at them from under a sweep of raven-black hair, pulled into a ponytail by two monk-orange headbands.

'Hello, Naomi,' Dorothy said. 'Congratulations. It's a boy. Meet Luke.'

'We missed you!' the woman said to Dorothy, then turned to inspect the new arrival. 'Oh dear, Luke, these dreamy green eyes. Joel won't be pleased. Dorothy was under strict instructions to recruit an ugly one.'

He couldn't place the woman's accent. Her vowels were long and meandering, making him think of hay and honey. Dorset, maybe, but with a hint of Estuary? She appeared almost stereotypically hippie. Her giggles were more punctuation marks than laughter, but her smile was sincere. He repaid her with an awkward, unpractised grin.

'You're just in time for dinner,' Naomi said. 'Stella made salty, too-bitter bean stew. Very apt. Tells you everything you need to know about our ginger, Welsh ice queen.'

'Naomi! Dear me,' Dorothy said.

Naomi responded with a wide, toothy smile.

Dorothy stopped in one of the cabins and dropped a parcel wrapped in brown paper on one of the beds. Then, they entered the roundhouse, which was warm and smoky from the cooking hearth at the back of the room. An odd collection of people sat on battered wooden chairs around the communal dining table. They wore the kind of clothes you'd find on a charity shop rack: mismatched colours, odd layers, and the fallback of T-shirts and jeans.

Dorothy introduced him, pointing at each commune member in turn, and Luke made an effort to remember their names. The three men: Joel, Slevin and Michael. The two women: Stella and Faye, in addition to Naomi, whom he'd already met. They all looked to be over thirty, except for the woman with blonde pixie hair, Faye, and the brown-eyed man built like a rugby player, Michael, seeming to be younger, maybe in their twenties. They both had that fresh twinkle in their eyes, as though life's machinery of drills and hammers had not yet had its way with their dreams.

Luke hesitated, placed his backpack and Dorothy's bag against the wall and joined the table to sit between Naomi and Dorothy. A tight-lipped Stella served up metallic bowls of steaming bean stew while Faye poured water from a jug into tin cups, which she handed around.

'Is Lilian not joining us?' Dorothy said.

Forks screeched against the metal of the bowls. The silence thickened with something unsaid. Most of the commune's members looked away, seeking distractions, suddenly interested in the basket of kale and potatoes, the flour store, the charred hearth and pots and pans, the beaded macrame strings that curtained the door, and beyond them the quilts of rain that had started to fall again.

'Did anything happen?' Dorothy asked.

Stella looked up, her stern eyes harsh, like they could pierce through granite. She opened her mouth as if to speak, but then said nothing.

Slevin, who wore no shirt, the outline of his skeleton showing under thin, spotty skin, stood up and went to stare at the torrents outside.

At last, Joel cleared his throat and spoke. 'Lilian decided to leave.' Then, in a put-on American accent, he added, 'Commune living wasn't for me after all.' His tone was sarcastic, but Luke detected something else within it. Worry? Guilt?

Dorothy frowned. 'She couldn't wait until I got back? I would have talked her out of it, or at least listened to her reasons. I mean, was she in such a hurry, she couldn't wait for a ride? It's a long way to walk.'

'She was dead set on leaving,' Stella said.

From his position at the door, Slevin coughed, then echoed Stella's words, 'Yeah. Dead set.'

Dorothy looked around the table. Her eyes settled on Joel, then travelled to Naomi. 'Oh well, at least we don't have to debate where to put Luke. He can use Lilian's bed. You don't mind, do you, Naomi?'

Naomi said nothing, forking beans into her mouth. Her almost permanent smile now lowered to half-mast.

Slevin returned from the door and came to stand by the table. With forced cheer, he said, 'Isn't it time for the welcome ceremony?'

As if to the baton of an invisible conductor, everyone at the table reached for a drink from their tin cups, lacking even the pretence of enthusiasm.

'I got 'em,' Stella said. She left the table, rummaged in a wooden box that was set against the wall and returned with a pair of bright red Wellington boots, which were clearly not new. Luke wondered who had worn them before.

Stella held up the boots. 'Welcome, Luke, to our little commune. May you prosper here, et cetera and all the rest, and may you prove worthy to stay. Sorry about the colour, but that way we'll never lose you and, you know, you can't escape.'

A token round of applause and welcomes followed. With finger and thumb in his mouth, Slevin produced a half-hearted wolf whistle.

Stella handed the boots to Luke, who set them on the floor and thanked them all as graciously as he could. *Remember to smile.* This lukewarm reception couldn't be about him. They didn't know him yet. Maybe it's just how they usually behaved and, after all, he was a stranger.

They returned to their meal, and Luke set to work on the stew. It wasn't exactly tasty, with a rich, bitter aftertaste, but it was hot, and he was hungry. Food was food. He'll get used to it. *Food is sustenance* was probably one of their slogans.

When all the bowls were empty, all clean, as if every morsel counted, Joel tapped his fork on his cup. 'The Synner's Crag Commune meeting is hereby convened.'

'If we're observing welcome ceremony formalities...' Slevin said and held up a bottle of tequila and a small canvas bag, from which he drew shot glasses that he lined up on the table. He poured a shot for each of the assembled and handed them around. Then he poured himself one, drank it with an *ah!* and filled himself another. 'Cheers!'

They raised their glasses and drank. Luke shivered at the drink's sharp kick.

'Only three items on the agenda today,' Joel said. 'Item one: welcome back, Dorothy.'

'You can call her *mother*,' Faye said. 'We won't judge.' She turned to Luke. 'He doesn't like to mention it, like it's a dirty secret.'

Faye was holding Michael's hand now. A couple, Luke noted. Or just close? He stole a glance at the remaining two women. Stella had a freckled face, a forceful jaw and a don't-mess-with-me stare. Naomi, on the other hand, with her softness and curves... *Don't think of other women. Don't you dare look at them.* He shook his head to free himself of Karla's voice.

'Item two:' Joel said, 'welcome, Luke. I guess we already did that. Item three: food supplies. Faye, you want to take this one, as Chancellor of Food and Grand Keeper of the Kale?'

The title sounded like a well-worn joke. No one laughed, and Luke belatedly reined in his smile.

'We're low on everything,' Faye said. 'The veg we have will last a couple of meals, but flour, sugar, beans, rice, everything else, is pretty much gone. We need a supply run. It's kind of urgent.'

'More booze,' Slevin added, 'definitely.'

Dorothy sighed, but then quickly softened her face. 'I'm shattered, but if we need food, I'll rest tomorrow and then, the day after, I can collect my pension for a supermarket run. Can we last that long?'

'A few potatoes,' Faye said, 'handful of beans, four or five small bags of flour and some kale, but it's on the verge of turning mouldy. Don't know if we can use it. Tonight's stew with some bread will be enough for breakfast. We'll ration, but we'll live.

'Another round?' Slevin said, holding up the bottle.

'I think I'll go to bed,' Dorothy said. 'But you youngsters carry on, and please make Luke feel welcome.'

'Don't you want some dessert first?' Stella said. 'We still have rice pudding leftovers from lunch.'

'It's very tempting,' Dorothy said, 'but at my age, you have to watch your figure. Eating healthy can add years to your life, mark my words.'

'You'll live to bury us all,' Stella said.

'I can barely carry a shovel, dear,' Dorothy said with a faint smile, 'and there's so many of you. See you in the morning.' She pushed herself up from her chair with both hands and left the table in slow, determined steps. Exhaustion had made her look older, her eyes sunken like dark hollows. When she reached the door, she picked up her bag, turned back and spoke to Luke. 'Don't worry. The commune can be gruff and not much for manners, but you'll get to know us. You're one of the family now – mud, banter and all.'

As Dorothy spoke, Slevin refilled everyone's shot glasses. When she had gone, he raised his overflowing tequila shot, splashing some in the act, and toasted Luke, 'Mud, shit, beans and tears.' Still holding up the glass, he looked around. 'And Dorothy. She's the glue that binds us. Don't know what we'd do without her. And now you, Luke. Welcome to our marvellous, effing commune.'

Luke raised his drink, downed it in one, and set the glass on the table. If Karla had witnessed him that night, sharing dinner and drinking with these people, there would have been consequences; they'd all be at risk. It didn't bear thinking about, yet still he did, incessantly, at the same time counting the fingers and thumbs of each hand.

CHAPTER FOUR

Dorothy left the door of her cabin rolled open to let in the dying light of dusk. Come darkness, a chill would fill the air, but she'd keep warm, wrapped in her parka coat inside her mountaineering sleeping bag, which, after years of use, carried only a hint of the familiar plastic scent and whispered the occasional rustle of nylon: *sah-seh-sah.*

She cocooned into a snuggly bundle, but only up to her neck. A cold head was always preferable. It made her feel connected. She could breathe fresh air and wake up with the first rays of dawn, smell the forest and feel alive. Those precious moments of a new day were her favourite – the thick webs of sleep melting into the joy of early birdsong. *I chose this life*, she would tell herself. *I live here, in the woods, with my son and our commune friends, singing around the bonfire and breaking bread together. Yes, they have their petty grievances, of course they do, but then I remind them of what they left behind: millions of knives punching through plastic covers of microwave meals, transient relationships, soulless jobs and miserable commutes. To what end? To bring up children like pups in a kennel while wasting mindless hours in front of illuminated glass rectangles that suck out your soul?*

She heard footsteps and turned her head to the door. By now, there was barely any light, but she thought she'd seen a hunched figure creep past.

'Hello?' she called out. Her cabin was behind the roundhouse and close to nothing useful. There was no reason for anyone to pass it unless they deliberately came to see her. Maybe Slevin got too drunk again. So quickly? She wished he would wear a shirt rather than walk around half naked, even on the coldest days.

'Well, good night then,' she said out loud, more to reassure herself.

She faced the ceiling again and wiggled her body little by little until her position within the sleeping bag was just right. It was then she realised she had forgotten to brush her teeth. She considered getting up, but fatigue weighed on her limbs, keeping them still, like a rag doll finally set to rest after being shaken by the slog of the long journey. *Oh, to be old in the presence of the young who see their time on earth as infinite*. She didn't think she would ever again drive all the way to London and back. It was an arduous journey, only undertaken to see Sandra one last time. Her younger sister was diagnosed with stage-three cancer and was waiting in anger at the slopes of stage four. She had only seen her once before since she'd left to set up the commune, and that visit ended worse than bad.

In a moment of misguided hope, Dorothy decided to bury the hatchet of their long estrangement and try one last time. Who cared about their ancient arguments? As it turned out, Sandra did.

'Shall I make us a nice cup of tea?' Dorothy had offered, measuring the emotional chill under the high ceilings of her sister's stuffy lounge. Piles of unwashed mugs had multiplied in the kitchen. Apples and clementines rotted in an oak fruit bowl, growing furry beards of mould. A faint smell of decay and urine and Sudocrem hung in the air like a shroud of tiny droplets. Dorothy held back a cough and repeated the question. 'Tea?'

'Come to gloat?' Sandra said. 'Sorry to disappoint you. I'm not quite on the final stretch yet. I have an excellent oncologist. Slovak, I think, or Serbian, maybe? Wears a bow tie. Always looks dapper. "There's treatments, Sandra," he says. "We have options, and we will try all of them." Nice man. His secretary says when one of his patients dies, he always sends flowers.'

'He must send a lot of flowers,' Dorothy said.

'You sound jealous.'

Dorothy coughed and suppressed a bitter giggle. 'Every woman should have flowers sent to her at least once. I'm pleased you'll finally get yours.' She regretted the words as soon as she said them. It was Sandra's fault. Her sister brought out the worst in her.

'You never know,' Sandra said. 'I might outlive you. Life's so unpredictable.' She drew an oxygen mask to her face, took a breath, removed it, but kept it in her veiny hand. 'I thought you'd show up at some point, to pontificate. Can't help yourself, can you? How's Joel?'

Dorothy glared at her sister. 'He's fine.'

Sandra licked her chapped lips and avoided Dorothy's eyes by pretending to inspect the dial on the oxygen tank. 'I got him a present, a set of hunting knives. Tried to send them, but Royal Mail doesn't think you exist. They're in the hall. Remember to take them before you leave.'

'You got him knives?'

'Joel was always fascinated with murder weapons. Takes after his father. The set I got him is very sharp. There's a whetstone, too. I'm sure he'll put them to good use.'

Dorothy shuddered. 'This is new,' she said.

'What is?'

'You, pretending you care about your nephew. It's touching. I'm touched.' She sighed. 'Knives? Really? You know what?

Never mind. Are you sure you don't want a hot drink? Can I make you something to eat before I go? When did you last have a meal?'

'Why are you here?'

'I was in London anyway,' Dorothy lied, 'and thought I'd come to see you. I have to recruit a new member for Synner's Crag.' That last part was true, but she would not have travelled to London just for an interview. In the past, she had asked potential commune members to meet her somewhere closer, like Newcastle or Berwick-upon-Tweed. In a phone call from the road, she'd dictate an internet ad to her friend Martha, who also did an initial screening of those who responded and set up the interviews.

'No one up north wants to join your commune of alfalfa munchers? You had to travel hundreds of miles to find a fool who will?'

Dorothy inhaled stale air and counted to ten. She gathered saliva to moisten the dryness in her mouth. *Don't rise to her provocation.* She would answer the question in a measured way. 'It's easier to commit when your old life seems a long distance away. They know the deal: no phones, no bank cards, leave your possessions behind. It makes it easier to let go, makes the commitment more honest.'

'Less easy to escape, you mean, from your little dog shelter. I know you, Dorothy. The ones you choose will all have emotional wounds and battered personalities. You can't help yourself. Not so much sainthood as safety in numbers.' With three fingers, Sandra touched her pursed lips. 'Anyway, thank you for your visit, but there really was no need to bother.'

It was hopeless, utterly hopeless. Against her better judgement, she tried to be grateful for the opportunity to say goodbye. *This is how I'll remember you*, she thought but did not say. *Bitter and angry, without an ounce of kindness.* When they were girls, they used to play together in the meadow for hours, building nests for their dolls to sleep in. As grown-ups, even minutes together were painful. If Sandra had died as a child, Dorothy would have loved her forever. What a sobering thought.

Dorothy stood, looked down at her wheezing sister and thought of something more to say.

Sandra shook her head, soured her face and raised the oxygen mask for a few laboured breaths.

'Well, goodbye then, and good luck.' She picked up her hat and purse, turned her back on her sister, collected the brown paper parcel that contained Joel's present and walked out.

At a retro-style café near Borough Market, she sat in a quiet corner and finally allowed herself a muffled cry over a cup of milky tea, using folded napkins to wipe away her tears. In the background, Louis Armstrong and Ella Fitzgerald sang *Dream a Little Dream of Me*. A woman typed numbers into a spreadsheet on a laptop. A suited man with a grating trumpety voice ordered a *decaf-soya-latte-to-go-and-make-it-hot*. There, in that moment at the café, she had a sudden longing to be back in the forest, away from the noise and grime and the atrocious hiss of the milk steamer. Peace was the sound of nature, the clean air, the absence of those walls of noise, the pressure closing in to flatten her to nothing on the dirty urban pavements that collected dog poo and wrappers and discarded chewing gum.

An owl hooted outside her cabin, and Dorothy noticed a fresh tear in her eye. She was back at camp. It was all done. Both Sandra and the new recruit. In hindsight, Luke's arrival was good timing, what with Lilian leaving. Oh dear, Lilian, a lost soul from Minnesota who'd travelled all the way from the States to hike around the UK. One day she showed up at the commune, stayed for a night, then another. Joel seemed to take an instant shine to her, and by the end of the week she was approved as a member. Joel and his silly infatuations. Lilian was only twenty-one, fresh out of an accelerated nursing programme. She was half his age and seemed savvy enough to keep him at arm's length. Other than that, Lilian fitted right in and had recently been keen on reviving their failed vegetable patch. Now she was gone, maybe Luke's allotment experience would be good for that. A strange boy, that Luke. Beneath his piercing green eyes, she could tell he was hiding something, yet she felt in her bones he was right for the place.

A strange, melodious howl sounded outside, like a person imitating a wild animal. It felt close, as though a person was standing just out of sight to the left of the door. *Awhoo!*

'Go away! I'm trying to sleep.'

She licked the veneers of her teeth to remove the day's furry accumulations, though without much success. She placed her palm flat on her belly and shivered at the touch of cold on warm skin. *Deep down, we're all afraid of the dark. Shadows scare us. It's a primal thing. But this is Northumberland. Nothing bad can happen here.*

A pleasant brush of wind stroked her face. Despite her weariness, sleep was elusive. Thoughts and thoughts and thoughts. *Come now, sleep! I'm ready.*

And then it happened, without warning, as sudden as an earthquake. A sharp shot of pain jutted along her left arm, up to her neck and jaw.

She caught her breath, light-headed. Her sweaty forehead felt icy against the tendrils of the breeze. She tried to reassure herself. *Old age brings ailments and pains. In the morning, I'll be fine. It can't be serious.*

Should she take an aspirin just in case it was a heart attack? It couldn't be. She'll take one anyway. No, two. *Bugger, bugger, bugger.* Her chest constricted as if caving in on itself – pain! – like the tightening jaws of a vice, squeezing, squeezing. She tried to move. *No. Stay still. Stay calm. You'll only make things worse.*

Was this it? The end?

Silly cow. It's probably a panic attack. She'd had one once when

Joel's dad, her ex-husband Jimmy, was arrested for murdering his new wife. Then, too, Dorothy thought she was dying. *Oh, the amateur dramatics.*

Pain! She exhaled a minuscule smidgen of air, though the breath somehow sounded loud as a whistle.

I need to settle myself. Calm down, Dorothy. In the morning, I'll wake up as usual, drink coffee, wash my face and wonder at my stupidity – such a silly hypochondriac cow. Heart attack? Whatever next? Tomorrow I'll laugh about it and won't breathe a word. At my age, health should stay an entirely private thing. Let this be a lesson: not every ache means death. There's no need to panic. I still have time.

Not every ache meant death, but this one did.

A final spasm ran through her, like searing lightning. Then it stopped, accompanied by a thought: *When you die alone, your death is a story no one ever gets to tell.*

All aches were gone, replaced by floods of warmth and calm.

She checked her breathing. It had ceased entirely. She no longer felt her body. Where were her arms? Her legs? The palm that rested on her belly, the belly upon which rested a palm? Her eyes may have been open or closed, yet they no longer saw.

A strange, unexpected relief was followed by an ultimate comprehension. She knew with pure clarity there was nothing left but her thoughts, the last seconds of brain function before the lack of blood would cease her entirely: a girl playing in the meadow, building nests for her dolls, a teenager sneaking out to smoke with her friends and experiencing her first clumsy fumble in the back seat of a car with a boy called Thomas, a woman in a terrible marriage that gave her a strange, beautiful boy and the address of a prison she never visited. The freedom of divorce and the two unsatisfactory men that followed. Then the inheritance, the purchase of land in the woods, the commune, five happy years.

Seconds stretched like hours. Time on the outside no longer held meaning. On the inside, all she saw, if seeing was the word, was bright milky white, exactly as advertised. She thought of her sister and hoped that Sandra wouldn't find out that she, Dorothy, had died before her. Petty, she knew, but in this place of warmth and light, there were no ill consequences for honesty. It was better for her sister not to have the satisfaction.

The milky light began to dim, and her thoughts turned to Joel. Will he be sad at her death? Will he say nice things at her graveside? What will he become without her tempering influence? If she was being honest, there was also that awful business with– No. Even at death's door, she couldn't think it. *Don't worry. Joel will be fine.*

And then a final thought, like a distant, tinny voice whispering in the night, *I really should have brushed my teeth before I died.*

CHAPTER FIVE

Naomi led Luke to their joint cabin. Along the way, she showed him the essentials in the bare light of the moon: the black plastic water tank that had a small thumb tap and an enamelled metal mug attached to it with a length of rope. *We fill it with water from the spring. It's hard work, so be sparing.* The trail leading to the toilet: *We use those big rolls of blue cleaning paper. It's rough, but you'll get used to it. Throw some sawdust in the hole when you're done on number twos. For the rest, feel free to find a friendly tree.*

She pulled aside the cabin's carpet-fabric door, and Luke followed her into the utter darkness. He stood still, taking in the musty smells – his sweat and hers, and earth and sodden forest. Naomi scratched a match against a matchbox. Its flame illuminated her face like an apparition coming to the fore from the shadows. Luke tried to remember the last time he'd seen a match lit or smelled its phosphorus smoke. Not for a long time. They were magical technology, forgotten by those with self-lighting hobs and microwaves and central heating.

Naomi put the flame to the wick of a fat candle that stood on an upturned metal bucket, and the room showed itself to him in muted gradients: two beds and some crates on cement flooring that was partly covered by a raffia rug. T-shirts, knickers and bras hung on a makeshift washing line. The walls were hidden by fabrics printed with colourful mandalas, their shapes dancing to shadows born of the flickering light. *Hippie decor*. On the bedside crate lay a book – *A Voided Youth* by Ashleigh Boroughs. Luke remembered the anonymous quote at the start of the novel: 'One must enjoy his days on earth, for one never knows if they are his last.' It was used ironically, or at least that's what Luke thought. He laid his rucksack on the floor and nodded at the book. 'Hits hard, that one,' he said.

'Just finished it,' she said. 'Glad they ended up together, but the whole thing's fucked up.' Her eyes landed on his chest, then travelled to his biceps. Her lips parted a sliver.

'Well, fiction,' Luke said.

'You work out?' she said.

Luke raised his chin and felt his face tighten.

She shook her head. 'Sorry, starvation breeds hunger. Someone hurt you, right? I can tell. Takes one to know one.'

He rubbed the back of his neck and looked at the beds. 'Which one's mine?'

She pointed to the bed on the right, a mattress over a pallet-wood base. 'We'll wash the sheets in the stream on laundry day. I hope you don't mind. I left Lilian's on, in case she came back.'

'I thought she was gone.'

'That's what Joel said, but look, all her things are still here, even her baby blanket. She couldn't sleep without it. It's odd, and I'm not sure what to think. Lilian was our latest recruit. She seemed so happy here, and she baked the most amazing bread.' She smacked her lips. 'Crispy crust and the centre all soft and fluffy. We ate it warm, straight from the clay oven. Faye's version doesn't come close.'

'How about you? When did you get here?'

'Been here a year. Best thing I ever did. Escaped prison by chance and a little cunning. Good luck to them finding me.'

Luke approximated a chuckle, though it came out dry. He wasn't sure if she was joking.

Naomi started to unclip the laundry pegs, folding the T-shirts and underclothes into two neat piles on her bed. 'Don't know why I told you that,' she said. 'Haven't told anyone else here, except Lilian. She got the whole story, but she's, you know, not here.'

'Your secret's safe with me.'

She grunted her thanks, preoccupied with the folded clothing before her. 'Not sure what to do with Lilian's. She's a tiny waif of a thing.' She held up a bra by its straps. 'Couldn't fit my equipment in this. Microscopic. Maybe it'll fit you.' She looked up at him. 'Massive personality though. Her trainers were all pink, but that was the only girly thing about her, like a statement to confuse the enemy. I'll miss her.'

Luke scratched his head. 'So, prison. Can I ask?'

'No.'

He showed her his palms in apology. 'Sorry. Just making conversation. I know I'm the new guy.' His face felt hot. He hoped the candlelight hid his blushes. In the roundhouse, the group had made him feel like an outsider with their in-jokes and innuendos and references to things he knew nothing about. It felt like they were doing so on purpose, to exclude him, just like school.

'What do you think, so far?' Naomi said.

'About the commune? I feel lucky to be here.'

'You said that, like, fifty times in the roundhouse.'

'Must be true, then.'

'Who was she? Or he? The person who…'

He suddenly felt cold, as if the temperature in the cabin had dropped below freezing. He crossed his arms, then uncrossed them. 'She,' he muttered, and hurried to change the subject. 'Dorothy said there's some bad blood with the farmer?'

'Yeah. Stella and Slevin have a habit of *borrowing* food from his fields. He made threats, showed up with a gun, said he has a licence to carry for pest control, and we shouldn't be pests on his land. Didn't help that his strawberries were there on the table like evidence, all nicely presented in a basket for him to scowl at. He's now got razor wire over the stone wall boundary. Not that it'll stop anyone. He was here again a few days ago. Timed it perfectly to catch us eating his veg. I guess he noticed Stell and Slev's incursion and came by for a final warning.'

'Why steal from him if we have food?'

'Well, you've tried Stella's stew. There's no budget for tasty things, and fruit doesn't last long. Anyway, Dorothy will sort it out. She's good at making peace, bless her.' She stretched and yawned. 'Right, bedtime. We get up early here.'

He sat on Lilian's bed, his bed. It bore a feminine scent, like a mix of vanilla and carob with a hint of pine.

Naomi kicked off her boots and wriggled as she pushed down her jeans. She removed her jacket and hoodie, and then, without warning, pulled off her T-shirt, leaving her in nothing but plain black knickers and an off-colour bra.

'You don't have to look away,' she said.

He tried to focus on her face, her white teeth, her dimples, anything but her nearly naked body, her breasts, the light of the candle dancing on her skin. His mouth dried to sand while he controlled his facial muscles, attempting to convey disinterest. Other muscles, too, awakened in him unbidden. Then, the most unsavoury thought came to his rescue. What if Karla found out he was here, in a cabin, alone with another woman wearing next to nothing? A glacial waterfall of fear doused his arousal in an instant. A lump formed in his throat, and he suppressed a cough.

He looked down at the raffia carpet. 'Stop me if this is off-limits, but the thing with Lilian… Joel seemed, I don't know, weird about it.'

Naomi grabbed an oversized T-shirt from her bed and slipped it on like a nightgown. 'Perceptive,' she said. 'He had a crush on her, if you ask me.' She sat on her bed and seemed to consider this for a moment. 'Something went down. It's all a bit suspect. Lilian loved the commune, so no, I'm not believing the story that's being spun.'

'No one contradicted Joel.'

'Oh, don't worry, baby communard. Eventually, it'll all come out in the wash. It always does, here.' She lay down and pulled the blanket all the way up to her chin. 'Most secrets, anyway. Dorothy will prise it out.'

'I enjoyed my time with her on the drive up.'

Naomi sighed and closed her eyes. 'Heart of gold, will of steel. Don't know what we'd do without her. Go feral is my guess.' She yawned. 'I'm shattered. Blow the candle out before you go to sleep.' She turned on her side, her back to him.

Luke lay down on his bed's thin mattress. He stared blankly at the beams and green tarp ceiling of his new home and listened to Naomi's gentle breaths, along with the background rustle of the leaves against the wind. After a while, he pushed his hand under the pillow to adjust it and found something hard hidden there. It was a notebook, the word *DIARY* written in capital letters on its cover. He glanced to confirm that Naomi was asleep and opened it. All the pages had been torn out, except for the last entry, written in neat childlike script over two double-sided pages.

CHAPTER SIX

Dear Diary,

Angry storm clouds are gathering over the commune, which is to say, things could get ugly mighty fast. There are two communes in Synner's Crag: the one you see and the other one that hides beneath the surface. It lurks. Yes, "lurks" is a good word for it.

I'm sorry I had to tear out the rest of you, my dearest, dear Diary. Now the vultures are circling and ready to feed, I'm scared they might read you, and then all hell will break loose. Thing is, I think they already know about… (won't write it down). But, honestly, it's none of their fucking business. I may be the youngest here, but they have no right, no right at all. What are they, the morals police? And whose morals? Joel's? Stella and her animal familiar, Slevin? I don't think so.

Yeah, they probably know. You should have seen how nobody spoke to me at dinner, like I wasn't even there, and now Joel informed me I have to meet him and Stella and Slevin at the cave tomorrow, but go by myself. Basically, I have to leave after lunch and wait for them there, like I'm waiting at the principal's office until they design to see me. No, we can't all walk there together because this is "a secret meeting", like, give me a break, that makes no sense.

If it's as bad as I think, you and I know it's all because of Joel's obsession with me. He doesn't know how creepy it makes me feel, but I can't talk to him about it. Maybe in front of Stella and Slevin I'll have the courage, and then see how high and mighty he acts. It colors everything he does. Creepy, creepy, creepy.

Well, I can handle myself, as you well know, but there are three of them, and it might get heated. When I get angry, I say things I don't mean, hell hath no fury, and it will escalate and they'll ask me to leave and never come back, and Stella will tell me to wait outside the camp and throw my things in a trash bag and then throw it at me and tell me to start walking, like what happened when Dorothy was away and Damien had to leave. They poured water on his clothes before they gave them to him. Stella will invent a rule. Thou shalt not whatever. Begone with you and never come back. They can be petty and hateful. I mean, I'm not saying Damien was right to steal the booze and have his little party. Even so, it's not a capital offense, right? They waited for Dorothy to be away this time too, the scheming bastards.

Dear Diary, if you could speak, you'd ask me why, then, am I going to meet them. You know why. Because deep down I'm hoping I'm totally wrong about this. They're so weird here about things sometimes. Maybe when they gave me the silent treatment at dinner, they'd just had enough of my chatty American ways. I mean, I can hear them mocking me, like when Joel does his fake (terrible) American accent and keeps saying "you betcha" and "oh ya" like he saw on that Fargo show (OK, points for knowing that Minnesota borders North Dakota, but that's no excuse), or they laugh at me when I say eggplant instead of aubergine. And because I'm young and American, they seem to think of me as some cheerleader type. They have no idea what I've been through. All I wanted was for them to get to know me, really know me, and then, maybe maybe maybe, I'd have the courage to tell them the truth about my life.

So, back to the question: why am I going? Because I hope I totally misread the situation, and they just want to talk about something else, like food plans or the vegetable patch, and they don't want to raise everyone's hopes up, like a surprise. Maybe Joel wants to revive the project to have a second camp in the cave? Maybe the way they asked was just their silly British way and they can't help it.

That's what I hope, despite my gut feeling. Silent prayers. Loud prayers. Every kind of prayer. And if they say I have to leave, I'll tell them I want Dorothy to be here. I have to talk to her and explain before I go. I owe her that much. They won't allow it, though, will they?

These last pages I'll leave here. If they banish me, they won't pack the bedding. It's commune property and all that.

Naomi, pretty please, if you find this, then they sent me away. Even if you're angry with me, I don't deserve to be thrown out like garbage. Please speak to Dorothy and tell her what happened, not like the lies they sold her when Damien left. I'll wait a little and then come back and speak to her. I'm begging you!

Goodbye, Diary (what's left of you). So long. Here's hoping I'm just a silly American girl and I'll see you tomorrow. Then I'll burn these pages and ask Dorothy to get a new notebook and we'll start again, OK?

xxx

Luke tore out the pages as quietly as he could and folded them into a small square. Naomi was still asleep, her back to him. He reached down to his backpack, placed the folded pages into a side pocket, shoved his dirty socks on top and zipped the pocket shut. The diary's cover he hid under his mattress. The next day, he'd dispose of both the pages and cover. It was too early to be part of any drama. If he shared Lilian's diary, they'd know he'd learned of what happened, or some of it.

He blew out the candle. It took him a long time to fall asleep. Whatever happened at that meeting, Lilian never got her things. Best not ask questions. Not until the vote. At least Dorothy was with them now, and everything would be fine.

CHAPTER SEVEN

SEVEN DAYS BEFORE THE RECKONING

'Every morning,' Naomi said as she tied the laces of her tan leather boots, 'the first person up makes coffee, which is usually our resident ginger, Stella. I don't think she ever sleeps more than four hours a night. No wonder she's got a face on her like cracked leather. Forget I said that, sorry. To be fair, she's been getting up later. Anyway, before we go to breakfast, each of us carries one jerrycan of water from the spring to fill the water tank. I'll show you. It's a five-minute walk each way. Good, easy muscle work.'

'Even Dorothy?'

'She wants to, bless her, but we voted an exemption. The commune agreed.'

'The commune votes on every decision?'

'Technically, yes, but that's exactly the argument we had when Michael and Faye wanted to move in together. Joel raised it to a vote, and him and Michael nearly came to fists, like, *you can't tell me not to live with my girlfriend*. Joel made it about "the soul of the commune", said that if you're a couple, *you're committed to yourselves more than you are to us*. His jealousies are predictable, mostly. If he had his way, we'd all be sister-wives.

Anyway, Dorothy took a ninety-minute round trip to buy the bell tent, and that was that. They moved in the same day. Joel and Slevin got more room when Michael moved out of the crowded boys' cabin, and Faye left Dorothy to some privacy in hers. Everyone's happy. Well, almost everyone. Joel still mouths off about it sometimes, and Dorothy has to calm him down and wipe off the spittle from his emotional bib. It's lucky he's channelled his obsession into the new cabin he wants to build. It'll keep him busy and off everyone's backs.'

'We expecting more people?'

'Not really, but if you get Joel started on the subject, you'll get a lecture about how he wants this commune to be *the beginnings of a movement*. His delusion is that people from Synner's Crag will some day go out into the world and start new communities everywhere, practising our superior form of… whatever. In the plan, there's probably a marble statue of Joel for each commune.'

'Not a fan, then?' Luke said.

'Joel's Joel, which is fine, but to be a prophet, you need charisma. I don't think anyone will follow him to the other end of camp, let alone world domination. I suppose he could build his new cabin from all the bargepoles people won't ever touch him with.'

Luke pressed his hands into his pockets, angled his head and looked away.

'What?' she said.

He shrugged. 'Nothing.'

After the jerrycan water run, Luke stood outside his cabin door and admired the idyll around him. Every group of people will have tensions bubbling under the surface, and sometimes above it. It was the natural course of things and a small price to pay for where he was, for the safety it promised. And that's all he wanted, more than anything: safety and peace. He thought about Lilian's diary and vowed to watch his every step, never give them cause to be upset with him. When he was younger, going through teacher training for his first career, he'd shared a flat with two others. It was always the little things that caused resentment: unwashed pots and dishes, overheard gossip, taking the bins out.

Mellow rays of sun bathed the encampment in light, the grass and tree leaves glistening from the night's raindrops. Smoke rose from the roundhouse's chimney and from the clay oven outside it, caressed away by a gentle breeze. Faye was kneeling in front of the oven, spatula in hand, carefully retracting bread into a wooden bowl, one fist-sized bun at a time. Then she covered the bowl with a flannel and loaded the oven with another batch of dough lumps. Under her pointy ochre hat, Faye's face was a picture of apathy, like she hadn't a care in the world.

'Good morning,' Luke said to her from afar with a carefully placed smile.

She looked up from her baking but did not respond or meet his eyes. Then, she carried on with her work, as if she hadn't heard him. Luke kept his smile firm and then let it drop. He closed his eyes and breathed in the scent of fired bread and woodsmoke. A wind chime that hung above the bell tent's door tinkled a soothing tune like a fairy's xylophone. The scene had the aura of a pleasant midsummer's dream.

A plump pigeon waddled across the cut grass before him, unafraid. It stopped, turned its head to him and cooed. He tried to imitate the soft murmur of its call. The pigeon stared at him, its head rotating in curious jerks. The world was as it should be. Small niggles weren't worth the bother.

A bell rang, followed by a throaty shout from Stella, 'Breakfast!'

The pigeon flapped its wings and took flight.

At the communal table, the cauldron of the previous night's bean stew took pride of place, reheated. As Luke sat down, Stella handed him a cup of coffee and one to Naomi. Then she looked at them both and angled her head with a smirk. 'Already?'

'Already what?' Naomi said.

'You two look very comfortable together. There's sort of an... afterglow.'

Joel crossed his arms, squeezing his shoulders with his fingers. 'You slept together? On his first night?'

Naomi glared at him. 'What if we did? I mean, look at him: these eyes, chiselled chin, nice body. Wouldn't you?'

Luke stared ahead. Naomi could afford to play these games, but he could not. On the other hand, he didn't want to contradict her and risk what could become his first real friendship in this place.

Joel shoved his chair back and stood, the resulting screech grating the air. He pounded his fist on the table, causing the crockery to shudder. After a moment, he slumped back into his seat with a huff, picked up his coffee and took a long, slow sip, his eyes never leaving Luke. Then, as if a switch had reset in his mind, his manner changed, and he was calm again. The tight lines on his face melted into something akin to resignation.

Faye entered with a large bowl of slightly charred bread buns. 'Baker's two-dozen,' she said. 'Eat 'em while they're hot.'

'Where's Dorothy?' Naomi said.

'Probably sleeping off her wild partying in London,' Joel said. 'Leave her be.'

'She'd want us to wake her,' Faye said. 'Plus, there's no work rota. Toilet needs cleaning, wood needs chopping, lunch will need–'

'Nonsense,' Stella said. 'I propose a commune holiday. Who's with me?'

'To celebrate what?' Michael said.

'In honour of... of Dorothy,' Stella said. 'She could hardly object, and we deserve a day off. The toilet will take ten minutes. We have enough wood, and the vegetable patch can wait. Everything's dead anyway.'

'That's circular logic,' Joel said.

'You what?' Slevin said and scratched an angry spot at the centre of his bare chest that looked like a third nipple. 'Anyway, if we replant veg, the farmer will only sneak in again with his weed killer. Why give him the satisfaction?'

'There's no evidence it's him,' Naomi said. 'I reckon we're just crap gardeners.'

'It should have worked with the compost and fertilisers,' Slevin said.

Naomi shrugged. 'Lilian thought we over-watered, at the wrong times. She had a little more experience than us city folk.'

'Beans,' Joel said. 'Breakfast, lunch and dinner. That's why we need to regrow. We can't just rely on Dorothy's pension.'

'All right,' Stella said, 'here's what I think. Celebrate during the day and then go on a requisition mission tonight beyond Adrian's Wall. Last time I looked, his cabbages looked nice.'

'Cabbages!' Slevin said with a sly grin and cupped his hands suggestively over his chest.

'Jesus!' Stella said. 'Don't you start and all, you filthy dog.'

Slevin's grin remained at full beam. 'All I'm saying is, I'm in favour of said mission and will partake, unlike mummy's boy, here. *I'm appalled by what they did, Mummy. I'm Saint Joel, me. I would never, ever, borrow some necessary produce from the farmer's fields.*'

Joel stared into his mug, as if puzzled by the constitution of the coffee. Then he looked up, not at Stella or Slevin, but at Luke. 'I'm not scared of anyone,' he said.

'Of course you aren't,' Slevin said. 'I'm not for a minute implying she'd spank you on your massive bottom.'

'All right, all right,' Stella said. 'Enough, children. Commune holiday. Show of hands. Who's for it?'

Slevin and Stella held up their hands.

Faye's hand rose, and Michael followed her lead.

Stella stared at Joel, who was again inspecting his coffee with great focus as if it contained an important message. She turned to Luke. 'You with us, new guy?'

'Too green to vote on anything,' Luke said.

Stella flashed him a stiff smile. 'That's fine. If you're not keen on a holiday, you can clean the toilet. Naomi is also against, so she can show you how.'

'I'm happy to clean the toilet,' Luke said. 'Really, it's no problem. I should start pulling my weight.'

'You'll do a great job,' Stella said. 'I noticed you count your fingers all the time. OCD cleaners are the best.'

Luke stopped his counting mid-hand.

'Who died and made you queen?' Naomi said to Stella.

'I don't see what's unclear,' Stella said. 'You don't want a holiday, suit yourself. You don't have to have one. Motion passed by a majority. Today is declared Dorothy Day. Let's eat.'

Naomi shook her head. She leaned towards Luke and whispered in his ear. 'I choose my battles carefully. It's no big deal, don't worry, but I don't think Dorothy would be best pleased. You'll see.'

'It's fine,' Luke said to her, quietly but loud enough for the rest of them to hear. 'I'm the new guy. I don't mind.'

The toilet was a cubicle built of old plywood that was imprinted with concentric patches of damp. A frayed, floral shower curtain acted as its door.

'The shit composts,' Naomi explained, 'so we can't clean with anything harsh. The big job is to empty the container every couple of months, but that's Slevin's chore. He doesn't mind shovelling shit. I think he actually likes it. Smells of it for a week or two until he finally decides to wash. All we have to do is wipe the seat, the bowl and the floor. Then we take the liquid collection tank and empty it away from the trail. We all do the toilet chore. Well, except for Joel. Somehow, he managed to get out of it. No one wants to press the point, because he's, you know…'

'A bit on the spectrum?'

She thought about this. 'Not sure. I'd say Joel has a spectrum all of his own.'

Naomi took him through the toilet routine. It wasn't too bad, except for the urine on the seat and floor, the buzz of irksome flies, and the nauseating smell that held a faint aroma of regurgitated beans. Still, it was just a chore.

When they were done, they walked down the leafy trail to the stream. After washing their hands, they sat together and watched the twinkling flow of water. Naomi pointed out two dragonflies that glided above it like dancing hovercrafts.

'Why did you let them think we slept together?'

Naomi picked a yellow flower and threw it into the stream. It sailed away until it snagged against a branch. 'For entertainment value. Sorry, couldn't help it.'

'Joel didn't seem pleased. You think he's into you?'

'Nah.'

'Isn't he?'

'Okay, maybe he was a bit interested once, not that I gave him any reason for it. But when Lilian got here, he only had eyes for her, and when I say *eyes*… Honestly, it was like a bull wanting to mount a schnauzer.'

A branch snapped behind them, and they both turned in unison. Joel was looking down at them.

'Speak of the devil,' Naomi said.

'What?' Joel said.

'You come to apologise?' Naomi said.

'Apologise for what?'

'Many, many things,' Naomi said.

'I came to tell you: you need to come back to camp.'

'Is that an order or a request?'

'Dorothy's dead.'

Naomi rushed to her feet and brushed her hands on her jeans. 'What?'

Luke pushed himself up and stood beside her. His throat constricted. *Dorothy's gone?* It didn't seem real.

Joel's face was rigid and chalky as limestone. 'Faye found her. She died in her sleep.'

'I'm so sorry, mate,' Luke said.

Joel crushed a bug on his shirt. It left a black dot where it perished. 'Would have been better if she waited to collect her pension. Not much food left.'

'You okay?' Luke said.

'I have a headache. I'm tired. To be honest, I could have done without this today.' He looked from Naomi to Luke. 'You're bang out of order, you two.' To Luke, he said, 'Be careful what you reap, mate. Be careful what you sow.'

'Honestly, I...' Luke said, then stopped himself.

'You're upset,' Naomi said. 'I'm not going to judge you today.'

Joel kicked a rock into the stream. 'Nobody cares,' he said, though it was clear to Luke that he did. He cared a great deal.

CHAPTER EIGHT

Luke had to admit that digging a grave was infinitely more challenging than it appeared in the movies. Michael and Slevin did battle with the frustratingly tough Northumbrian soil, their shovels striking rock after rock, each needing to be dug around and under until it could be extracted like a tooth. Luke offered to take his turn, but was refused, a kind of snub that he read to mean *it's not your place. You hardly knew her.* He wished they'd let him help.

Joel stood above the digging operation, offering unsolicited advice that Luke thought on any other occasion would probably have been rebuffed, but at his mother's grave was gracefully listened to with nods and mostly ignored. His voice was dry, devoid of emotion. It must have been his way of coping.

Luke had no reference point. His own mother died when he was two. He wasn't even sure if he'd attended the funeral. When he was twenty-seven, his father died some nine thousand miles away in Australia, in a suburb of Alice Springs. At the time, it didn't even occur to him to embark on an expensive twenty-six-hour trip just to attend a ceremony for someone who wouldn't take the tube from Putney to come and see him.

'But mate,' his Australian half-brother Bruce had said on a WhatsApp video call, 'don't you wanna say goodbye?'

'He's managed without me so far,' Luke said. 'I think he'll be fine for this one.'

It occurred to him that if the kind social worker from his teens had died, he might have been a little sad. But when it came to his father, a foot deeper in the ground was a foot closer to Hell where he belonged – notwithstanding that being in the Antipodes, it also made him a foot closer to Luke. *He'll have to go through the devil to get to me.* Strangely though, as he looked at Joel's expression, he somehow understood it, an instinctive perception that dug beneath the rubble of words. Joel was scarred, like him. Maybe they could even become friends? Maybe. If the jealousies about Naomi could be overcome.

Eventually, they reached the six-foot depth that Joel demanded and checked with a tape measure, though the hole was shaped more like an uneven blob than a rectangle. Joel and Stella walked across to Dorothy's cabin and returned with her figure wrapped in a turquoise blanket, the fringes of a coat's fur hood escaping from the folds. As they laid her next to the open grave, the edge of the wrapping fell from her face. Naomi looked away, but Luke held his breath and observed the pallid, dry skin, the bloodless lips, the shrivelled face that had retained little of Dorothy's ever-kindly expression – the woman he had spent an entire day in a car with, a woman he thought was on his side in this strange group that had not yet come to accept him, the key to a favourable vote. Although his work at the crematorium entailed dealing with the dead, Luke never got to see them there, only their coffins, which were rolled on well-oiled wheels to the business end of the operation, where he waited to 'process' them. Yet, this was not the first human body he'd seen. Karla had made sure of it.

Faye cried silently, wiping her tears with the sleeve of her jumper. Michael choked when he tried to speak. The two youngest members of the commune held onto each other while the others seemed to make do without the comfort of human touch.

The consensus around the graveside was that death was part of the circle of life. They repeated this mantra as if to convince themselves it was true, but their gestures were uncertain, their voices often stifled or off-pitch. Luke did his best to pretend their insecurities were also his. *Blend in. Pretend to be one of them until they accept you.* Every day counted, every interaction, every word. At least here, at the graveside, he didn't have to remember to smile.

They lifted, then heaved Dorothy into the grave.

As she fell and settled, face down, on the hard soil, the blanket retreated from the back of her head, revealing a bald patch, the shape of a duck's foot.

'We can't have her face down,' Slevin said.

Joel shook his head. 'It doesn't matter.'

Slevin spat on the ground, wiped his mouth with the back of his hand and approached the grave. He set his hands on either side of the pit to ease himself down, but slipped to land ungraciously on top of Dorothy. There was a cracking sound, as if he'd broken her. A burp rose from her mouth, choked by the earth, but still unnaturally loud. A collective shudder seemed to pass through their little group.

'Stop it!' Faye cried out. 'What are you doing, you idiot?'

'Don't interfere,' Stella said. 'He needs to turn her over. Show some respect.'

Joel looked ahead with a vacant expression, his shoulders slumped.

Slevin planted his feet wide over the body and, with difficulty, turned Dorothy onto her back. Her cheeks and forehead were sullied by dirt. She looked like she was smiling now, laughing at their efforts. Slevin tugged on the blanket until he had enough material to cover her face, which he did with a gentle sway of the hand, like a magician hiding a rabbit. He stood, his fists at his sides, and looked down as if admiring his handiwork. Then he nodded and reached up with his hand. Michael grasped his wrist and helped him climb out, back to the world of the living.

They all stood and stared into the hole in the ground, Luke a step further back. He felt like a stranger, intruding on their grief.

'Would anyone like to say some words?' Stella said.

They all looked at Joel.

He blinked, then shrugged. 'Goodbye, Dorothy.' His voice was level and empty.

Naomi retreated and came to stand next to Luke. 'Twat,' she whispered. Then she spoke out, her voice breaking. 'We'll miss you, Dorothy. Thank you for bringing us all here, to this place. Thank you for helping us. I don't know what we'll do without you.'

'We'll live,' Joel said. 'Let's cover her.'

At sunset, they lit a bonfire, centred within a circle of stones at the edge of the camp's clearing. As the kindling ignited and brought flames to the logs, Slevin passed around shot glasses and opened the first of three bottles of tequila he had lined up. Each *to Dorothy* toast made the blaze seem brighter and loosened their tongues. All except for Luke's. He kept his drinking in check, one shot to each of their three. Sobriety was a necessity, to avoid any missteps.

Naked of all but short, orange shorts, Slevin danced in circles around them, ululating and singing in tongues.

'Sit down,' Joel said after Slevin's volume increased, and his chanting grew more frantic.

'Why?'

'If we make a bonfire, we play Truth or Truth,' Joel said. 'That's the rule.'

'Not sure that's appropriate, mate,' Faye said.

'She was my mother,' Joel said. 'I get to say what's appropriate.'

Slevin stopped mid-dance, his hands still in the air. 'Did he just call her *my mother*?'

Stella caught Slevin's eye and shook her head.

Slevin shrugged. 'Fine.' He took a rubber band out of his pocket and used it to bunch his curls into a ponytail. Then he sat down, the coarse, dirty skin of his bare feet pointing to the fire. 'Who gets to call the question?'

'Not me,' Joel said. 'Faye?'

Faye looked into the flames, then her eyes circled the group. 'All right then,' she said. 'Truth or Truth: what was your first ever sexual experience?' She turned to Luke. 'We all have to tell the truth, the whole truth, and nothing but. You want to start?'

He shook his head and bit his upper lip. 'Maybe later.'

'It's compulsory,' Faye said. 'Everyone has to answer.'

'I'll go first,' Slevin said and scratched his groin. 'I was sixteen. My biology teacher, Jane Marsden. She gave me an anatomy lesson. Eight months later, she went on maternity leave. Saw pictures of the baby on Facebook. I'm telling you, the little dude didn't have her husband's eyes. His name's Arthur. Good solid name, Arthur. Truth or Truth, Joel.'

'Age twenty,' Joel said. 'At home, with a family member. I hated it, but she insisted.' He hugged himself and stared into the fire.

A log crackled into the silence. No one dared look at Joel until he spoke again, almost in a whisper. 'Truth or Truth, Faye.'

Faye didn't hesitate. 'Age seventeen. I was a late bloomer compared to the other girls. Samuel and I were boyfriend-girlfriend for a week, and I kept pushing him to do it. I didn't want the sex as much as I wanted *it* out of the way. Peer pressure, you know? It's not just boys that talk about it.'

'Really?' Slevin said. 'Wish I'd known.'

'We drove to the back of an industrial estate and did it in the back seat of his second-hand Ford KA. He cried. Then he drove me home, and I never saw him again. Okay, well, maybe I didn't want to see him.' She squeezed Michael's hand and looked at him. 'Truth or Truth, Michael.'

When it was Luke's turn again, he looked at their expectant eyes. 'I honestly don't remember,' he said.

'Foul!' Slevin cried out, his speech slurred. 'Everyone remembers their first time, even my nan when she got dementia. Only thing she forgot was that she wasn't supposed to talk about it. Prim and proper lady she was, my nan.'

Luke sensed danger but found he couldn't say another word. It should have been easy to talk about Rosie, his girlfriend in sixth form, his first, when love was a *forever* that lasted two months. With Karla, even the mention of sex with others could unleash dire consequences. He braced himself to push through. *She isn't here. She wouldn't know.* The vote depended on it. His life depended on it.

Before he had a chance to speak again, Slevin pointed a finger at him. 'I call foul! You play the game.'

'Leave him alone,' Naomi said. 'He's not a member yet. He doesn't have to. It's my turn.'

'Foul!' Slevin repeated.

Naomi ignored him. 'Truth or Truth. My first time was—'

'Well, this should be good!' Slevin said, rubbing his hands and slurring even more. 'She said she's Catholic and doesn't believe in sex before marriage.'

'No comments allowed,' Faye said.

'It's all right,' Naomi said. 'It's a fair question. For a long time, I didn't believe in sex before marriage. Far too long.'

'Oh, wow wow wow,' Slevin said. He raised his glass to Luke and downed the tequila in one. 'Ah! Luke, my friend, it would appear you took our Naomi's virginity on your first night. Well done, mate! Kudos. Was it your first time too, virgin boy? Is that why you,' he formed air quotes with his fingers, '*don't remember*? Or was it just not that memorable?'

Joel wiped his face with both hands as if washing it, got up, sat down again, and stared at Naomi.

Naomi smiled. 'No. It wasn't Luke.'

'Explain yourself,' Slevin said. 'I know it wasn't me, as far as I can remember. I'll have a fair guess it wasn't Michael and definitely not Joel.' He burped. 'Definitely. You said you were Catholic all your life. Who, then?'

'You're right, Slev,' Naomi said. 'I didn't use to believe in sex before marriage. So, Truth or Truth, my first time was with my husband.'

'You're married?' Luke said.

'Sorry mate,' Slevin said to Luke. 'Naomi has a secret husband, which makes you... Let's see. No, not an adulterer, 'cause that's her.' He counted to three on his fingers. 'You're *the other man*.'

'I didn't,' Luke mumbled, but no one paid attention.

'I'm a widow,' Naomi said. 'He was murdered.'

The fire sent a flare of sparks into the air.

'What the fuck?' Stella said.

'Truth or Truth,' Naomi said. 'Just playing the game. You asked. I answered. He's long dead.'

'Who killed him?' Stella said.

Naomi used a stick to upend a log, causing the flames to engulf it. 'The person who did it got sent to prison, but they escaped.'

'You're safe here,' Faye said.

'Yeah. Definitely safe.'

CHAPTER NINE

SIX DAYS BEFORE THE RECKONING

Luke's slightly sore head was reflected back at him in the weary, bloodshot eyes around the communal table, hollowed out of any joy, struggling against the harsh morning rays that shone through the east-facing door despite the beaded strings that curtained it. They were suffering badly, and Luke was grateful for his moderate intake of booze the night before.

Stella had made two pots of coffee and prepared their breakfast: a whole boiled potato each, cut in half, sprinkled with rough salt and eaten without cutlery. Sustenance. No one moved more than necessary, not even to swat the fly that buzzed around them, landing on Slevin's face, on Stella's shoulder, then on the back of Luke's hand.

Luke gargled coffee to wash away the tastes that rose up from the night's mild fermentation in his stomach. He hoped the lukewarm liquid would temper his breath, which smelled to his own nose like rotting fish.

They ate in a silence that was uninterrupted until, with sudden force, Joel's hand crashed onto the table in an attempt to flatten the fly, causing the plates and cups to jump and jingle.

'Ow!' Faye said. 'My head.'

'You missed,' Stella said.

'At least I got your attention,' Joel said. 'Decisions need making. We have to–'

'Can't it wait until lunch?' Stella said. 'Can't you read the room?'

'He can't read rooms,' Naomi said.

'Don't interrupt me,' Joel said.

Stella gave him an arm salute. 'Yes, sir!'

Joel stared at Stella. She glared back with a defiant pout.

'Look,' Joel said, his tone softer. 'I know it's a tough time, and we're all feeling a bit off, but we need to discuss how we carry on, so there's no anarchy. We have to be organised and disciplined.'

Michael ran his fingers through his hair, which was thick with sweat. 'Listen, mate,' he said. 'We're all sad about your mother, but nothing's changed with the day-to-day stuff. The commune will carry on. We'll vote on things, like before.' He shrugged. 'No anarchy.'

'You're a clueless, stupid child,' Joel said.

'What did you call me?'

Faye squeezed Michael's shoulder. 'He's in mourning, hon. Don't get upset.'

'In case you haven't noticed,' Joel said, 'after this breakfast, we have a few potatoes left, a little bread, less than a meal's worth of flour, one bag of sugar, some coffee and tea, and no more pension money.'

Slevin grinned. 'And five bottles of tequila. Just saying.'

'I have a fiver left,' Naomi said. 'We also need soap and tampons. And no, Stella, menstrual cups won't do it.'

'I have ten quid,' Luke said, following Naomi's lead.

A couple of others around the table offered their fivers. The total sum pledged was twenty-five pounds. Mindful of the rules, the commune's members had kept little money for a rainy day, or perhaps they were not willing to volunteer it.

Slevin shook his head. 'That'll cover the lady sticks and maybe a couple of days' worth of food for the seven of us if we go for flour, beans and rice. Not worth the trip. Anyone maybe under-reporting their treasure?'

The room was silent.

'We have to be smart,' Joel said. 'If we start growing veg now, we'll have some to eat in a few weeks. Until then, we need to forage: pick berries and mushrooms, make nettle soup, survive on what we can find. It's what we tried to do when we started here. We can do it again.'

'Yeah,' Stella said. 'That worked wonders then, didn't it? Anyway, Joel, no need to stress. There's fields and fields of food.'

'No one is going into Adrian's fields,' Joel said, 'and that's final.'

Stella crossed her arms. 'Says who?'

'I do. And if you don't agree with me, remember it was also my… my mother's wish. I'll draw up a rota.'

Stella stood, her eyes narrowed. 'Your mother's wish? Forgive me if I don't have the patience, but my head hurts, and no one wants to have this conversation now.'

'Some people are more persuasive when they're dead,' Joel said.

'This meeting's over,' Stella said. 'In fact, it never really started. We can discuss it later, when we're all a bit more with it.' She marched out of the roundhouse.

By lunchtime, Joel had pinned a new rota to the stained corkboard above the near-empty food boxes. In that day's column, under *Afternoons*, Luke and Joel's names were written next to *Foraging*. Luke wondered if anyone would pay attention to Joel's dictates.

There was no formal lunch gathering. Instead, a tray of sliced bread lumps was left on the communal table with a cup of olive oil and a ramekin of salt. A sign written on a torn cardboard square read *one and a half each (only)*. Commune members alternated between naps in their cabins and coffees and teas in the roundhouse, or in ones or twos out on the unkempt grass under the hazy sun. Naomi was absent, gone away into the woods. Luke sat on the mossy patch of grass at the front of their cabin, catching the occasional murmurs of speech: *Joel, Dorothy, food, idiot, sad, Stella, democracy, farmer.*

As the warm sun emerged behind a wolf-shaped cloud, Luke dozed off. He was awakened by a shadow that loomed over him. Joel was dressed like a survivalist in camouflage trousers and shirt, a khaki multi-pocket safari vest and a wide-brimmed bucket hat that was crumpled and had clearly seen better days. He carried a brown backpack. A sheathed knife dangled from his belt. The effect was like a mix between Bear Grylls and Winnie-the-Pooh, readying for an expedition.

Joel followed Luke's eyes and grinned. He did not seem like a son in mourning. 'It's an eighteen-inch Parang machete,' he said with uncontained excitement. 'I already had a collection, but this is new, a set of hunting knives I got from my aunt. They're excellent, excellent.'

Luke shuddered.

'Right, it's foraging time,' Joel said. 'You ready? Dress warm. We'll be away for a while.'

Joel led him to the nearest trail that did not require crossing the encampment's centre, probably wishing to avoid talking to anyone. *Not exactly Mr Popular*, Luke thought. *Not a prophet by anyone's standards.*

As they trekked through the woods, it occurred to Luke that

if Joel abandoned him, he'd have to find his way back to the camp. He tried to pay more attention to the path they took.

Unlike his gruff demeanour at breakfast, Joel was jovial and talked at length about plants and berries, but Luke couldn't shake off the feeling that his commune mate was putting on a show, and not a very good one at that. There was something not quite right about the way Joel looked at him, the way he kept touching the sheath of his blade, his eyes darting to Luke and then back. Or was it his fertile imagination again? He didn't know these people, other than a slightly closer acquaintance with Naomi. Dorothy was the one who brought him here, and Dorothy was gone. Could they decide by a count of hands to send him away? It was unthinkable, the prospect of going back, finding a job, living in a dreary bedsit somewhere until he remade his life, the anonymous loneliness of city life, and worse, much worse, if Karla and her family found him, which invariably they would: perdition and violence and harm. He shivered.

'Threats of violence are worthless,' she had told him once, 'unless you're willing to follow through. Believe me, I have eyes on you, and I have the resources. 'Til death us do part, remember, my lovely? 'Til death us do part.'

Luke forced himself back to the present. *I'm safe here. She can't find me.* Still, before catching up with Joel, he counted his fingers three times. Then he did it again.

They settled before a wild thicket to collect a crop of blackberries, spending half an hour, the result of which barely filled their Tupperware container. Luke's hands were purple with juice. Joel had a smear over his chin from his frequent bites for *quality control*.

'All right, that's enough for a little dessert,' Joel said. 'We'll get mushrooms, but not now. It's getting dark. We should have left earlier, sleepy head. Follow me. We've got some distance to cover.'

Joel marched at a steady pace, his steps determined, his eyes set forwards, not looking back at Luke, who followed a few paces behind. The canopy of trees became thicker, filtering the reds and yellows of an obscured sunset, then the remnants of fading light.

The path sloped upwards. Luke's damp shirt clung to his back as they climbed. His gut told him to be alert, that they were going the wrong way.

'I thought we were heading back to camp,' he said to Joel's back.

Joel stopped and looked back, his face unreadable. 'No time to explain. Sun's setting and then it'll be pitch dark. You're slowing us down, city boy. I don't want to have to wait for you, all right?'

Luke drew in a long breath, exhaled it, then nodded. Where was he being led? He matched Joel's stride and counted his fingers incessantly.

The woods thinned, then ended. At a fork in the barely visible path, Joel stopped briefly, pointed to the right and said, 'Synner's Crag cliff is that way. It's very muddy this time of year, and we don't have time anyway, but I wanted to point it out. That's where people end up if they don't behave. We'll take a left here. Keep up, yeah?'

The landscape before them was sloped and rugged. Boulders jutted from the ground like giants.

Luke looked at Joel's backpack as the large man marched ahead, feet stomping, knife tilting back and forth with every step. He stopped for a moment, pretending to tie his bootlaces, picked up a rock and hid it in his jacket pocket. Then he rushed to catch up.

At last, Joel stopped before a cave the size of an elephant, like a gaping mouth in the hillside. They were standing in a clearing at the cave's entrance.

'Wait here,' Joel said. 'You can sit.'

Luke did not sit.

Joel went into the cave. When he returned, he carried a large plastic box in his hands, on top of which lay a stack of chopped wood. 'We'll camp here tonight,' he said. 'That way, we can do some more foraging in the morning. More chance of finding mushrooms in this area. I'll build a fire. Watch and learn.'

'What is this place?'

'Synner's Crag Cave. We keep some stuff stashed inside. It's like an away camp. Sometimes all of us come here. Well, except for Dorothy. She doesn't like to...' He corrected himself. 'She didn't like the climb, and she complained about the sleeping bags. Too damp. Don't know what her problem was. They're perfectly dry when you fold them properly into the boxes and keep the lids shut.'

Joel built the logs into a misshapen pyramid, then tore some paper from a blue roll in the box, squashed it into a loose ball and placed it under the wood with a helping of dry leaves on top. He lit the paper with a match. It took three attempts and several more balls of paper for a smoky fire to start. Shadows danced at the cave's mouth, though Luke could see nothing beyond it other than utter darkness. He imagined a demon with fiery eyes emerging from the cave to claim them.

Joel sat in front of the fire and ordered Luke to do the same, as though commanding an underling.

'Don't sit so far,' Joel said. 'Come closer, so I can see your face. That way I can tell when you're lying.'

Luke shuffled forwards and noticed Joel had his hand on his machete's hilt.

'Closer, mate,' Joel said.

'What's this about?'

'You and I are going to have a little chat, like a personal Truth or Truth, and remember the rules, so you better cross your heart and hope to die.'

Luke put his hand in his jacket pocket and closed his fist around the rock he had hidden there. In what he hoped sounded like a lighter tone, he said, 'Isn't there a rule about drinking tequila when you play Truth or Truth?'

Joel shook his head. 'This one is going to be completely dry and completely honest. Do you understand?'

CHAPTER TEN

The small bonfire sent bitter smoke this way and that, forcing Luke to close his mouth and eyes whenever it blew at him, though the taste of charred wood still lingered on his tongue. Unseasoned wood produced thick, tarry smoke. It was one of the first lessons he'd learned at the commune. The cooking in the roundhouse was all done on a wood-burning stove with an inefficient chimney, and so they all smelled of smoke all the time. He wondered if, after a while, they no longer noticed it as he did. It certainly covered up some of their body odours, though not entirely. Luke had been alert to the natural smells of the people in the commune. As soon as he arrived, he decided it was best to leave his deodorant stick hidden in his rucksack. Fitting in was the priority.

'Truth or Truth,' Joel said. 'Now we play.'

Luke wet his lips and took his time, letting Joel's words hang in the air. His teaching days had taught him about bullies. Some were experienced tyrants who had mastered manipulation and knew the exact buttons to push to inflict the most misery, demeaning their targets with expert skill. Then there were amateurs like Joel who meted out their oppression through a vague bully's intuition, not entirely aware of the pattern they followed. Joel didn't seem like he could read others and only understood his own conventions. The best way to manage his kind was not to yield everything, to negotiate and use their own rules against them. But this strategy was risky. Amateurs could be unpredictable, especially when they were armed with a blade.

'If we play,' Luke said, trying to inject a mix of confidence and innocence into his voice, 'then I should be able to ask questions, too. That's the game, isn't it? The rules?'

Joel drew his machete from its sheath and plunged it with force into the ground before him. 'No,' he said. 'You know there's a vote coming. You do what I say.'

'You're threatening me with a knife, so I don't think I have your vote, anyway.'

'It's not a knife. It's a Parang machete.'

Luke found it hard to count fingers with one hand gripping the rock in his pocket. For the count to be valid, he had to touch each finger with his thumb, then the thumb with his index finger. He held Joel's gaze. 'A good point well made,' he said. 'Still, if you want to do this, we both play.' He readied his legs for a backwards scramble, but then thought, *It would be hard to run in complete darkness through rocky terrain.* No. He was done running. He would stand up and fight, rock in hand, machete or not.

Joel's lips parted slightly as he considered Luke's demand. His face was like that of an irritated child. He sighed, looked from his machete to his feet and then at Luke. He shrugged. 'All right, then. I'll allow it. Truth or Truth. Did you sleep with Naomi?'

'We slept in the same cabin.'

Joel huffed out a frustrated grunt. 'She cultivates your

emotions like they were her darling roses. Then she comes back with a scythe to reap them.' He made a reaping motion with his hand along his neck, tilted his head, closed his eyes and stuck out his tongue, playing dead. His words and overacted theatrics seemed rehearsed, not something he'd come up with there and then.

'Joel. I'm not sure—'

'You slept with her. I can tell. You have to be careful with these women.'

'These women?'

'Don't play dumb with me, Lukas. You know exactly what I mean.'

'My name is Luke.'

'Is it, though?'

With his free hand, Luke tugged on his ear and took a deep breath. 'Mate,' he said and looked straight into Joel's eyes, speaking with the authoritative voice of a teacher telling off a pupil who was out of line, 'what the actual fuck?'

Joel was silent for a moment. Then, he raised his palms. 'Sorry. I get inside my head sometimes.'

Luke struggled to contain a little smile that hid behind his lips. This small, assertive victory was new and not entirely about Joel. Distance from Karla had allowed him to lay a small foundation of confidence and rebellion. He tried to imagine her as a figment, a hallucination, something unreal from a life he no longer lived. He returned his focus to the smoky fire. Joel was the more pressing problem, and his knife had not yet been sheathed. The weather of his commune mate's emotions was unpredictable. He'd have to be careful.

'I swear. I didn't have sex with Naomi. I like it here. I'd like to stay. The last thing I want is to complicate things.'

'Why are you lying to me, Lukas?'

Luke took a breath. Maybe if he distracted Joel, he could

lower the heat and prevent the conversation from boiling over. 'I answered your question, truthfully,' he said. 'It's my turn now. Truth or Truth, Joel: why did you call your mother Dorothy, not mother?'

Joel pouted. Then his face cycled through several different expressions. 'I can't talk about it.'

Luke decided to take a risk. 'You know what everyone's thinking, right? After what you said happened with a family member.'

Joel's eyes widened. 'What? With Dorothy? Is that what…? No!' He kicked the ground, looked at his shoe as if it were someone else's, hesitated, then shook his head. 'No.'

A log crackled, and the fire's pyramid crumbled.

At last, Joel said, 'I know she seemed motherly to all of you, the great maternal leader, Saint Dorothy, but she never cared much about her own son. I read somewhere that love reveals itself in the little things, bothering to show an interest. I made my own lunch boxes. I had a key to a house that was hers, really, never felt like mine. I was an inconvenience, so I hid in my room. Or maybe she hated my dad too much to like me. Then, when I was older, other things happened, unforgivable things.' He hesitated, then quickly added, 'Not what you think.'

'Well, that's honest,' Luke said, thinking, *but is it?*

'Truth or Truth, Luke. Have you ever killed anyone?'

'What a question,' Luke said, then lied. 'Of course not. Truth or Truth, Joel, have you?'

Joel's eye twitched. His right hand reached for the machete's hilt and tightened around it. 'I did. We did. Didn't mean to. It happened so fast. You know what? I think that's enough games for tonight. Time for you to sleep.' He drew the blade from the ground.

Luke readied himself, his palm firm around the rock, every muscle in his body tensed, his head clear and alert. He could feel his heart thumping. A metallic taste like rust filled his mouth.

Calmly, as if he hadn't a care in the world, Joel cleaned the dirt from the machete's blade with the sleeve of his shirt.

Luke got to his feet and took a backwards step.

Joel looked up at him, his brow furrowed, the edge of his tongue showing through tight lips. Then, something seemed to dawn on him. 'You thought I was going to stab you?' He sheathed his blade and shook his head.

'Why have you brought me here?'

'You're here because I wanted to get to know you. Now that Dorothy is gone, it's only natural they'll look to me to decide things.'

'I thought this was about Naomi.'

'I forgive you.'

'You forgive me?' Luke said and immediately regretted it. He should have let things lie.

Joel was suddenly friendly, his voice light and calm. 'No, actually, I don't, but she'll cast you aside soon enough. I'm warning you, though, never lie to me again. Now, food and then bed. We've got some sleeping bags stashed here. I hope you don't sleepwalk. There's a deep shaft just inside the cave. It's like a hole that goes straight down. It's very deep. You fall, you die. Let's eat. We'll have half the bread now, and the rest will be breakfast.'

The sleeping bags were musty, but at least the ground was even and dry under the rock canopy at the cave's entrance. The night sky was clear and full of stars, the air cold and saturated with moisture. Moonlight illuminated the borders of the cave's mouth. Beyond them, there was only blackness.

'What's that sound?' Luke said. 'Like a fluttering.'

'Just bats, don't worry. They don't bite or suck your blood or anything. They never come near me when I sleep here. I guess if they did, worst case scenario is rabies.'

'Rabies can kill you if it gets to your brain.'

'Calm down, Lukas.'

'Just saying. So, you're interested in Naomi? Have you told her?'

Joel laughed, perhaps for the first time since they left the camp. 'Nah. It's not about that.'

'It's not?'

'The idea of the commune is that we're here together, living as a group, doing things as a group. Couples ruin it. Suddenly, you have people more dedicated to each other than the group. We already have Faye and Michael together, and everything feels different. It's such a shame.'

'What if they decide to stay and have children here?' Luke said.

'If there's a child, it should become a child of the commune, and we all get to raise it together. We can take turns looking after it when everyone does their chores. I don't think Faye and Michael will last, though. They'll be back in their old cabins soon enough. You'll see.'

'What makes you say that?'

'They think they're in love, but love is, like, temporary hormones. It spoils things, makes them harder. In any case, they're too different from each other. I'll make Michael see reason. He listened to Dorothy, so he'll listen to me. I'm the father of the commune now. It's my job to take care of them.'

'Really? That's how you think they—'

'It might take a little time, but don't worry, they'll see sense. They have to.' Then, in a formal voice, as if reciting a speech, he added, 'Communes aren't just a way to live. They're an ideology, best when they're pure. That's why we came here and started all this, Dorothy and me. That's what we're trying to build, a better way of life. Otherwise, it all falls apart. I promise you, Lukas, I won't let it.'

Luke scratched his left arm, which felt like it had developed a blotchy rash. *You'll convince them like you did me?* he thought, *with a machete and threats?* He made a point of yawning loudly. 'I think I'll go to sleep now. It's been a long day. Good night, mate.'

After the draining excitement of the day, Luke had no trouble falling asleep, his nose filled with the smells of smoke and the mouldy sleeping bag that Joel had given him. He dreamed of his trip with Dorothy and an imagined conversation that never happened. One in which he confessed to his crimes and the misery that followed. 'It wasn't my fault,' he kept telling her. 'I had no choice.' In the dream, Dorothy had left him at a service station. Her parting words were said in Joel's voice, 'You should be ashamed of yourself. There's always a choice. You should have stood up to her, not let her emasculate you like some wet rag. Are you a man? No, really. Are you a man? Someone like you could never join our commune.' He woke up startled. She was right. He should have stood up for himself. At the time, he was blinded by passion and then fear. Getting away meant he could see things more clearly. But seeing was not the same as doing. *One step at a time.*

A bleak, grey dawn was followed by feeble rays of sun. Luke got up and folded his sleeping bag. Joel was still asleep on his side, his thumb in his mouth. Luke stepped quietly to the cave's entrance and took a few steps into its shadows. To the side was a stack of firewood next to three large clear-plastic boxes containing camping equipment: more sleeping bags, two blackened pots, a folded tent, blue paper rolls, matches, a windup torch. To his left, he saw the deep, dark shaft that Joel had mentioned. He gave it a wide berth and took a further step inside. Under a rocky ledge, he spotted a single pink running shoe with white laces. Luke shuddered as he remembered Naomi's comment about Lilian. *Her trainers were all pink, but that was the only girly thing about her, like a statement to confuse the enemy.*

He lifted it, smelled it for no reason, then returned the shoe to the exact spot where he found it. Being careful not to make any noise, he stepped out of the cave and came to sit beside Joel, waiting for him to wake up. He wouldn't breathe a word about seeing the shoe, certainly not to the man with the knife.

CHAPTER ELEVEN

FIVE DAYS BEFORE THE RECKONING

Stella's stomach ached as though a clump of wool had lodged itself inside her gut. She recognised the sensation as worry rather than the result of meagre food and hunger pangs. After her wood chopping duties, she lay sprawled under the intermittent sun on what they called *the best grass*, a small square of lawn that Slevin had cultivated from domestic grass seed at the western end of the commune's clearing, and which he tended to regularly with their rusty hand-push lawn mower. This spot was mostly used by Stella, and she had come to think of it as her private retreat, somewhere to sit in peace when she felt antisocial. The others seemed to respect her claim and not bother her there, not even Joel.

Slevin approached, bottle of Budweiser in hand. The bottle had become a staple of commune lore. Slevin would fill and refill it with water, saying he liked to pretend he was drinking cold beer. It certainly looked the part that day, sweating droplets in the heat over the remaining shreds of label and glue. Stella suspected he sometimes spiked the water with tequila from their reserves. Maybe more than sometimes.

'*Bore da*,' he said.

'Don't,' Stella said. She knew he meant well, but it was usually Joel who greeted her in Welsh, intended as a kind of slight, the same way he used to copy Lilian's American accent. It riled her every time.

'Feeling edgy?' he said.

'Edge of a volcano. Might erupt.'

'Hungry?'

'More like the Hunger Games.'

He scratched his naked chest, looking uncertain. 'Full of clever comebacks today.'

She patted the grass beside her. 'Come, sit with me.'

Slevin folded his lanky frame into the lotus position next to her and took a sip from his bottle. He smelled of clean sweat, having bathed himself in the spring earlier. About time, too. He said nothing more and waited for her to speak.

Stella was grateful for his patience, for their unspoken understanding, and tried to organise her thoughts into something coherent. Unlike the rest of them, she'd experienced the angry recriminations that could escalate into nasty tit-for-tat warfare when a commune unravelled. She had grown up and suffered adolescence at the Chestnut Farm Collective in North Wales. In that commune, their 'family' of twelve off-gridder adults and four children lived in a dilapidated, always-freezing farmhouse in a lush, remote valley and attempted to survive on their own polytunnel produce, a small brood of laying hens and two underfed milking goats. At one time, there had been pigs and a dream of a cow.

After an especially grim winter, the collective's members reluctantly conceded that they needed a stable source of income to keep them fed. Stella's father volunteered to take up an insurance sales job in Penrhyndeudraeth, a town whose name, as an Englishman, he could barely pronounce. He'd spend his weekdays there, staying in a low-rent room at an old widow's house. Stella remembered her excitement when he'd arrive on Friday nights with supermarket bags of food and a plastic box of pick-and-mix sweets for the kids.

With the inflow of money, the collective found itself arguing over whether to save for a rainy day or purchase some solar panels to heat water and power some essentials. Maybe they could even have a laptop and dongle to connect to the internet. Battle lines were drawn, and Stella, twelve at the time, listened to the zealot Mairead, decrying the death of their purpose, the slippery slope down which they were sliding towards assured ruin. '*Off-grid* means just that,' she kept repeating like an excitable parrot. 'Before long, we'll have a television, and then what would be the point?' Over many nights of impassioned debates, voices were raised, and relationships grew bitter. One time, their weekly meeting nearly turned into a brawl.

The argument was swiftly resolved when it turned out Stella's father had used creative licence when he described his landlady as an 'old widow'. The widow, whose husband had died in a fishing accident a few years earlier, was young enough to steal her tenant's heart and the collective's only source of income. Solar panels were out of the question. Even so, the sediments of anger remained, and Mairead did not speak to Stella's mother for a month other than in occasional spitted words to liaise on chores and the preparation of meals.

Stella had pleasant memories from her younger years and bitter ones from the moment she was old enough to understand. Living so closely together with others created a cycle of tension that, like a weathervane, pointed at different members for their transgressions, depending on the way the collective's winds of grievance blew.

Roger and Nikki were incensed when Gary let the children go for a swim in the pond by themselves, including their own five-year-old, Rory. Mairead, who had no children of her own, had taken Gary's side. 'The collective's children,' she said, 'should be allowed to grow up organically, the way nature intended, not wrapped in cotton wool.' After several vocal and silent dinners, the tension died out, only to be rekindled when the fingers of blame turned to point at Stella's mother, Lorna. They called her lazy for failing to clean the chicken coop one morning, as prescribed by the rota. Everyone in the collective should pull their weight, they said, ignoring Lorna's constant slaving in the kitchen to prepare most of their meals.

On and on it went, the cycle, cliques and camps forming and dissolving, tempers flaring with misgivings about one person, then the next. Collective meetings were mostly used for talking. Listening had swiftly gone out of fashion at Chestnut Farm.

From what Stella remembered, it hadn't always been like that. There were good, idyllic years, jovial communal dinners made with eggs she herself had collected. There was singing around fires, Kev playing his acoustic guitar and leading them in out-of-tune renditions of *Hey Jude* and *Bridge Over Troubled Water*. There was joy and hope and a smug feeling that even the collective's children could sense and mimic: we've been lucky to escape the rotten lives that others *out there* are forced to endure. With hindsight, Stella thought that perhaps communes had limited lifespans – enthusiastic at birth and spiteful as they neared their ending.

By the time Stella was fourteen, the collective's good times were all but replaced by arguments and vicious whispers. Despite her mother's objections, Stella went to live with her father and his widow, enrolling in an actual school. This was a significant improvement, even though she had a target on her back for her thin nose and ginger hair and for her odd pronunciation of Welsh, which she had half-learned from her mother. When her school years were over, she escaped Penrhyndeudraeth as soon as she could.

After years of false starts, Stella settled into a stable

customer service job with Cardiff Council. Working to live in a city, at the beck and call of tyrannical bosses, was a level of drudgery she had never imagined for herself when she fed the chickens and milked the goats at the collective. Her nostalgia fought harsh battles with her less appealing memories.

At one of her many low ebbs, she saw a small internet ad seeking members for the Synner's Crag commune and applied with bated breath. As soon as she met Dorothy, she had convinced herself, *this time will be different*. After all, wasn't a commune's spirit the product of its members?

But now Dorothy was gone, and Stella recognised the familiar patterns she knew so well from her childhood. Joel was Synner's Crag's Mairead, wanting rules and regulations and a dogged pursuit of purity. Stella, like her mother, was the opposite. A good life was the purpose. A commune was a means, not an end. Live together, enjoy simplicity, contribute, share meals. Don't get too close. Don't have arguments. Don't be like that other commune, its members now disillusioned and dispersed.

Stella looked up at the cloudy sky, lost in thought. When she still said nothing, Slevin placed his hand on her shoulder and gave it a gentle squeeze.

She brought her fist to her mouth to muffle a sob.

Slevin gave her a sympathetic smile. 'Dry your eyes. We'll sort them out. Naomi and Faye will be with us. Michael does as he's told. What do you reckon to new guy?'

'I don't trust him,' Stella said. 'Something's off.'

'Oh no,' he said. 'You fancy him.'

'Shut up.'

'Worry not,' he said. 'Jealous Joel will probably kill him. He's got form.'

She shook her head. 'Don't joke about that. I keep thinking about Lilian. I can't sleep. If only we—'

He raised a finger to his lips to silence her. 'What happened, happened. Nothing we can do about it now. Let's take a breath and focus on the present, how things should work after Dorothy. The commune will carry on, and we'll make sure there's no weird changes or anything.'

She dug her fingers into the earth between the blades of grass. The soil was moist and cool. Mud lodged itself under her fingernails. 'Joel's going to be a pain,' she said, 'and I'm not sure about Luke. My gut says we should vote him out.'

'I can get close to the guy,' Slevin said. 'See what's what. Joel took him on an away mission, probably to recruit him to the dark side. Saw them come back. Luke couldn't get away from him fast enough, so maybe he's okay.'

She sighed. 'What do we do about Joel?'

'You want me to kill him? Any preference how?'

For the first time that day, she giggled. 'Only if we run out of food. By the size of him, we'll have plenty of Joel to go round, but I bet he tastes sour.'

'Just like chicken, I promise.'

Stella bit her lip. 'You know what my mother told me, the last time I saw her before she died? She said, "Do you really like living this lonely life in the city?" I was in Cardiff then, in a pokey flat. I told her it's better to live alone than be together at each other's throats, like her lot did at the collective. And look where we're at now.'

Slevin rubbed his hands together. 'I know what will make you feel better. A fat chicken from the farmer's coop. And that, m'lady, will taste *just* like chicken.' He held his smile firm for a moment, then frowned and looked at her, suddenly serious. He placed his bottle on the ground, pressed it down and turned it until its base was buried a couple of inches into the ground. 'Stell,' he said, 'look at me, not at your feet.'

She met his eyes and gave him a brief nod to go on.

'You know my story – what happened to me at the research station.' He took a deep breath, held it, then released the air with a whooshing sound. 'They underestimated me, thought they could lord it over me. When they were stuck in an ice crevasse and desperate for help, I rescued them, and still they treated me like shit. Well, they found out, didn't they?' He looked down at the sunken bottle. 'What I'm trying to say... I understand you're worried, but when it comes down to it, I won't take any shit from anyone. Not for you, not for me. I promise.'

'Good thing they all think you're a clown.'

'Yeah. Won't see me coming.'

Stella prised the bottle from the ground and took a long swig of water. No tequila, unfortunately.

'I'm serious,' Slevin said. 'Trust me. We'll sort them out, by force if necessary.'

Stella remembered her mother's indignant, angry complaints after she'd been accused of not pulling her weight at the collective. 'You know, Stella,' she said, her voice carrying within it a shade of unexpected darkness, 'if Mairead disappeared suddenly, for example, if she fell and broke her neck, the collective might survive this.' When she saw the shock on her young daughter's face, she quickly added, 'Of course, I wouldn't wish death on anyone. Forget I said that. It's unkind. We must never be unkind.'

'I'm hungry,' Stella said to Slevin.

'We'll go raid the fields as soon as it's dark.'

She smiled and raised the bottle for a toast. 'Skol, clown!'

Slevin met her toast with an imaginary tankard. 'What happened to that woman your mother hated so much? What was her name?'

'Mairead,' Stella said. 'She killed herself, two months after the collective dissolved. Hanged herself from a rafter with an extension lead.'

'Good for her,' Slevin said.

PART TWO

AND SO, IT BEGINS

CHAPTER TWELVE

TEN DAYS POST DISCOVERY

'Sit down, Mr Czerniak,' Sandra Saint-John said to the private investigator. 'All this stomping around is making me dizzy.'

'Call me Alex, please,' he said, still pacing the shaggy carpeted floor of her lounge. He wasn't sure how to broach the subject of payment. Dealing with rich clients was one thing – a sickly member of the ordinary bricks-and-mortar class quite another. He wished he hadn't come.

Alex's mother was a Polish immigrant who talked about money incessantly. Maybe it was the hereditary effects of the war, the fear of having none, or maybe her own mother was the same. For this conversation, Alex wished he could channel her fierce, direct manner. His last job, for five billionaires whose children had been kidnapped, had paid him well. So well, in fact, he'd thought he would never have to work again. But then came the purchase of the too-expensive house in Richmond, the extensive renovation project and, to his shock and horror, the oversight. He and Mary had forgotten to plan for the taxman. About half went to the state. Before long, the windfall from that lucrative job had dried out. Mary wanted to send the girls to a good private secondary and then a good university.

Sandra waited for him to complete two further laps. 'I thought what I offered was generous, especially the final bonus. It's a good sum, a very good sum. What seems to be the problem?'

'If I may be so bold,' he said and cleared his throat. 'I appreciate your generosity, but my investigation could take weeks, maybe months. As you've already explained, you have a cancer that, erm, well… It could end our arrangement early. It's uncomfortable for me to say this, honestly, it is, but I have children, bills to pay. I'm not a gambler. I should remind you that you came to me because of my reputation. My connections with the police and my sources are second to none. If you want the best private investigator, me, then we have to reach some kind of better arrangement. My fees reflect my reputation. I get results.'

Alex wiped his brow, unsure how well he'd delivered his grandiose sales pitch. He lowered himself onto the ragged chair opposite Sandra and smoothed the edge of its brown felt upholstery with his fingertips.

She leaned forward. 'Let me explain a bit more about the assignment.'

He knew this tactic. Draw the investigator in, whet his appetite with details until he became invested. Alex vowed to humour her but stand his ground. He discreetly pressed the *Record* button on his phone – insurance, to avoid arguments later.

'You want me to find out what happened to your sister, Dorothy,' he said, 'and the other members of…' he took out a little black notebook from his jacket pocket, opened it and glanced at the three circled words, 'Synner's Crag Commune. Odd name for a place.'

'When our parents died,' Sandra said, 'they left their grand house in Highgate to Dorothy.' She looked up as though she was calling on memories, perhaps of her younger years in that house. 'Our pig-headed father had a fixed sense of what a daughter's duty should be. He didn't allow you an inch left or right. So, you see, once I escaped my parents and got on with my life, I didn't want to subject myself to... Never mind. Over time, we lost touch. I don't think they liked me much. As you can probably tell, the feeling was mutual. By the time they died, the self-important toads hadn't heard from me in a decade.' She shrugged and brought her hands to rest on her knees.

'Okay,' Alex said, 'so Dorothy got the house.'

'And their life savings, which she threw away on the land for the commune. It could take years to resell that worthless plot of nothing. The house, on the other hand, I had it valued at five million pounds. Maybe more, if there's bidding.'

'But you came to me, so I assume there's some kind of problem. Aren't you your sister's only surviving relative?'

'The will is the problem. Dorothy left her entire estate to the members of that cunting commune. You would have thought the problem is nearly solved, what with most of them dead. The only slight snag is...' she pursed her lips, 'they didn't all go then and there.'

Sandra paused, and Alex realised he was holding his breath.

'Sorry, I'm not being unkind,' she said, not sounding in the least sorry. 'Every death is tragic and all that. Still, there's one member remaining, that Luke Bridestone, and he might just pull through. If he does, he gets to have it: a house worth millions from people he didn't even know. Just a random stranger, taking away my inheritance.' She scratched the protruding hairy mole on her cheek. 'And that, Mr Czerniak, will be an absolute travesty. Something needs to be done.' She bowed her head a little and looked up at him, her eyes narrowed. '*If* he survives,' she said slowly.

Her words hung between them like poisonous pollen in the airless room.

Alex shook his head. 'I'm sorry, madam, but I don't think I can take this assignment. I know PIs have a reputation for being ruthless and doing what it takes, but I draw the line at–'

She interrupted him with a stream of fake giggles that rolled from her mouth like an engine refusing to start. As she did so, she raised her hand and gave him a dismissive wave. 'If I wanted a hitman,' she said, 'I'd look in Directory Enquiries under H, not under P.'

Alex relaxed a little, but his guard was still up. His instincts told him to be wary of this woman. Still, she was a potential client. He pasted an understanding smile on his lips.

'I need to know what actually happened,' she said. 'My nephew, Joel, is also gone. I liked him, despite his strange… Anyway…' She exhaled a long sigh. 'This man in the hospital, I'd like you to find out his role in all this.'

With sudden comprehension, Alex knew what Sandra wanted. 'The forfeiture rule,' he said. 'I've had a case about that once. If Luke's a criminal, if he killed any of them, he can't benefit from their deaths. Your sister's last wishes then become obsolete, and you can inherit the house.'

Sandra rewarded him with an appreciative smile. 'Very good, Mr Czerniak. Very good. That's precisely the question I'd like you to answer. If that rule applies, if he killed even one of them, it can all go to me.'

'I only deal with the truth, yes?' he said.

'Of course, of course,' she said with an unconvincing shake of her head. 'The erm… truth, yes.'

He closed his notepad, clasped it between his palms and waited. Silence was his answer. Let her fill the silence.

At last, she spoke. 'I'm in part-remission. I hope to be here for years.'

'Forgive me, your… situation, it means you're a risk to take on, not just for me, but for any investigator. I'd like to help you, but the compensation needs to reflect... the uncertainty.' He looked at his briefcase. This job wasn't going to work out. Alex didn't like turning down a client, but he had to think of his family. 'I have two wealthy clients with cheating husbands who'd like to retain my services. Stakeouts could keep my team busy for weeks. To take on your case, I'll have to turn at least one of them down.'

She wagged a finger at him. 'You're very good at this, aren't you?'

'My mother doesn't think so.'

'I'm going to win this argument,' she said. 'I've decided you're going to work for me, and that's final.'

He clasped his hands and waited.

'I'll increase your bonus to £500,000 and give you a £30,000 retainer to start. There. Now, tell me the best investigator in London won't work for me.'

Alex kept his face neutral, or at least he hoped he did.

'In my condition and age,' Sandra said, 'financing is hard, but I should be able to release equity from this house, definitely enough to cover your bonus. My savings will take care of your retainer. I can get you the thirty thousand as soon as we start.' She raised her chin and looked at him triumphantly, as if she'd achieved some impossible feat.

Alex forced himself to hold her gaze. Half a million was an unheard-of amount to pay an investigator for a private matter by someone like Sandra, not super-rich by any measure. Even the original price they'd discussed was high to begin with, and he only wanted to increase it a little because of the risk that his client might die before he got paid. He never expected her to counter with these enormous sums.

'You must think I've lost my marbles,' she said. 'I can see it in your eyes. Why not use all the money I have access to now instead of paying you? I have no children to leave it to.

With the extra half-million, I could live it up like a duchess, right?'

'Of course I'm happy to take your money, but I won't pretend it hadn't crossed my mind.'

'I don't want to live like a duchess. I want to live like a queen. My parents' house is worth ten times more than what I can release from this one. Ever since my health improved, I got a glimpse of the possibilities, and I have bigger plans, much bigger. There's a luxury cruise ship only millionaires can afford, not half-millionaires. And then, I'd like to see the pyramids, sip a cocktail on a beach in the Maldives, charter a private jet to the south of France if I fancy it. The millions from that house are like a lottery win, my opportunity to live *the life*, for once. And my death, even if it comes early… it won't seem so much like a drag.' She reached for his hand and held it, her eyes pleading. 'Will you help me?'

'And if we discover the gentleman in the hospital isn't a killer?'

She let go of his hand. 'You'll still get your bonus. I guarantee it. As long as you find out what really happened.'

He couldn't shake the feeling that the generous payment was meant to dictate the result of his investigation. If that's what she thought, she was very much mistaken. Still, there was no reason to discuss it now. For a moment, he considered countering with a discount, a more affordable fee, but then he thought of Mary and the girls, of the possibility he'd be tied up in this case for weeks on end, with Sandra succumbing to cancer before he was paid.

'Thank you,' Alex said, keeping his cool. 'Guaranteed bonus. I'll put it in my contract.'

'Of course you will,' she said. 'One more thing.'

'Yes?' he said, thinking those *one more thing* statements, uttered just before he left, were often the client wanting to tell him how to do his job. They were usually wrong.

'If you're looking for a place to start,' she said, 'look at his background, this Luke. Aren't people drawn to those who are like them or the exact opposite? Dorothy was the one who recruited everyone to the commune. I'm pretty sure they'd be abusers like her ex-husband Jimmy, or victims like she was.' She shook her head theatrically. 'She did wallow in it well enough, the poor woman.'

He stood and nodded. Sandra was yet another client who watched true crime documentaries. 'Thank you,' he said. 'I'll get on it right away. I should have no trouble getting the inside track on the police investigation. We can use their information to widen our net.'

'Good,' Sandra said. 'The sooner you start, the quicker we'll get that bastard, thieving scum.'

'By the way, it was good of the lawyers to let you see your sister's will so soon. They didn't have to, considering you're not the beneficiary. You must have been very persuasive.'

'Nah,' she said, sounding less formal, like they were a team now. 'That wasn't necessary. Dorothy told me about her moronic plan as soon as she made the will, just before she moved to the commune. Even gave me a copy. Said it was to protect her legacy.' She shook her head. 'See how that turned out? Crime of the century. Some legacy, eh?'

As Alex shut Sandra Saint-John's front door behind him, he straightened his jacket collar and tried to contain his doubts. The pay for this case could be excellent. However, there was always a chance Sandra Saint-John wouldn't last long enough to make good on it.

He walked to the main road and hailed a cab. 'Met Police HQ, mate,' he said. 'Quick as you can.'

CHAPTER THIRTEEN

Alex sat patiently in his wife's Met Police office while a uniformed officer waited for her to read and then sign some forms. The place had that peculiar police smell, like old files and a whiff of cooking gas. Detective Chief Inspector Mary Czerniak was a busy woman, and Alex tried not to burden her at work. On this occasion, though, they were investigating the same case, the deaths at Synner's Crag. They could help each other. More likely, she could help him. He sipped on vending machine coffee in a polystyrene cup, its sharp acidity tempered only by a dusting of powdered milk.

'School run go okay?' Mary said, once the officer had left.

'Miss Baxter wanted a word.'

'Oh?'

'A girl in Poppy's class stole her pencil case. Poppy tackled her to the ground, arrested her and recited a full and proper police caution. Apparently, it was faultless.'

Mary rubbed her hands together. 'That's my girl!'

'When the teacher intervened, Poppy threw a skipping rope at her and shouted, "Taser! Taser! Taser!" Miss Baxter wasn't best pleased.'

Mary covered her mouth, overcome by a fit of giggles. She recovered and blew her nose on a tissue. 'You look a little stressed, hon. I take it you've met Sandra Saint-John?'

He nodded. 'Not my favourite client, but she'll pay well, if she survives long enough. Cancer, prognosis unclear. I guess you've spoken to her? You know about Dorothy's will?'

'My team conducted an initial interview to get a sense of her, so yes: Dorothy's will and the incessant finger-pointing at Luke Bridestone. Because of the money angle, we'll need to do a bit more digging, rule her out.'

'Her? Really?'

'She's a sickly woman, but you never know. Conspiracy? Sandra sent her nephew Joel a set of hunting knives. Dorothy visited her in London and took them to the commune with her. This only happened about a week before the bodies were found.'

'Sandra told you?'

'Probably thought we'd find out anyway.'

'Any progress on the bodies?'

'Ninety per cent identified. There were personal items in their sleeping cabins and the tent. All we're waiting for are some dentals and final DNA confirmations. Nearly there. I'll get you the list once it's conclusive.'

'Post-mortems?'

'Look at you, all business,' she said. 'I didn't even get a hug.'

'Here?'

'Okay, maybe not here.'

'I need to keep Sandra sweet.'

'How much is she paying?'

'A decent retainer and then half a million on completion.'

Mary whistled her astonishment. 'She wants you to find him guilty of something, doesn't she? Very badly. Forfeiture rule?'

He nodded. 'And if you find out Sandra's involved, could you try not to arrest her before I'm paid? Pretty please?'

'Alex!'

He shrugged and glared at the ceiling. 'For the benefit of the tape, I would never suggest my wife could be swayed by financial considerations. And she's got a lovely figure on her. And her hair's so soft.'

She looked at him thoughtfully. 'Maybe we need to put an officer outside Luke's room in the hospital. I know it sounds paranoid, but if Sandra's willing to pay you these ridiculous sums…' She picked up a pen and scribbled on a sticky note. 'Okay, so, post-mortems. We've had the results from the first one, Dorothy Saint-John. She was found buried.'

'Violence?' he said.

'I don't trust this pathologist. A bit sloppy. Unfortunately, he's all we have.' She rummaged through the pile of files on her desk, extracted a brown folder and leafed through it. 'There were signs of a blunt force strike to her back, like someone jumped on her and broke her spine, but that might have been post mortem. Inspection of her organs suggests the primary cause of death was a myocardial infarction, a heart attack, probably caused by the violence. Probably. We can't know for sure.'

'You're thinking Joel?'

'No evidence as yet, but it's early days.'

'A child's anger towards a parent… well, it can be brutal.'

She tapped her fingers on the desk. 'I'm not usually rattled, but this case… all these deaths. And none of it makes sense. We spoke to the farmer next door, Adrian Kyloe. Nice man, salt of the earth. Said he didn't have much contact with them, but from what he saw, the members of the commune seemed happy and normal. No tensions he was aware of. Someone's fuse must have blown.' She looked up from her desk. 'But Joel's not the only suspect. There are some other interesting characters in the mix, dangerous ones.'

'Oh?' he said.

'I'll give you the lowdown once we confirm their identities. Better you don't waste your time chasing phantoms. I know what you're like.'

He pointed at his chest and feigned offence. 'Me?'

'Workahol consumption is a leading cause of death in this country, more than murder.'

Alex brushed his hand over his wife's knuckles. 'I'll look into Luke first. You got anything on him?'

'Not yet. We've been focused on the crime scene and identifying the victims. Then, we'll have to notify the families. Well, officially. Some of them have already come forward. I really hate that part.'

CHAPTER FOURTEEN

FOUR DAYS BEFORE THE RECKONING

Breakfast was scrambled eggs with beetroot and spinach, alongside an apple each. Lunch was an even mightier feast, and Naomi couldn't resist a fresh strawberry before devouring the slices of fired aubergines and the thick stew of chicken, carrots and potatoes. She felt happy and contented. A full stomach would do that, especially after the meagre rations of the previous days.

Stella and Slevin's nocturnal tour of duty beyond Adrian's Wall had taken them to the fields, the orchard and polytunnels, collecting a hen and some eggs from the coop on their way back. A basket of celery, marrows and spinach promised more variety at dinner. The bounty on the lunch table yielded a series of delighted gasps and shrieks as each member entered the roundhouse.

Slevin genuflected, rotating his hand in a grandiose flourish to a round of applause from everyone. Everyone, that is, except for Joel, who looked like he was struggling with the effects of a mild laxative, keeping his arms crossed and his facial muscles tense.

Hunger did away with morality, though Naomi had no

issue with the venture to begin with. The farmer wouldn't notice the missing produce, but even if he did, it was only a tiny fraction of what his vast farm yielded. To them, it meant survival, a point brought into sharp focus by the previous night's soup of nettles, mushrooms, and the few remaining beans, floating like fish turds in the thin concoction. 'Flavoured hot water,' Stella had called it. It was consumed in sullen silence, except for Slevin's noisy slurps. Joel's so-called 'dessert', the few blackberries he'd collected with Luke, was hardly enough for a few tiny mouthfuls.

Naomi's only reservations about the previous night's mission were that Stella and Slevin had not thought to bring more. With seven mouths to feed, the remaining food could stave off hunger until the next day, which meant another trip to the fields and more risk. Before they went out again, she would have a word, maybe help them make a shopping list. They should plan what they needed and consider the kind of produce that would last longer.

But for now, Naomi was happy to eat. She passed the strawberries to Joel, who made a face as he took them, held them up, then placed them back on the table, a look of disgust on his face. He hadn't touched the food and restricted himself to the cold slop from the previous night's dinner. *Joel can suit himself, be as prissy as he likes. Starve, if that's what he wants.* Naomi would have liked to kick him in the groin once or twice, though court evidence suggested her actions were likely to be more calculated than that.

She stole a glance at Luke. *He should stop showing them his teeth with those forced smiles.* His insecurity unnerved her. What did Joel say to him when they were away? She remembered her first days at the commune, how she'd wanted to please everyone, to make sure they liked her. Luke, however, took this to another level. What was he running from that made him so desperate to stay? *Probably something mundane, like wage slavery or city living.*

She had tried to prod him, but he was guarded. *Maybe a mythical ex or nasty parents?* But there was help out there for people like him. He could talk to friends or even a professional. No such support was available to escaped murderers. They had to keep their counsel and fend for themselves.

She wished her crime was robbing a bank vault, her escape funded by gold bullion and bundles of tens and twenties. She'd go on the dark web and buy a fake passport, charter the yacht of a corruptible captain and sail to Tahiti, or past the Cape of Good Hope and eastwards, find a good base, bribe some officials and make a new life for herself. But Synner's Crag would have to do and, dramas aside, it was a good option for someone like her. And no, not in a million years could they send her away. She wasn't Damien or Lilian. If someone messed with her, she'd show them what's what. Prison had been a good training ground for actual violence. Her commune mates were all timid, whatever their veneers. She could crush them if she wanted to. Even the formidable Stella with her pretend toughness, or Joel with his entitlement and his bush knives and his Dorothy complex.

She stole a glance at Luke. Last night, she'd seen him undress to his underwear, his near nakedness showing off tightly defined abdominal muscles. She sensed he was reluctant, but was there any chance she could ask for a favour? She had an almost instinctive need to make the sign of the cross but then stopped herself. Any shred of her Catholicism was long gone. She picked another strawberry from the basket and bit into its sensual flesh, sending sweet, tangy juice onto her tongue. *Stop it!*

'I don't agree with this,' Joel said, abruptly ending Naomi's daydream.

Slevin picked a strawberry's green stem from his teeth. 'We know, mate. If you don't want to eat, don't eat. More's the pity for you, more's the food for us.'

Joel turned to Luke. 'It's stolen,' he said. 'You shouldn't be eating this.'

'Leave him alone,' Naomi said.

'It's not right,' Joel said and pounded his fist on his flat palm. He'd been pounding his fist a lot these days. 'I say it stops. We can live off our own food. Dorothy wouldn't have—'

'Well then,' Stella interrupted him. 'Instead of trying to put people off their food, why don't we put it to a vote?'

'No vote. You can't vote on the law. Theft is theft.'

'Thou shalt not steal,' Slevin said and started laughing, his giggles turning into a fit of hiccups.

Without warning, Joel lunged at Slevin, throwing him off his chair and onto the ground with a side punch. Then he jumped, belly first, on top of him, Slevin trying to fend off the barrage of blows. They fought on the floor, fists, teeth and hair, but Joel's heft and incandescent fury kept him on top. It certainly stopped Slevin's hiccup attack.

I think I'll just watch the show, Naomi thought, reaching for another strawberry. *It's a good thing Joel doesn't have one of his knives on him, though.*

'Hey, hey, hey, stop it!' Michael called out and rushed to separate them. Stella joined him.

Michael placed Joel into a headlock and dragged him backwards along the floor.

'Scumbag,' Slevin shouted. 'You pulled my hair, you wuss.'

Joel tried to escape Michael's hold and lunge again, his face erupting in crimson blotches of fury, but Michael didn't let up and tightened his grip.

At last, Joel gave up, his breath heavy, his arms slumped at his sides.

'You gonna behave, mate?' Michael said. 'If I let you go, you won't start again?'

Good for Michael, Naomi thought. Usually, he just observed and said little. *The boy becomes a man.*

Joel nodded, and Michael released him. He sat up, dragged himself away from the table and remained seated on the floor, leaning his back against the wall, panting, staring at them, his eyes moist and serious.

'You're right,' Stella said to Joel. 'This needs to stop. It's difficult for all of us without Dorothy, and we can't fight over every decision. Until things settle down, maybe what we need is a leader, just for the time being. Once we're back to normal, we can reinstate the old commune rules. Otherwise, it'll just be chaos. But it's not just you, Joel. You can't be the default. Any nominations?'

'It should be me,' Joel said. 'You know it's me.'

Without looking at him, Stella said, 'We're not a hereditary monarchy.'

Slevin got up from the floor, righted his chair and sat down, his palm on his cheek. 'I nominate Stella,' he said through a bloodied grin.

'Thank you, Slevin,' Stella said, feigning surprise but looking very much like she expected the nomination. 'Anyone else?'

Naomi saw through the set piece being enacted before her, but there was nothing for it. In the scheme of things, it didn't matter as long as the commune persisted. With Stella in charge, at least they'd eat well.

'You know I can get us through this,' Joel said. 'I was here from the start. If I'm in charge, we'll be ethical and do it right. What's the point of pretending we're self-sufficient and then be robbers? It's not a good look. A commune needs to act like a commune. Proper rules.'

'True to form, Mairead,' Stella said to Joel.

'What did you call me?' Joel said.

'Nothing. For a minute, I confused you with someone else.'

'What's your pitch, Stella?' Naomi said.

'We do what we need to survive,' Stella said. 'We're here to live, have fun, enjoy ourselves. Not starve like abandoned dogs.'

'Is that all you think about, fun?' Joel said. 'That's not a commune. It's bloomin' anarchy.'

'Hell, yeah!' Slevin said and clapped. 'Those in support of Stella, please raise your hands.'

Naomi saw the raised hands around the table: Slevin, Faye and Michael's, and joined in with hers. She could see where the wind was blowing, and it was out of Joel's sails.

'Who's in support of Joel?' Stella said.

Joel sat deflated on the floor. One hand rose: Luke's. *Well, that's a surprise.* Whatever else Naomi might have thought of him, he had the spine to show courage. Or reckless stupidity. She fancied him a little more.

'Motion passed,' Slevin said. 'All hail Stella.'

'Why, thank you,' Stella said. 'Joel, chill. It's all right. Nothing bad happened. Will you join us at the table, please?'

Joel shook his head. 'Don't play all benevolent with me, Mary Queen of Thieves.'

A loud voice roared outside. It was the farmer. Naomi shuddered. *Not this again.*

'Dorothy! Come out here! We need to talk, right now! Without your kids. You hear me? Come out!'

CHAPTER FIFTEEN

Stella made a point of taking her time, strutting to the door as if she hadn't a care in the world. Naomi had to give it to her: less than two minutes as leader, and she already behaved like one. Stella leaned her hand against the door frame, parted the beaded threads that shielded the door, angled her head and spoke with complete calm. 'Well hello, Adrian. It's so nice of you to drop by.'

'Where's Dorothy? She was supposed to come by the farm. She left me a note saying we were gonna sort things out.' He spat. 'You people. Nothing means anything to you, does it? Nothing. Where is she?'

'I'm afraid she can't talk to you right now. Whatever you have to say to her, you can say to me. I'm in charge while she's away.'

The farmer grunted, came to the door, and shoved Stella aside with a forceful hand. He looked in. His eyes surveyed each of them in turn as if to verify they weren't Dorothy. Then, his gaze landed on the baskets of fruit and vegetables, the bucket of plucked chicken feathers and their half-eaten lunch. His eyes widened. His mouth dropped open, baring big nicotined teeth. He exhaled an angry snort and took a further step inside.

'Can I help you?' Stella said, still standing at the door, her hands on her hips. 'You seem interested in our shopping. Would you like to join us for lunch?'

'Shopping my arse,' he said. 'I'd recognise my produce anywhere.' He spat at the floor. 'Lying bastards is what you are. Common thieves.'

'Meaning no disrespect,' Stella said, 'but an aubergine is an aubergine. Beetroot is beetroot.'

'You got yourselves a live chicken from the supermarket and plucked its feathers?'

The farmer was shaking now, his nostrils flaring. He reached back and drew a pistol from the back of his belt, circling it so it pointed at each of those seated at the table, then at Joel, who was still on the floor, then at Stella. Finally, he settled his aim on Luke.

'What's your name, pretty lad? You'll be first.'

'Luke. You want to kill me, go ahead.'

'I don't want to, but I will if you don't tell me the truth.'

'There, there,' Stella said, still cool as an ice lolly. 'I don't particularly like Luke. I mean, I don't know him that well. He's a bit slippery when it comes to…' she looked at Luke, 'loyalties. Still, there's no need to kill him, and there are six witnesses. You'll be growing lettuce in the prison greenhouse. I'm sure you don't want that.'

The farmer held his gun fast, still trained on Luke, but turned his head to Stella. 'You think you're so clever, don't you? I can make it so there's no witnesses. No one knows you're here. No one will miss you.'

'Dorothy will know,' Stella said. 'Or do you plan on killing an old lady too?'

Well played, Stella, Naomi thought. *Well played, but don't push him too far.*

'You know what?' the farmer said. 'I don't need a confession. You're guilty bloody thieves, the lot of you.'

'I object to your accusation, sir!' Stella said with a snarl, her accent ever so slightly more formal and English, as if she were playing a role in a period drama. 'We're no such thing. Now, please leave us alone and crawl back to whichever dung hole you came from. I'm warning you.'

The farmer turned his gun to Stella, came within a step of her and used the weapon's muzzle to lift her chin. 'You're a feisty one, aren't you?' With his free hand, he grabbed his crotch. 'Maybe we can come to some sort of arrangement, eh? You give me melons, and I'll give you my carrot and sprouts.'

'You should leave,' Stella said, her voice a crack less confident. 'You're making a fool of yourself.' Then, she howled at him with the entire capacity of her lungs, 'Leave!'

For a moment, the farmer seemed taken aback by her cry. He retreated a step and lowered his gun. Then he spoke to the room. 'Here's what's gonna happen, and thank your lucky stars I'm in a generous mood. You have exactly four days to clear off. On Wednesday, I'll be back, and I won't be so forgiving. In the meantime, I'll be patrolling the fields. I shoot vermin on sight, ask questions later. Am I clear?'

'You're very clear,' Stella said, 'and let me return the favour. You will leave us alone and never set foot here again. We did nothing to you. Your accusations are ridiculous, and this violence, it's... it's unbecoming. You will leave us be, you hear?'

'The fancy words of fancy ponces,' the farmer said. 'I'm sure your parents can feed you. That's not my job. Now, you have my terms. Can't say I didn't warn you. Make your last four days at Synner's Crag count. Either way, they'll be your last here. How it ends is up to you.'

The farmer turned to leave, and Naomi was about to

breathe a sigh of relief when Stella spoke, her voice confident again. 'I'm sorry, but we're not leaving. This is our land.'

Stupid sow, Naomi thought. *Can't she be quiet? Why provoke him?*

The farmer waited a moment, his back still to them. Then he turned to face the room. He took two steps forward, looked to his left, and his eyes met Michael's. He raised his gun, pointed it at Michael and pulled the trigger. The shot's sharp *bang* reverberated in the roundhouse. Michael looked down, on his face a mix of confusion and surprise. He didn't cry out but simply stared at the blood oozing from his thigh.

'No!' Naomi whispered. 'What the fuck?'

The expression on the farmer's face was strange, as if he, too, was surprised by his actions. He looked at Michael's wound and then at his gun, like he found it difficult to reconcile the connection between the two. He paused, shook his head, and swallowed twice. Then, he seemed to recover himself and puffed out his chest. 'Don't even think of telling the police. My brother works for the force, and he's very senior. If you try, it won't go anywhere. He'll tell me you grassed, and that, my friends, is going to be bad for you, very bad.'

By the time Adrian walked out, Michael had fallen sideways from the chair to the floor, his face ashen. Stella and Faye rushed to his side. Everyone at the table stood up, unsure of what to do. Joel remained seated on the floor, staring ahead.

'I'll get him,' Michael said. 'I'll get the bastard.' Then the delayed pain seemed to hit him like a mallet, and he groaned through gritted teeth. 'Ah! Ow, ow.'

'We need to stop the bleeding,' Faye said. 'We need to wrap it.' She held one hand to the wound to stem the blood and, with the other, touched Michael's cheek. 'Don't worry, baby. It'll be all right.'

'I wish Lilian was here,' Michael said through rapid breaths. 'Nurses are good at lying.'

'Get me a paper roll,' Faye cried out. 'Now!'

Naomi shuddered, shook off her shock, and sprang into action. She rushed to one of the plastic boxes stacked along the wall, threw off its lid, and hurried to Faye's side with a roll of the blue paper they used for the toilet. Then she moved the chairs out of the way to clear the area next to Michael and give Faye some space.

'There's no first aid kit?' Luke said.

No one answered.

'Here, baby,' Faye said. 'We'll stop the bleeding. You'll be fine. Just breathe.' She tried to compress the wound with a large ball of crumpled paper, but it quickly became soaked. Blood was still pouring out of Michael and onto the floor. 'Just need to stop the bleeding,' she muttered. 'Hold on, honey. Hold on.'

Michael took short, noisy breaths. He looked at Faye. 'Do you think we could have had babies? I would have loved some babies with you.'

Faye grabbed the roll of paper and started wrapping layer after layer around his thigh. 'It's fine. You'll be fine. I'll wrap it tight, and we'll get you to help. We'll have beautiful babies. I learned at school how babies come, and it's definitely not from your leg. You have to trust me. I got an A in anatomy.'

Michael smiled through the pain. 'You definitely get an A for anatomy, darling.'

'Humour,' Faye said. 'That's a good sign. Let me just finish dressing this, baby, and I'll explain about the birds and the bees. Naomi, can you get me another roll? No, two. Get more. Someone get me a T-shirt, anything we can use to wrap this.'

'I'll go,' Luke said and rushed out.

'I'm not stupid,' Michael said. 'We can't disinfect it properly, and there's loads of blood.' He turned to Stella as if their newly installed leader might have more conclusive answers. 'I'm going to die, aren't I?'

'Don't ask her,' Faye said. 'She's the bitch who got you shot. He should have shot her, not you.'

'She did?' Michael said, his eyes becoming distant.

Stella looked pale, struck dumb by Faye's accusation. *Quite right*, Naomi thought and shook her head. *Quite right*.

'Don't worry, sweetheart,' Faye said. 'You'll be fine. I think we've stopped the bleeding.' She looked up. 'We need to get him to a hospital. Slevin, get the car keys.'

'Are you sure it's a good idea to move him now?' Naomi said, then paused and turned to Stella. 'And the hospital will report it. It'll be all over the news. We'll be overrun.' To Faye, she said, 'Don't tell them it was a gunshot.'

'There's a fucking bullet hole,' Joel said. 'Of course they'll know it's a gunshot.'

'Shut your mouths, all of you!' Faye said. 'Just be quiet.' She looked up and spoke to the group. 'Keys. Now!'

No one moved. They seemed frozen in their places.

Faye's bloodied hands started shaking, and the vein on her forehead pulsed. When she spoke, her voice was cold and level. 'If the police come, they will arrest Adrian. He'll go to prison. We'll be able to stay here. Isn't that what you all want? I don't know why I even have to justify this. Get me the keys now! Now!'

Slevin looked to Stella, and she nodded.

'I'll help him look,' Naomi said.

CHAPTER SIXTEEN

Faye kept her bloodied hand firm on the coarse blue paper that was wrapped in layers around Michael's leg. As she applied pressure, she could feel his pulse thumping in beats. Thump-thump, thump-thump, thump-thump. Dark red blotches seeped through the surface of the makeshift bandaging. Not enough. She'll have to use more. Luke returned from his cabin with two white T-shirts. Faye wrapped them around the wound. They, too, became soaked.

'Michael, look at my face,' she said. 'Not down. At my face. I love you.'

He grunted through gritted teeth. 'You do choose your moments, don't you?'

Would it be so hard to say it back? The thought was selfish. She shook her head at her own neediness. She imagined him dying, buried next to Dorothy. Her throat constricted. It was difficult to breathe. Over and over, despite herself, she couldn't help but picture a funeral and the words she would say. *I'd only just found you, Michael.* Her entire imagined life would break without warning, and with it the dream of giving birth in their bell tent. She knew being broody so young was unusual, but both she and Michael were meant for each other. No question about it. Their child would have been a happy little girl – in her dreams, it was always a girl – in a cute floral dress with Faye's hair and Michael's deep brown eyes, blowing raspberries at nothing in particular at the roundhouse's communal table, or sitting between her parents in front of the bonfire, clapping her tiny hands as they sang. She tried to curtail the incessant thoughts, tried to wish him well again. *We'll look back on this time and reminisce about how bad it was and how it all turned out okay in the end. Please!*

With her free hand, she cupped Michael's cheek and looked into his deep, lost eyes. They were barely focused. 'It's all right, baby. We'll get you to a hospital. It's only a leg wound. It's treatable. You'll be fine, I promise.'

She looked down at his thigh. Blood was pooling under it. The exit wound. He was bleeding from two places, and whatever she tried wasn't enough. 'Where are those keys?' she shouted. 'We need to get him out of here!' She reached for another roll of paper, frantically wrapping more and more over the bloodied T-shirts. *It's not working. I don't know what I'm doing. Maybe I should apply more pressure? It's a mess now, such a mess.*

'Slevin's on his way,' Stella said. 'He's coming. Then we'll carry him to the car.'

Faye squeezed Michael's hand. It was clammy.

Slevin entered. 'No keys,' he said. 'Naomi and I searched Dorothy's cabin, all the usual places. They're gone. Luke, you were with her in the car. Any ideas, mate?'

Luke took a moment to think. 'We got out of the car. She locked the doors. Then... then she put them in the pocket of her coat, the parka. Maybe they're still there.'

Joel chuckled like a deranged idiot. 'She took them to her grave.'

Faye's head was spinning. Her nostrils flared. She hissed at Joel. If she were not holding the bandaging on Michael's leg, she would have lunged at him, throttled him, squeezed until his eyes popped out. 'I hope you rot in hell,' she said to him. Then she spoke to the room. 'We have to dig her up.'

Joel was on his feet in a flash. He crossed his arms. 'No one is letting her out.'

'Shut up,' Faye said. 'Slevin, please!'

'Not going to happen,' Joel said.

'Stella?' Faye was now pleading in a high-pitched cry. 'I'm begging you. Help him. Please, Stella.'

Why are they even thinking about it? Why are they wasting precious time?

Stella half nodded. 'Let's go. Let Faye look after Michael. The rest of us will sort this out.'

Joel glared at the room but left the roundhouse, saying nothing, his eyes narrowed as if preparing for a showdown. The rest of them followed.

The roundhouse became quiet. *Quiet as a grave*, Faye thought, despite herself.

Michael's lips moved. Faye hunched forward to hear his whisper.

'Water,' he said. 'Water, please.'

Faye wrapped more paper around his thigh, the red stains slower to permeate it now. *Have we stemmed the bleeding?* She touched his forehead. It was cool and damp. His eyes fluttered.

'I'll be two seconds,' she said, then rushed out with a jug.

The thumb tap on the tank yielded a painfully slow trickle, and Faye wished the water would fill the jug faster. In this moment of forced contemplation, she looked up at the bright blue sky. The sun was shining with not a single cloud to shield it. She lowered her gaze to the treetops and then the camp itself. Not even a wisp of wind passed through the perfect silence. Not a single bird chirped. Complete and utter stillness and striking bright light. A vacant world. She longed to get back to Michael, but a part of her now willed the water trickling into the metal jug to take its time. If she didn't face Michael, if she didn't see the blood and his pale, fallen face, maybe the horror wouldn't be real, just a bad dream she could wake from.

She imagined herself waking next to him in their tent, the morning sun heating the canvassed interior. 'Good morning,' he would say to her, his voice hoarse from sleep, his head raised as he gave her the first angelic smile of the day. 'Sleep well?' Then she would say yes and not mention the nightmare, the awful events that made her wish she'd never dream again. Michael would wear his ripped jeans and the stained grey T-shirt he loved so much with the inscription *NASA* over its front, and she'd wear her comfy sunflower dress, and they'd walk over to the roundhouse for breakfast, holding hands.

Her escape to pleasant thoughts was interrupted when she thought she heard a sound. Footsteps? Were they back already? Did someone find the car keys elsewhere? She looked around for movement. Where had it come from?

Then, *thwack!* She jumped back in fright. A rock had hit the water tank, the resulting thud so loud in the silence, it sounded to her ears like a firing cannon. The surprise caused her to stumble and fall, losing her grasp on the jug, which was now on the ground, its contents spilled to form a muddy puddle.

Faye picked up the empty jug, stood, and scanned the camp. She could see no one. *Who would do such a thing?* She had to get back to Michael, but he needed water. She placed the jug under the tap and pressed the thumb tap again, her eyes flitting from one side of the camp to the other and back. The trickle of water was even slower now.

When the jug was a quarter full, she thought she caught a glimpse of someone in the corner of her vision. She turned her head and, for a moment, thought there might have been a figure at the edge of the clearing, behind their bell tent, running into the woods. The sun's bright rays obscured her line of sight. She couldn't tell for sure who, or what, it was.

The water in the jug will have to do, she decided, and rushed back to the roundhouse.

Michael was barely conscious. He was trying to speak, the look on his face urgent, as if he had something important to tell her.

'What is it?' she said. 'Here, I got you water. You've lost a lot of blood. You need to drink.'

She filled a cup with water and tried to hold it to his lips, but he turned his head aside, still mumbling, his words incomprehensible, 'Th... Th... Came... Heah...' He looked frightened.

Faye smoothed his hair and checked the room around her. Something was out of place. Something had changed. She racked her brain and looked again. Then she saw it. While she was away, a chair had been set next to Michael, as if someone had moved it there to sit beside him. She'd been so frantic to get back to him, she hadn't noticed it at first.

Michael was no longer mumbling. There was no time to dwell on who had come into the roundhouse while she was away or who might have thrown the rock at the water tank. Faye tried to offer Michael the water cup again, but by now he was barely able to open his mouth, let alone drink. She wet the end of her hoodie's sleeve in the jug and squeezed water drops into the small gap between his lips.

'Stay with me, baby,' she pleaded. 'Stay with me. We'll get you out of here. We'll get you to help, I promise.'

CHAPTER SEVENTEEN

By the time they had gathered the two shovels and reached the site of Dorothy's grave, Joel was standing before it, his back curved like an angry cat's, the hunting machete in his hand, its blade pointing forwards. Luke stood a pace behind the rest of them and observed, unsure how the tense stalemate could be resolved.

'I'm warning you,' Joel said. 'No one comes near her.'

'What's your problem?' Stella said.

'What's *my* problem?'

'That's what I asked. She's dead, Joel. If she was alive, she'd want us to get the keys and help Michael. He could die. Do you want that on your conscience?'

'She always puts the keys in the basket next to her bed,' Joel said. 'They're not in her pocket.'

'She didn't this time,' Stella said.

'You didn't look hard enough.'

'Slevin and Naomi both searched her cabin,' Stella said. 'They weren't there. Maybe you'd like to go and look for yourself?'

'Nice try,' Joel said. 'Nobody moves.'

'I'm just going to come closer,' Stella said, 'so we can talk like grown-ups, okay?'

He seemed to hesitate, and Stella took a step towards him.

Joel shook his head. 'Not gonna happen, Stella.'

'Why this sudden loyalty?' Stella said and took another step. 'You didn't like her when she was alive. You didn't even call her *mother*. Now she's dead, you're the devoted son?'

Joel imitated Stella in a shrieky juvenile tone, 'You didn't even call her *mother*.' Then, in a loud voice, bitter and sharp, he added, 'You all keep saying that. You sound like a broken record. It's boring. Don't you dare come closer.'

'It's not love, is it?' Stella said, still taking slow, careful steps forward. 'It's something else.'

Joel nodded, seemingly unaware that he did.

Stella was nearly upon him. 'It wasn't your fault,' she said. 'You were young, I'm sure. Whatever happened, it wasn't your fault.' She raised her hands to him, palms open. 'Let us get the keys. She's not coming back. We'll bury her again straight away. Think of Michael. We've got to help Michael. There's no need for you to be here.'

Joel raised his knife in the air in warning. If he slashed forward, he could stab Stella. Luke worried things could quickly go from bad to worse.

For a breathless moment, nothing happened. Stella and Joel looked each other in the eye, in a hostile standoff. Neither of them moved.

Surprising even himself, Luke spoke, his voice raised as if speaking to a class of pupils. 'Remember what you told me at the cave, Joel? You said you had to be the father of the commune now, that it's your job to take care of us.' He didn't look to see the effect of his words on the others and hoped they wouldn't laugh at Joel's ridiculous statement. 'Michael is one of us,' he said. 'Would you really leave him to die? His life is in your hands now, yours and no one else's. You can save him.'

Joel's left eye twitched, and his face softened a little. 'I don't... I don't...' he said, unable to complete the sentence.

'It's all right,' Stella said. 'You don't have to be here. It's all right, Joel.'

With the knife still in his hand, Joel fell to his knees, his head bowed. He started crying, the wails of a boy, emerging from deep within him. Tears and snot covered his face.

Stella came to stand beside him and patted his head as you would a pet's. With her head, she signalled to the group to bypass them and approach the grave. She caught Luke's eye and gave him a nod.

Luke and the rest of them gave Joel and Stella a wide berth and took the shovels to the graveside.

Joel stood, his head still bowed, not looking at them. Then he sheathed his knife and walked away into the woods.

Slevin turned to Luke. 'Dude, did he really say that?'

'That, and a lot more besides,' Luke said.

'Jesus,' Slevin said and shook his head.

This time, no one objected to Luke digging alongside Slevin. Naomi and Stella stood by the graveside, hands on their hips, their faces sombre, not speaking.

They dug silently, the mound of earth beside the grave rising like a dark reflection of the hole it came from. As the excavation grew deeper, without saying a word, they both slowed the rhythm of their shovels, conscious they were getting close. Luke shuddered at the thought of his shovel hitting Dorothy's body. When Slevin found a patch of coat, Dorothy's left sleeve, they abandoned the shovels, instead pushing earth with their bare hands towards the location of her feet until they unearthed her upper half and with it the muddy parka. Neither dared move the cloth that lay over her face. Luke noticed an earthworm by her ear.

Luke left it to Slevin to check all of Dorothy's pockets, the parka, her trousers, her shirt, then check them again. They looked at each other, and then Slevin looked up at Stella and Naomi. He shook his head.

'We'll head back,' Stella said. 'You okay to cover her?'

After the two women left, Slevin searched Dorothy's pockets one last time and ran his fingers through the earth beside the pockets in case the keys had fallen out. It was strange to think that they were standing over her, a person. Luke didn't know how he felt, except that he was cold and muddy and drained to his core. But then he thought of Michael. How bad was it? If they didn't get him to a hospital, would they be able to stem the bleeding and avoid infection? What would happen to them if he died? Will the slogans hold: dust to dust, the circle of life, nature's course? But gunshots weren't part of nature's cycle. And what about the farmer's threats? *One problem at a time*, he decided. If they all left, maybe he could pretend to leave and then stay. The cave could be a good option. *Thank you, Joel, for showing it to me, despite all the weirdness.* Maybe he could live there on his own, picking berries and mushrooms, perhaps a little from the farmer's fields. Be a wild man. Be a safe man. It was not an unappealing plan.

'I heard you ask, mate,' Slevin said, as he and Luke shovelled earth to cover Dorothy again.

'What?'

'I always thought we should have a first aid kit,' Slevin said. 'No way to sanitise or dress wounds. There's such a thing as being too close to nature.' He looked down at the half-refilled grave. 'Dorothy was usually sound, but every time I asked her about getting a kit, she said she would, but never did.'

'What about tequila, to sanitise?' Luke said.

'Maybe,' Slevin said, then shook his head, 'I don't think sanitising will be enough now. Not when he's lost so much blood.'

'Can't we hot-wire the car and get it to start?'

'I wish,' Slevin said. 'It's got an immobiliser. No chance.'

When they were done, they said a clumsy goodbye to Dorothy but stayed at her graveside a little longer. It seemed like the decent thing to do.

CHAPTER EIGHTEEN

Michael was no longer responsive. Judging by the amount of blood that had pooled on the floor, Naomi did not rate his chances. As she looked down at his listless body, she felt the dark edges of grief tighten her chest and shorten her breathing. She liked Michael, the least complicated member of the group. He and Faye seemed like the only ones among them who'd joined because they wanted to live in a commune, not because they were social rejects, on the run from their lives. Them, and Dorothy, now sadly gone.

Michael always had a friendly smile for Naomi, given freely, wanting nothing in return. In truth, she wouldn't have minded if he had wanted more, but he was dedicated to Faye. This hadn't stopped her admiring his Herculean figure as he chopped wood or fixed a roof or dug holes in the hard soil to anchor the last cabin they built a few months back, his sweaty top clinging to his chest, his bulging biceps barely contained by his sleeves. He was Naomi's definition of manly. As manly as Luke, but that one seemed like a non-starter. Even now, with his face dripping wet and his pale complexion, Michael still looked sweet: the face of an angel, the body of a warrior.

He won't last the day, she decided. There was nothing for it. An ambulance crew wouldn't get to Synner's Crag in time. If the police got involved, they'd interview them all and ask questions. If she made a run for it before they arrived, they'd still know she'd been there. Dogs and drones and roadblocks. It was only a matter of time until she found herself handcuffed in the back of a police van, returned to walls and razor-wire fences, tiny cells and meals of soggy pizza slices on lukewarm chips, or rice with an approximation of a curry. Above all, losing hope for years and years to come. They'd never again let her anywhere near an opportunity to escape. She'd be done for.

It can't happen, she thought. *I'd rather die.* Some prisoners acclimatised to the smelly, hollowed-out-soul experience of being locked up. Some even relished it, especially hardened criminals who'd spent spells in and out of captivity from an early age. Prison felt like home to them, a familiar place with predictable routines and the occasional excitement of violence or even a riot. Not Naomi. For her, every day behind bars was an excruciating form of torture. *Never again.* Her most vivid nightmares made her relive the cruelty of her nightly confinement in the cell, the stench of the toilet like rancid lemons, the lump of disgusting dinner still weighing on her stomach. She'd catch her breath and stare into the eternity of time ahead of her.

A month before she escaped, Naomi had tried to kill herself. It was a rational, well-balanced decision. Ending it was better than carrying on. She waited until the prison's halls were as quiet as they'd get. Then, she brought out the contraband razor blade that was lodged in the sole of her shoe and made a deep cut to what she hoped was an artery in her leg. It's possible wrists would have been a better choice, but she didn't fancy the cliché. As a trained project manager, she felt compelled to account for contingencies. If she survived, she didn't want the telltale marks on her wrists to give away the obvious story. She later reflected that this was a serious flaw in her plan: believing in the possibility of failure.

The unsuccessful attempt had left Naomi infuriated and more rebellious than ever. Her original crime, such as it was one, should have earned her a medal, not a life sentence. Still, nobody cared, and nobody visited. Since her incarceration, she'd received no letters, no phone calls, no interest or concern. The jury of her family and friends had been as harsh as the one at the trial. She was dead to them, and so she tried to make the figurative expression literal. *I'll make myself entirely dead. They might even get off their high horses and come to my funeral.*

As it turned out, her failed suicide attempt had turned into a blessing. It bought her a few days in a hospital and the opportunity to flirt with the guard assigned to her on the final night before her scheduled transfer back to C Wing. The pot-bellied man was giddy after winning £500 at the races and trusted his luck was holding firm that day. After a snog with an implied promise of more, he took off his jacket and went to fetch her a sandwich from the vending machine. The jacket held the key to her handcuffs and his wallet. Naomi appreciated him for being a textbook fool, though the vanilla taste of his vaper's tongue lingered on hers as she freed herself, stole clothes from another patient's room and then used the cash winnings in his wallet as her getaway ticket. The news reported that the guard had lost his job for dereliction of duty. She didn't feel sorry for him.

They will never again get their filthy paws on me. Not a chance in seven hells.

Joel walked into the roundhouse. 'I'm sorry about earlier,' he said to Stella, almost casually, as if it were a small spat not worth dwelling on. 'How's he doing?'

'We didn't find the keys,' Stella said. 'I don't know where they could be.'

'I told you not to dig,' Joel said.

Faye was becoming more frantic, her eyes darting from Michael's face to the bloody mess of paper and T-shirts bandaging his thigh. Her hands trembled, as did her voice. 'I'm going to run to the road and get help. It's the only way to save him. I'll stop a car and get them to call an ambulance.'

'That road leads nowhere,' Naomi said. 'It doesn't see a car for days.'

'I have to try. I have to. Or I'll get to the houses near the bus stop and knock on doors. We can't just wait and let him die.

'It will take you hours,' Naomi said. 'Don't you want to stay with him?'

'Will you run instead?' Faye said, then looked around. 'Any of you?'

No one met her desperate, imploring eyes. Naomi's words had had the desired effect. It was pointless. Could Faye not see it was a waste of time? Hours and hours would pass before anyone could reach them. Michael would be long gone.

Faye rasped in frustration, and then her expression changed. Her eyes were filled with a renewed purpose. 'Stella, here, hold the bandaging, tight as you can. I'll get help if it kills me. Hold on, Michael. Please, hold on for me, baby.' She smoothed his hair and kissed him on the lips.

'I'll go let the boys know,' Joel said, looking uncomfortable. Why he had to tell Luke and Slevin about Faye's decision was unclear. He was probably just looking for an excuse to make himself scarce.

As soon as Stella took over, kneeling by Michael's side, Faye sprinted like a startled deer out of the roundhouse, her hands still bloodied. She looked determined, unstoppable, running for Michael's life.

Love, Naomi thought. *And decency. What a pity. What a shame.*

'Just going to the loo,' Naomi said. 'Be back in a sec.'

CHAPTER NINETEEN

Naomi made a brief stop in Joel's cabin and selected a bush-knife from his collection, which she tucked into the waistband of her trousers, the hilt hidden under her T-shirt. The sheath felt tight against her skin, and she adjusted it to her side, so it wouldn't slow her down. She looked around, checked that no one was watching, then rushed to catch up with Faye.

The trail was muddy, and the vegetation overgrown. Naomi wondered how long it would take Faye to reach its end, where the path met the dirt road. It was better to tackle her while she was still in the woods. Less exposure was safer, even if the likelihood of anyone seeing her was small.

Naomi dreaded what she had to do. Michael was as good as gone. There was no point in all this running and trying. If Michael couldn't be saved, why sacrifice Naomi as well? They'd lock her up and throw away the key. Faye didn't know any of this, of course, but she had left Naomi with no other option, none. If only there were another way. If only. It couldn't be helped.

I'm so sorry, Faye, she thought. *You should have stayed. This mission you're on, it's hopeless.*

The act of killing was not something Naomi considered lightly. Criminality was not written into her life plan. Quite the opposite. After graduating with a first-class degree in computer science, she quickly landed a well-paid job at a trendy Hoxton web agency. Her tiny flat on a leafy street in Islington contained lava lamps and a galley kitchen and house plants. She'd go on first dates in the quirky independent café with the '50s theme that served responsibly sourced drinks with the option of soya or cashew milk. For second dates, she'd always suggest Thai. After years in the insipid shallows of the dating pool, Des came from the deep to snag her. He was everything she had dreamed of: a handsome, successful accountant with a slightly crooked nose, bright-red designer glasses, a dashing beer belly and wide shoulders.

The first dance at their wedding was one of her last happy memories. Des had been sweet, caring and supportive – a great catch, everyone said. It was only much later, ruminating the night away on the sweat-soaked sheets of her prison cell bed, that Naomi realised how her life had seamlessly mutated from one worn cliché to another.

Within the first month of their marriage, the jealousies began. She came home after work, and Des asked her where she'd been.

'I went out for a drink with the guys from the office,' she said. 'I only stayed for one.'

'I can smell his stink on you. Who was he? I want his name.'

'Des, I would never–'

'Liar!' he growled at her in drunken anger. That was the first time he hit her, a stiff-handed slap in the face and a punch to the gut. From then on, she always kept ice in the freezer and ibuprofen in her bedside table drawer. She'd try to get home early, before his drinking turned suspicions into fury.

Afterwards, he'd apologise. He always apologised. 'I'm

sorry, No-na,' he'd say in sober morning-after regret, using the pet name that made her cringe. 'It's like something gets hold of me when I drink, and I get so angry. It's not who I am. I'll do better, I promise. I won't drink as much.' His avowed moderation never lasted the week.

At first, she tried to forgive him, to understand. People were complicated, and alcoholism was an illness. She loved Des. Together, they could work this out. Unfortunately, sober Des proved more loyal to his drunken self. 'I love you so much, No-na,' he'd say. 'Please, don't tell anyone, or things could get worse. My anger, it's… Anyway, it doesn't happen too often, does it? I'm cutting down.'

One time, she had called the police. The Met officers who came, two men, showed no interest. They took some details and left after Des told them it was just a domestic argument, nothing more. The coppers seemed more eager to listen to him than they did her. He appeared reasonable when he wanted to, a decent man with an unhinged wife.

'I'm sorry we wasted your time,' Des said as he showed them out, somehow faking sobriety. 'I'm sure you have better things to do than blue-light to a couple's home just because she's upset he didn't stack the dishwasher the way she likes it.'

The final straw came on a stormy October evening. Naomi got home late after a longer day than most. A project she was managing had been delayed because of a mistaken server setting on her team's part. The client wasn't happy. After she dealt with a protracted Zoom call featuring a group of furious faces, she stopped at a small café on her way home to calm herself with a latte and chocolate muffin.

When she got back to the flat, Des was sprawled on the sofa in his blue gym shorts, cradling the iPad, an empty vodka bottle discarded on the carpet next to him. Naomi realised with alarm that he had the Maps app open.

'Whose house did you stop at?' he demanded.

'You're tracking me?'

He slapped the iPad on the glass coffee table and pointed at its screen.

Her ordeal left her curled up into a ball on the bathroom floor, where Des had locked her for the night. *That'll teach you.*

She waited three days to exact her revenge and had planned it to the most minute detail, utilising all her skills as a project manager. This was also her downfall. The jury was not convinced she had acted in self-defence. In their eyes, the delay and meticulous planning were the marks of premeditation. Even before the verdict, she could see the questions in their eyes: why didn't she escape? Why didn't she go to a shelter? Why didn't she simply move out and divorce him? All good questions, for people who don't understand.

On the night of his death, Naomi made sure Des knew she'd be home early to make them both dinner. The day before, at work, she asked Adam for some ketamine. Adam was a regular clubber and talked freely about getting high with the horse-tranquillising drug. He was thrilled that she'd asked and only took a day to deliver it to her. He was like a missionary, recruiting others to join in on the fun. He gave her a gram in a small plastic pouch of off-white powder.

'This one's on the house,' Adam said, 'but be careful. Don't take too much. Otherwise, you'll go into a K-hole and won't be able to move, or worse. A dab is all it takes, nothing more. Promise me.' Adam ended up a star witness at her trial.

Naomi had originally intended to mix the drug into a tub of Ben & Jerry's cookie dough ice cream, Des's favourite dessert. However, despite the poetic appeal of this plan – revenge supposedly best served cold – she was uncertain how well the melted mixture would refreeze. It might just look too lumpy to be eaten. Instead, she baked it into a steak pie and served it with chips and a large dollop of ketchup, just the way

Des liked it. He arrived home after a stop at the pub, smelling of booze.

'I love you, Des,' she said, while he was eating the pie. 'And I'm sorry.'

'You're my world,' Des said. 'It's time for a clean slate, for both of us. A fresh start, my love. I just want us to be happy.'

She was almost ready to pull the plate away from him, give him another chance. She remembered the man she had fallen in love with, and the thought was like temporary amnesia for all that had happened since their fairy-tale wedding.

Then his manner changed. 'Yeah,' he said while chewing, pointing his fork at her. 'We have to be honest with each other from now on. Here's your opportunity. It's confession time.'

She knew that look, the frantic eye movements, the way he was just before he became vicious. For a long moment, she didn't speak, buying time. He was forking the last of the pie into his mouth, chewing, swallowing. When he'd consumed it all, she said a silent prayer of thanks, but then the doubts crept in. Adam had said the ketamine would kick in immediately. Maybe the batch he'd given her wasn't as potent as it should be, or even not ketamine? You couldn't really tell with street drugs.

But then she noticed his eyes. His pupils had grown into huge, dilated circles.

'You're right. I did betray you,' she said in a confident voice she had never dared use with him before, the voice of a project manager, speaking to an unruly client. 'But never with anyone else.'

He grasped the side of the dinner table, raised it a few inches and let it drop with a thud, causing the plates and cutlery to rattle. Her glass of Diet Coke toppled, its contents spilling to the floor. Des glared at her, bearing his teeth, his jaws tight with rage.

'You're a small man, Des, a violent and nasty bully, and I

blame myself for staying with you. I should have left a long time ago. I should have left the first time you hit me.'

At this, he laughed – a snarling, cruel cackle. He rubbed his hands in preparation, as he often did, but his movements were slow and uncoordinated. 'Found your courage, have you?' He seemed oblivious to his speech becoming slurred. 'Think you're too good for me?'

'Yes, I believe I am,' she said calmly. 'We're done.'

'You're not going anywhere.' He wiped his brow with the back of his hand, then looked at the hand as if he'd only just found it. Maybe being wasted had become so normal to him, he hadn't noticed the effects of the drug.

'Shh, Des. Don't waste time. Anything you'd like to say to me before we're finished?'

In an almost comedic way, looking like he was struggling to control his limbs, he pushed back his chair. It fell, its backrest pounding the floor with a bang. As he stood, his posture changed. He was wobbling. Still, he made a fist and raised it. 'You're not going anywhere, missy,' he slurred. 'By the time I'm done with you… If you thought in your silly little head you can leave me… Man and wife, for better or worse.'

'Quite right,' she said, exactly as she'd rehearsed, every moment of that day. 'I'm not the one leaving.'

His breath became laboured. He stumbled, then dropped to his knees, a look of incomprehension in his eyes. He gasped. 'What have you done?'

'What I should have done a long time ago. Goodbye, Des.'

Her words were timed perfectly. His eyes glazed over, and he fell on his back. Naomi remained seated at the table. She stuffed her mouth with chips and chewed slowly, looking at his inert body on the floor. *Too much salt*, she thought. *Won't have to use so much when he's gone*. For the first time in a long time, she felt calm. She washed down the chips with beer from his glass that had somehow remained on the table unspilled, then got up, walked over to the knife rack and selected the blue-steel chef's blade.

The court papers recorded only two stab wounds: one that punctured his heart's right ventricle and one to the neck, causing a vascular injury and perforating his windpipe. Either could have been fatal on its own. These facts, too, counted against her in the trial. Apparently, for it to have been an act of fearful impulse, she should have stabbed him many more times, in a less precise way. Her lawyer argued something called *Battered Wife Syndrome*, that she had been abused over a long period and finally cracked, but there was no evidence to support it. Des never allowed her out with visible injuries. By all accounts, and there were many, he was a perfect husband. Bespectacled accountants don't hit their wives. She often regretted not taking the time to consider what it would look like to a jury. Even experienced project managers sometimes overlooked a crucial detail.

And now, chasing Faye, she reminded herself of her capacity to act, to do what was necessary. After Des, she had sworn never to let anyone ruin her life. It was either Faye's or hers. In that equation, there was only one logical solution. She practised what she would say to Faye as she bled out. *I'm so sorry, sweet Faye. I'm not a bad person. Rest in peace.* Then she would hold Faye in her arms as her life ended, being careful not to dirty her own clothes with blood.

CHAPTER TWENTY

Faye knew with absolute certainty that she would run and run, through the woods, along the miles of dirt road, and then the endless tarmac stretch until she saw a car or, failing that, reached the line of grey-bricked houses. If a car came, she would force it to stop, stand in the middle of the road if she had to. If no one answered the door at the houses, she would break in and find a phone. There was no question of stopping or giving up.

What happened to Michael was Slevin and Stella's fault, both of them for the stealing, but Stella's in particular for provoking Adrian in the roundhouse after he'd already decided to leave. Why couldn't she just let the farmer go? And that hesitation before she agreed to search for the keys, it boggled Faye's mind. The decision required no thought, none at all. Faye expected a flurry of activity, people stepping in with offers of help. Instead, they all looked mildly bothered, like Michael didn't matter. It was how they usually treated the younger members of the commune: her, Michael and Lilian, as if their age made them less important, lesser members. It had always been annoying, but now, but now... Michael's life hung in the balance, and yet the way they reacted was beyond shameful. It made her blood boil.

Despite her anger, Faye did not consider herself blameless. Her own guilt lay heavy on her shoulders, at once crushing her and driving her forwards. She was almost certain that she herself had contributed to the farmer's rage. If Michael died, she could never forgive her commune mates, but, in equal measure, she could not forgive herself.

Her feet pounded the ground as she pushed herself onwards, the wind rushing at her sweaty forehead, her breath shortening with effort, her mouth dry and tasting of rusted metal. Marathon runners did it, and so could she. Six miles to the road. Another two if no cars came. Not even a marathon. *It's all in the mind*, she kept reminding herself, like one of those inane motivational speakers she'd always considered too enthusiastic, but whom she now had no choice but to believe, like gods accepted at a time of mortal crisis.

She bartered with the universe. *Tell me what to do to save him, and I'll do it. Never drink again? No, not enough. Cut off a finger? Two?* A thought occurred to her. *If I strangled Stella, will you make Michael better? No. What an odd idea. Still, if it made a difference, I'd do it.*

Only a few days earlier, the terrible events that had struck them like lightning would have been unthinkable. *Dorothy's dead, and now Michael was going to... No! Don't think it. But he was so pale. Hold on, baby. I'm getting help.* She imagined an ambulance, a medic leaning over Michael and reassuring her. *He's going to be all right, miss. We got here just in time*, her sobs of relief, holding his hand, sitting beside him as he woke up in a hospital bed. Then, they would return to the commune, lie together on their conjoined mattresses in the bell tent, her head on his hairless chest, listening to his heartbeat, smelling him, that peculiar

Michael scent of earthy sweat that was almost adolescently sweet, feeling grateful for every moment together.

When she arrived at Synner's Crag, the reality of commune living was a strange novelty, but she took to it quickly. Here, chores meant something. You weren't earning money to tick off a list of boxes of what you were meant to do or who you were meant to be. You carried water because they all needed to drink. You cooked to feed yourself and others.

Her mother was mortified. 'Have you lost your mind? What about your law degree and training contract?' She had said this while hugging a milk-no-sugar cup of builder's tea in their dilapidated council flat on the Isle of Dogs.

'Or maybe,' Faye said, 'I finally found my mind. Please don't give me *the speech*.'

'I thought you were smart,' her mother said, making an expansive gesture with her hand to encompass the entirety of their lounge, the tattered settee, the mouldy window frames. 'That's right. Spend the rest of your life on minimum wage like me. Go on, then. See how you feel when you're my age, pinching pennies and shopping at Poundland.'

I'll live on minimum wage for the rest of my life if you'll save Michael. Please!

In any other place, the Michaels of this world would have been blind to her existence. His perfect physique, the dimples and dreamy eyes, the deep Black Country accent that made her weak at the knees. But, and she had to admit this even if reluctantly, at Synner's Crag, there were not many other options, so she got a fair hearing. She was smart but not conventionally pretty, with her plain, shapeless face and her too-dry hair that couldn't be saved by any conditioner she tried. Never in a million years would he have given her a second look, not even a first.

Faye spent most of her time at the commune with Michael

and Lilian, *the youngsters*, against the backdrop of the staler lot: Stella, Slevin and Joel. Their little group came to each other's defence, at least long enough for Dorothy to douse the fires and smilingly remove the froth from any argument.

Naomi, for her part, was more playful but didn't choose sides. And Dorothy was Dorothy, the United Nations, striving for peace, dignity and equality on a healthy planet. She was her own unique grouping. The new guy, Luke, was yet to find his place, but he seemed to Faye to be a boring addition, probably a civil servant escaping paperwork. She hadn't really talked to him. He didn't seem worth it.

The youngsters had naturally formed their own clique and enjoyed each other's company, going on picnics together or exploring the woods and beyond. They stood up to Joel every time he recited his self-important speeches.

One day, shortly after Faye's arrival at Synner's Crag, a miracle happened. Lilian was busy baking bread, and Faye found herself with Michael, walking together, just the two of them, further and further from the camp. As they sat on a hillock and watched the sunset, he leaned in and kissed her. They made a fire and talked all night.

She could have been poring over contracts in a floor-to-ceiling glass-windowed office in the City of London instead, earning money she'd never have time to spend. She could have married a senior associate so they could both have dinner at the firm's staff restaurant and talk about their love of the law and what to pay the nanny. She could have given talks to underprivileged law students about their chances, lying through her teeth. She'd been a successful working-class candidate, but the law's slot machine only took a meagre few tokens. Instead, she rejected all the suffocating trappings and found the commune, and Michael, *my angel*. She shuddered at the word, imagining him spread-winged, sitting on a cloud in Heaven.

And now she was running for his life and running out of steam. Her mind told her she could run forever, but her body disagreed. Soon enough, she was gasping for air, her hamstrings locking up, pain shooting from the balls of her feet, through her spine to her neck.

She vowed not to stop. If it came to it, she would crawl to get help. Michael was bleeding out. *I'm so sorry, baby*. Branches hit her like flagellation whips. It was no more than she deserved. She thought back to what happened, how she had sown the seeds of calamity.

A week earlier, she had gone for one of her wanders, away from the commune. Despite how she loved spending time with Michael, even she needed time to herself, the birthright of a single child. On that fateful day, she followed her usual route, taking the eastern trail, which was more trodden and less muddy, to the edge of the woods. From there, she climbed the path up a moderately steep rise to the old, dilapidated ruins. The structure was a circular stone enclosure that must have been some kind of dwelling or silo. She liked to touch its ancient stones and feel connected to the people who had built it, many generations ago. She'd rest her back against the crumbling wall and watch the rolling green scenery that went on for miles.

As she approached, she heard a noise that, at first, she thought was animal grunts. She moved closer, trying not to make a sound that would scare away whatever was inside.

And then she saw them: farmer Adrian and Lilian. The farmer had his trousers down, thrusting rhythmically at her friend, who had her back set against the structure's wall.

With careful backwards steps, Faye retreated. She didn't think they had seen her. Lilian's eyes seemed closed, and Adrian had his back and hairy bottom to her. She returned to the camp, her head spinning, promising herself not to tell anyone what she'd seen. It was no one's business, and she liked Lilian, the closest to her in age. Lilian could do what – or who – she liked. Telling others about them would only stir up trouble, especially as Adrian was so unpopular in the commune. Over campfire drinks, his reputation had been forged in the fire from an unfriendly neighbour to a monster set on their destruction.

Still, she couldn't stop herself from confiding in Michael, swearing him to secrecy, but forgetting in the act that their bell tent was not soundproof, especially as it was so close to Stella's single cabin.

The next day, while Dorothy was away, Lilian had left the commune, probably expelled by Stella and her fellow elders. And this, all of it her fault, would have caused Adrian's anger. Lilian must have gone to him and told him of the latest thefts and her expulsion. If Faye hadn't shared her secret, he would not have barged into the roundhouse, he would not have shot Michael, and Michael would not be losing blood at a frightening rate. Of course, it was Stella and Slevin who were to blame for their thefts, but Faye was the catalyst. She had lit the match that started this awful, ruinous fire, a fire that would consume the person she cared about most, unless... Unless she made it and got help.

Was she getting close to the path's end, where it met the dirt road? It all looked the same: trees, trees and more trees. She was breathless. Her lungs burned hot. *I can't stop. I can't. I...*

Against her will, her excruciated body sent signals of surrender. Despite all the promises, the anger, the unbridled guilt, she was forced to a reluctant halt. *Only a little rest. Only a minute, then I'll carry on. Hold on, Michael.*

She drew in wheezing lungfuls of air as if she were drowning and crouched down, her hands on her knees. *I'll make it, even if it kills me.*

Then she heard something, like a foot trampling brush. She

didn't have time to turn her head, to understand, to think, before someone delivered the blow.

As she fell into darkness, her thoughts sped to a mix of incomprehension, sorrow and a bottomless pit of ire: a seething, all-consuming fury at an unjust world, and whoever had stopped her from calling for help.

CHAPTER TWENTY-ONE

The meanders of the trail snaked right, then left, and for a moment, Naomi thought she had spotted a glimpse of Faye's white hoodie ahead. She forced her legs to quicken. Faye was running long-distance, while Naomi had the advantage of only needing to achieve a final, fateful sprint.

As she ran, her hand brushed the sheath of the knife that bulged from her trousers. The back of her mind was readying itself for the encounter, rehearsing not so much the words she would say, but the movements of her limbs, the forward jump, the sudden thrust of the blade, designed to surprise and avoid any conversation. If Faye got a chance to speak, her last words might brand themselves onto Naomi's thoughts forever. Not that she hesitated over what she had to do. Sparing herself that burden was as much a practical consideration as the speed of her stab hand. Bringing about the death of another did not change her the way people always said it did, but there was always a risk: Faye was not Des. Would hurting her, *murdering her*, have a different emotional effect compared to the just dispatch of an abusive husband? She didn't think so, but a good project manager made contingencies for unforeseen outcomes. As the thick project management manual insisted, *you must mitigate potential risks.*

An unexpected thought crossed her mind. *What have I become?* Then came the sobering response. *I am who Des made me, who the criminal justice system made me, the result of what prison did to me. I didn't ask for any of it. I'm so sorry, Faye.*

Three quarters of the way down the path, she came to a sudden stop, startled by what lay before her. She hesitated, unsure at first what to make of it. She looked around with alarm, her hand reaching for the reassurance of the knife. Her heart thumped wildly from the effort. She was out of breath but now doubly alert.

On the ground, bunched into an uneven ball, was Faye's hoodie, dark stains showing in its folds. A log of wood the size of a bat lay beside it, its end stained brownish red. Naomi caught her breath and looked around again. *Can't see anyone, but I have to be careful.* She leaned down, touched the smear on the log's end and put it to her tongue. Blood.

She bent low and wrapped her hand around the knife's handle, listening for any movement. A sound like a branch snapping made her jump and draw the knife, pointing it this way, then that, unsure where it had come from. Her mind painted shapes into the forest, her heightened senses interpreting every noise as an assailant readying for an attack.

A few moments passed. Insects buzzed. Birds tweeted and flapped their wings. Her pulse sounded like a rhythmic drum in her ears. She allowed herself another glance down at the hoodie and the bloodied log.

Someone had got to Faye first. But who? And why? The answer to the second question was clear. Someone else at the commune did not wish the police to be involved unless, of course, it was Adrian's doing. The farmer had reasons enough.

Naomi puzzled over the discarded hoodie. Whether alive or dead, where was Faye? She looked for signs that might suggest her body had been dragged away, but Naomi was no detective. The forest bed with its undergrowth, branches and leaves was thick and unhelpful. It seemed able to swallow any attempt to disturb it without leaving a trace. Faye could have been pulled away or carried in any direction into the dense wooded surroundings. There was no way to tell.

She took a few steps into the woods to her right and scanned the forest. It was a futile mission. She could spend an entire day searching every which way and still not find a thing. If the stocky farmer carried Faye's feather-light weight over his shoulders like a lamb, he could make good time getting away.

She returned to the path, collected the stained hoodie, and wrapped it around the end of the bloodied log. Then, she hid the bundle a few paces away from the trail in a recess behind a tree and covered it with shrubs and leaves. No one would see it there. It wouldn't be found. Why was it left on the trail in the first place? A warning? Adrian in a hurry to carry his victim away?

For a long moment, she simply stared at her handiwork, the well-covered evidence, and tried to reassure herself. It was for the best that she did not have to stab Faye, but Naomi did not believe in guardian angels. If this person had no qualms about attacking Faye, then she, too, was in danger. They all were.

In a strange, unexpected way, being a potential target made her worry for Faye. Could she still be alive? Maybe someone struck her unconscious and took her. It was irrational, of course, worrying for the person she had intended to kill, but being in the same predicament, subject to the same prowling attacker, created a connection between them. If Faye was no longer running for help, Naomi hoped she was unharmed. She wished she could find her, perhaps hurt, but not dead. Then she'd take her back, and everything would be all right again. She'd nurse her back to health and make up an excuse about why she went after her. *I'd say I decided to run and help.*

Naomi returned to the path. She was spared killing Faye, but by being absent, stealing the knife, and running this way, something in her situation had irrevocably changed. These actions had made her an outsider again, scheming for her own survival above all others. Even if her long absence went unnoticed, she herself knew what she'd intended to do, and that knowledge was damning. Every dark secret formed yet another mask to be layered over those that came before it. She tried on an innocent, caring face to wear in the roundhouse. *Can the commune go back to some sort of normality after this? Is there a chance for us to return to how we used to be?*

She looked at her wrist to read the time, a habit she hadn't shaken, even though there were no watches in the commune. If she didn't get back quickly, she might be missed.

I'm sorry I couldn't save you, Faye.

She sprinted back the way she'd come, the knife clutched in her sweaty hand, all the while searching the woods ahead for any danger and throwing backwards glances for an attacker who might follow.

PART THREE

KARLA

CHAPTER TWENTY-TWO

FOURTEEN DAYS POST DISCOVERY

When Alex returned to Sandra Saint-John's lounge a few days after their first meeting, he thought it smelled marginally better. The previous scents of decay and emollients had been replaced by lilac air freshener and the sharp tang of bleach. Like the room itself, Sandra seemed neater, her dull grey hair brushed and pulled back. The ashen hue of her face had recovered to a healthier blush, though the expression pasted on it remained stern, her still-sunken eyes as demanding. He didn't mind. She had signed and returned the contract.

She motioned for him to sit and offered no refreshments.

'You've got something for me?'

He opened his briefcase, brought out his black notepad, and flicked through its pages. He knew from memory most of what he had to say, but clients liked to feel they were dealing with a professional. *The allure of the private investigator, the mystique.* He never carried the too-formal tan leather briefcase anywhere except for client meetings.

'Considering the number of casualties,' he said, looking up from his pad, 'the police have established a special operation. It's unusual to see so many deaths in one incident. The team is based in London, mainly because of resourcing challenges, but it includes a liaison officer from Northumberland, and they might move the operation north later.'

'I'm not interested in bureaucratic ins and outs,' Sandra said.

He was trying to set the scene for her, but decided to skip straight to the updates. The client was not always right, but the client was always *the client*. He supposed this client, for obvious reasons, felt a sense of urgency. He tried to imagine her sipping champagne on a luxury yacht, but couldn't fathom the severe, scowling woman before him content with anything, let alone enjoying herself. His rich clients had taught him an important lesson: misery could not be paid away. It followed you wherever you went.

'The police have the first post-mortem reports for the two members of the commune they found buried: your sister, and a man called...' he looked at his notes, 'Michael Bind. My source at the police operation says she doesn't particularly trust the lazy pathologist on the case, but budget cuts mean they'll have to make do. That's also why the other reports are delayed. They're being released in a staggered way.'

'Your source is a she?'

Alex didn't like her tone, but was not going to react, especially as the *she* in question was his wife. Officially, Mary could never tell him anything about an ongoing investigation, but their marriage bent the rules for what they justified to themselves was a mutual benefit. Alex often helped her with police cold cases, and Mary, in turn, gave him access to crucial information. It was a win all round: for the Met, Alex's clients, and their household income.

'Let me talk you through what they've found. Your sister's body...' He looked at her, seeking a reaction. When he found none, he pretended to consult his notes. 'She appears to have been the first to die. This confirms she most definitely did not lead them on some kind of death ritual.'

'More's the pity for her,' Sandra said. 'Better for the outcome we need.'

Alex nearly coughed but reined in the reflex.

'She's already dead,' Sandra said. 'Don't give me that face.'

Alex nodded without meaning to and shared what Mary had told him. 'She died of a heart attack. There were also signs of a blunt force strike to her back, but this might have been after her death. One theory is that the fatal heart attack was triggered by an argument or a scary event. Then, her dead body was assaulted. If that's correct, someone must have been very angry with her.'

'I don't blame them,' Sandra said. 'She could be quite annoying.'

Alex silently cleared his throat. 'It's only an initial theory. Considering the number of victims in this case, the police will hold back on drawing conclusions until they have the results of the other autopsies. Bottom line, the police think she died a natural death, but one that was brought on by some sort of nasty confrontation.'

'So, not actually natural,' Sandra said. 'Well, one down, as they say.'

For some reason, Alex noticed his client had painted her fingernails a vivid shade of red. The remission was doing wonders for her. It wasn't the illness that was making her callous. Rather, he decided, better health had returned Sandra to her authentic, hard-boiled self. He took another moment to pretend he was checking his notes. He had never before met a client he disliked so much from the very beginning. *Carry on and think of payday.*

'Michael Bind's autopsy concluded that he died from blood loss due to a wound inflicted to his thigh. His femur was partly shattered. The original report suggested a gunshot wound, but apparently, this was a mistake and was corrected after a senior officer from Northumbria Police questioned the findings. Usually, these things are cut and dry, gunshot residue, that sort of thing, but the pathologist was made to correct his report and admit he might have been wrong. No guns were recovered from the scene, and this scenario was highly unlikely.'

'What, then?'

'A sharp object, maybe a knife, used with substantial force. Michael's death was definitely the result of direct violence.'

She rolled her eyes.

Alex gave her a formal, straight nod. Clients loved that gesture. 'That's all I have so far,' he said.

Sandra tapped the fingers of her right hand on her knee. 'It's a start,' she said, 'and I suppose it bodes well. There was violence. They're all dead, except for the one person who did it. Do we know anything about him?'

'I don't have much yet, except for the basics. Luke Bridestone, thirty, the last one to join the commune. Your sister drove him up from London on July 24th. Her car was parked near Euston station. There's CCTV footage of their journey from motorway cameras and also from their stops at service stations.'

A glint came to Sandra's eye. 'They live in peace for years, and then, a few days after this person arrives, they're all dead?'

'The police are keeping an open mind,' Alex said. He didn't like how she kept repeating the result she wanted him to find.

'She came to see me, you know,' Sandra said, 'when she was in London to collect this man, Luke Bridestone. I mean, what kind of name is that, anyway?'

Alex knew about the visit from Mary, but he wanted to ask her about it, whether Dorothy had said anything that might be significant. The contented look on her face stopped him. He drew a pen from his pocket and made a note in his pad.

'Luke lived alone in a flat in New Cross. Kept himself to himself.'

'Hmm,' Sandra said.

'Worked at the Honor Oak Crematorium.'

'Honor Oak?' she said. 'Really?'

'Is that significant?'

She swallowed, then swallowed again. 'My funeral plan,' she said. 'That's where I'm headed, eventually. Can you imagine this... this Luke getting away with it and then being the one to burn me to ashes? He'll see my name on the worksheet and laugh. Oh, the irony.' She reached forwards and placed her hand on his knee. 'You mustn't let that happen. We have to stop him.'

Alex waited until she removed the unwelcome hand, consciously making sure he didn't move his leg away from her as his instinct demanded. He returned the silver Cross pen to his jacket pocket, making a show of not rushing, then placed the notepad in his briefcase and clicked its clasps shut.

'You do understand,' he said, 'if Luke is charged with a crime, a trial will take time. Courts are clogged with cases. Your sister's inheritance can't be released until he's convicted. And he's still in a coma. If he doesn't wake up, you might need to make an application to the court based on any evidence we find.' He shrugged. 'I'm not really clear on how that works. You'll need to speak to a solicitor.'

'I assure you, I have no intention of dying before I have some time to enjoy this money, and that's that. Make a note in your little notebook: Sandra will be here to the bitter end.'

'Of course,' he said and got up. 'Thank you for your time, Ms Saint-John. I'm staying on top of the police investigation and making my own enquiries. I'll come back as soon as there's something worth reporting.'

'You won't stay a little longer to discuss our findings? What to do next?'

'I have a meeting with my source at the police. I mustn't keep her waiting.'

This wasn't a lie. Not entirely. He had promised Mary he'd pick up the girls from school and then cook dinner. Her schedules were more rigid than his.

'Have a good evening, then,' he said.

'There's a cheque waiting for you on the mantlepiece. Your retainer.'

Alex nodded as if the cheque was just a formality, but in his mind, he had already revised his route. He'd stop at the nearest bank and deposit it, without delay. It should clear by the next time he saw her.

CHAPTER TWENTY-THREE

THREE DAYS BEFORE THE RECKONING

Michael had died overnight and, for a while, no one dared touch him. It appeared, Luke thought, that they were waiting for Faye, wishing for her to return and claim her lover, maybe jolt them into action. But as the hours went by, it seemed less likely. *Where was she? Had she tried to contact the authorities and was thwarted by the farmer's brother? Had something happened to her?* So much time had passed.

Michael's body was left on the floor of the roundhouse, his back leaning on an empty chair that was propped against the wall, his face pale and bloodless, empty eyes staring at the entrance, lips parted from what might have been his final word.

They all ate their breakfast while standing outside and away from the roundhouse's door, cold remnants from the pots of yesterday's food. Coffee was out of the question. No one would go in to light the stove. An outside fire was too much trouble.

There had been talk of sending someone to call the police, but Naomi argued this could make things worse. If the farmer wasn't lying about his brother being a senior officer, they'd get nowhere. Luke wasn't convinced by this argument but, like the others, didn't challenge it. If Synner's Crag became a media story, Karla might hear about it. Then, she'd come calling. Michael was already dead. There was nothing they could do for him except give him a decent burial.

After breakfast, Slevin signalled for Luke to come with him, and they both sighed in unison before taking slow, heavy steps into the roundhouse. Luke knelt down and closed Michael's eyes in a careful, tender motion. He had seen this done in films and on TV. It was one of those things everyone knew should happen. If it were up to him, upon his own death, Luke would like his eyes to be left open. It made the end seem less final.

Slevin came to kneel opposite him, and they each took a shoulder, raising Michael's rigid body to a curved standing position. He remained frozen in stature and was heavier than Luke had expected, but there was an unspoken understanding between them that Michael should not be lifted horizontally by his arms and legs. They carried him like a friend, like an injured comrade.

Michael was buried next to Dorothy in the peaceful clearing, not a ten-minute walk from the camp. The sky was cloudless and blue, a warm sun shining on them as if nothing had happened, a suggestion of an indifferent world that carried on with its business. Michael was to be cast into darkness on the brightest of days. This time, Luke found his heart heavy, anguish flowing down his cheeks in salty tears. At Dorothy's funeral, he was still numbed by the fear and trauma of his life in London. By the time of Michael's death, something within him had been released. The catch on his emotions had been unfastened, bringing him one step closer to the person he used to be, a person who could grieve.

Once again, Luke found himself digging alongside Slevin. Joel watched, standing slightly apart from Stella and Naomi. Unlike them, Joel was not courteous enough to offer his help, even for it to be refused. It was as if the rules that applied during his mother's funeral remained in force, and Michael was simply an extension of the same thing, or maybe he didn't want to get his hands dirty.

Digging graves was hard work, but Luke didn't mind. The two deaths, so close to each other, had left him in a sort of dazed, dreamlike state. He felt detached from time and place, heavy with sadness. He hadn't expected his first week at the commune to be about planting bodies in the ground rather than seeds.

'Faye should have been here,' Naomi said.

'I reckon she bailed,' Joel said. 'Couldn't deal.'

'You're probably right,' Naomi said. 'Still, it's sad she's not here to say goodbye. She loved him.'

'If you love someone,' Joel said with unexpected bitterness, 'you don't betray them.'

Naomi shook her head but did not respond.

The hard work of the burial was finally done, and they all stood around the covered grave.

'Our Michael,' Stella said, 'builder of cabins, West Brom fan, lover of Faye, friend to us all.'

'Wasn't really our friend,' Joel said. 'More interested in Faye.'

Stella ignored him. 'We'll miss you, mate. We'll miss your smile, your positive attitude, always helpful, never complaining, even about my bean stew, which, let's face it…' She choked, then recovered herself. 'Goodbye, commune friend. Rest in peace.'

When they all returned to the camp, Naomi and Stella set about cleaning the dried blood from the roundhouse's floor with brushes and a bucket of water. They worked in silence, Stella scrubbing so vigorously, she sometimes stopped to catch her breath. The water in the bucket had to be changed several times when it became too dark to be useful. They dulled the thickness of the stains, but Michael's blood had embedded itself into the MDF flooring, marking the place where he had lain, a final reminder that he had been there, that he'd never return. Still, they carried on, and Luke understood. What else was there to do about this senseless death but to scrub at it?

While the two women cleaned, the men stood and observed in solemn silence, Luke and Slevin covered in earth and mud from the digging, and Joel leaning his back against the wall, his arms crossed as usual.

After a while, Stella dumped her brush in the bucket, sat on the floor and wiped her forehead with the back of her hand. 'You two,' she said to Luke and Slevin, 'go clean yourselves in the stream.'

Luke didn't mind her command. Someone had to take charge. The sheep had lost their shepherd, and now they'd lost their friend. They all probably welcomed it, at least for now. *How long will it last?*

She turned to Joel. 'You've been a great audience, mate. Can you maybe go with them and wash the dirty pots?'

Joel shrugged but, for once, did not argue.

Back in the camp, after a wash in the freezing stream and a change of clothes, Luke sat with Slevin on folding chairs next to the clay oven. They were sipping sweet, black coffee from mugs that Naomi had handed them.

'You still wanna be in the commune?' Slevin said. 'I mean, two deaths, man, and then Faye running away. I mean, shit!'

'It's crazy, I know,' Luke said, 'but yeah, I do.' He sensed there was a new closeness between them, the camaraderie of gravediggers. Until now, Slevin had been distant, only speaking to him with a kind of humorous contempt. He wondered if his new-found kinship with the always bare-chested man meant that Joel would no longer see him as an ally when it came to the vote. *Will there still be a vote?* When they went for their wash, Joel had gone downstream to clean the pots, maintaining his distance. Could Luke keep himself above the fissure lines in the commune's relationships? They were a smaller group now. Whatever the rules were before, whatever the routines and hierarchies, there was a new world order, a world that seemed closer than ever to coming to an abrupt end.

Luke cupped his coffee mug, drawing warmth into his hands. 'What do you think about the situation with the farmer?'

'I know men like him,' Slevin said. 'Bark's worse than bite.'

'I'd say killing someone isn't just bark.'

'We had a chat about it earlier, Stella and I. We don't think he meant to kill Michael. He knew we had a car. Probably thought we'd get Michael to a hospital, and then his policeman brother would straighten things up. Murder, well, that's not something you can just make disappear, even if you're, like, senior police.'

Luke considered this. A theory, that's all it was, especially after Faye's failure to return. 'He sounded pretty serious about what he'd do if we don't leave.'

Slevin scratched his chin, then ran his fingers over his stubbled cheek.

'So, we're staying,' Luke said. The question, spoken as a statement, was about all of them, not himself. He would stay, no matter what. He realised, though, that after the last few days, he didn't mind being in the camp with Slevin and Naomi, and maybe even Stella. As for Joel, he wasn't entirely sure, especially after their overnight trip to the cave. The man was difficult and troubled. There was something dark and unpredictable about him. Maybe better out than in.

'Hope for the best. Prepare for the other thing,' Slevin said. 'But we still have a couple of days to make a plan. Today, we rest. Today is for Michael.'

He raised his mug, and Luke responded with his. 'To Michael.'

At that moment, despite all his anxieties and fears about

fitting in, about his past and the lies and prevarications, a warmth rose through his chest, a soothing calm. He was no longer an outsider. He was one of them now. He'd escaped fear and brutality. Not only was he safe now, but he had found the people who might become his mates – if they all made it past the threats from the angry farmer and what the man might do. And if there were still to be a vote, he felt he could count on Naomi and Slevin. If Joel turned against him, all he needed was Stella's support.

He sipped his coffee and looked at the lush greenery of the surrounding forest, the trees and wild vegetation bathed in the sun's golden rays. In this soothing warmth of new serenity, he allowed his shoulders to relax. For the first time in a long while, he didn't feel the urge to count fingers and thumbs.

CHAPTER TWENTY-FOUR

They sat around the bonfire, mostly quiet, with the occasional murmur. Luke found himself between Naomi and Slevin, his allies. It seemed natural that way – comforting, even. The very last of their remaining food was consumed with a large wooden spoon, straight from the stew pot that was passed around until it was empty.

'Where's Joel?' Slevin said.

'Who cares?' Naomi answered. 'Probably went into the woods to hunt squirrels or something. He wouldn't have liked our dinner anyway. Food's better without his speeches.'

'I guess,' Luke said, 'we might have to eat squirrels if we're avoiding Adrian's fields. Are we avoiding Adrian's fields?'

'Nah, mate,' Slevin said. 'It's empty threats. I reckon he scared himself shitless, shooting Michael. We just have to be double-careful. Right, Stella?'

'Stella?' Naomi said. 'You all right?'

At last, Stella spoke. 'I… I'm not sure. It's risky to go there. Look what happened.'

'So… what?' Slevin said. 'We just give up and leave? There's no food for tomorrow. *Nada.*'

Joel emerged from the shadows. On his back, he carried what looked like a scarecrow, dressed in a ragged old T-shirt and worn grey trousers that were fastened by a length of rope. The head was a filled pillowcase; a face painted on it in child-like strokes. In his other hand, he held a shovel. Joel looked jolly, energised, a complete contrast to everyone else's downcast mood. 'If we're going to honour Michael with a party,' he said, 'we might as well celebrate in style. This, my friends, is an effigy of the devil, farmer Adrian.'

'Dude!' Slevin said, suddenly cheerful. 'Way to go. Come on, let's plant him in the ground. Then we can drink and, once we're merry, we can burn him.'

With every round of tequila, the sombre mood turned livelier. Stella still looked solemn, but all the others were easing themselves into the fireside chatter: stories about Michael and Dorothy. *Remember the time when... Oh, I nearly pissed myself.* Luke allowed himself to let go and matched them shot for shot. It was fine. *These are my new friends. Well, almost. Drinking together will help. We're comrades, commune comrades, all of us.* He couldn't find fault in this argument, or he didn't want to.

Naomi took his hand in hers and laid her head on his shoulder. This both comforted and alarmed him. He was in that now familiar bind. From the corner of his eye, he saw Joel staring at them.

Naomi seemed to sense his inner turmoil. 'Relax, Lukey,' she said. 'Relax.' Then she looked at Stella. 'Why the long face, Stella? We're supposed to be celebrating Michael.'

Luke shuddered, still unsure what he should do. He now wished that he hadn't sat next to Naomi. *Too late.*

Stella whispered something that nobody heard.

Slevin, who had drunk more than the rest of them, using

his cunning method of pouring himself two shots for each of theirs, seemed a moment behind the conversation. 'Lukey?' he said. 'You called him Lukey?'

'Did I?' Naomi said and burped.

Joel got up and stood over Stella. His earlier joy seemed to have melted without warning. He looked down at her with a serious, tipsy glare. In a loud voice that no one expected, he spoke, almost shouting. 'It's all your fault.'

'Hey, hey, hey,' Slevin said. 'Don't do that, mate. It's sad enough as it is. We're all grieving.'

Stella seemed to awaken from her reverie. She met Joel's eyes. In a frail voice, she said, 'He's right. It's my fault. We shouldn't have stolen from Adrian's fields. I was wrong to stand up to him like that. I just… I was a fucking idiot.'

'Stop it,' Slevin said. 'You had no way of—'

She interrupted him. 'If I weren't such a cow, Michael would still be here, Faye would still be here. Maybe we could have agreed something with Adrian. Now it's all gone to shit.' Her face looked like she was crying, but without any tears. 'I'm sorry,' she said. She sounded broken.

'*Sorry* doesn't cut it,' Joel said. 'You can't be our leader. You have blood on your hands.'

'Oi!' Slevin said to Joel. 'Enough. I'm warning you.'

'You do choose your moments, Joel,' Naomi said.

Slevin shuffled to sit closer to Stella and put his arm around her. 'Don't listen to him, Stell. He can't talk, can he? Not after Lilian. You couldn't know what Adrian would do. You—'

'Lilian was an accident,' Joel said. 'And you two were there as much as I was.'

'What happened to Lilian?' Naomi asked. When no one answered, she repeated the question. 'I said, what happened to her?'

'Nothing,' Joel said. 'Commune life wasn't for her, and don't change the subject. We have important things to decide. Stella can't be our leader. We should vote for a new one.'

'Now?' Naomi said.

'Yes, now,' Joel said. 'We're all here. We can take a vote. I'm putting myself forward. Hands up if you support me.'

There was a pause. No one moved. A moth flew into the fire, its wings and body consumed in a flash by the flames.

It seemed like Joel's inability to understand context had dealt him another blow, yet still he waited, his hands on his hips.

To Luke's surprise, Stella was the first to budge. She raised a hesitant hand and held it up as though she was wishing for everything to stop: the arguments, the debate, the world.

Slevin shrugged and followed her lead, doing the same.

'You don't have a majority,' Naomi said. 'He's not elected.'

Luke waited a further few seconds, calculated the risks, and finally made his decision. He raised his hand to join theirs.

The grateful look he had expected from Joel didn't follow.

'First order of business,' Joel said. 'No more raids beyond the wall. Second order,'

'Don't give us orders,' Naomi said.

'Second order,' Joel repeated. 'Tomorrow, we start preparing for whatever the farmer's planning. We'll make sure he can't force us out. And no, Naomi, I don't want any more of your lip. Decision's made. We can carry on drinking for Michael.' He sneered at Stella. 'I'm sure we all wish he and Faye were both still here.'

When they reached the bottom of yet another bottle, tensions eased, and even Stella appeared cheerful. They all got up and danced around the effigy as it burned, with Slevin shrieking and performing his raucous ululations.

After they put out the fires in drunken, uncoordinated movements, they stumbled back to their cabins. Naomi held onto Luke as he led her. When they got to their cabin's door, he placed his hands on her shoulders and stared into her bleary eyes.

'I was wondering…' he said, then cupped her cheeks and kissed her.

'Ooh,' she whispered, 'come with me, baby communard. Come with Naomi.'

CHAPTER TWENTY-FIVE

TWO DAYS BEFORE THE RECKONING

When morning came, Luke was reluctant to open his eyes. His arm was wrapped around Naomi, their bodies squeezed together, spooning within the narrow confines of her single bed. He hoped they weren't loud the previous night, and he was thankful that they'd had the sense to roll down the carpet fabric of their cabin's door, despite the alcohol clouding their senses. He listened to her breathing, which perfectly matched his own. He could hear her heartbeat, feel her hair against his cheek, smell the sweet scent of their lovemaking. He wished he could stay like this forever, holding her. Life without tenderness was all hard edges. When he went out in the night to relieve his bursting bladder, it was only natural to come back to her bed.

And now he felt complete. The mould of pressure that had weighed on him was lifted, gone. He was his own man again. The past was in the past. The future, farmer or not, could only be better.

With a smile on his face, he finally opened his eyes. His mind was still bound by webs of sleep and the previous night's overindulgence. For that reason – that, and the tender warmth of Naomi's skin – it took him a moment to comprehend what he was seeing. The cabin was exactly as he expected it to be, tidy and neat, except for last night's clothes, discarded in haste on the floor. But there was something else, something unexpected. He rubbed his eyes and looked again. Nothing was wrong with his vision. On his own bed, on top of the pillow, lay a single flower, a white Madonna lily with yellow pollen brushes at its centre. It was artificial. He didn't have to check. He knew that flower well.

Luke held his breath and felt a chill run through him, as if submerged in glacial water, wrenching him into wakefulness. At the worst possible moment, Karla had found him. The flower was one of her props. A symbol of death she used to leave on his pillow as a reminder. *You sleep with anyone else, she dies, then you do. I will place this lily on your grave. It won't rot, but you will. 'Til death us do part. Make sure you remember this, my lovely.*

As if he could forget.

His thoughts spun in a merry-go-round of panic. Karla must have crept in when he went out for a piss, still drunk, his senses dulled – or worse, when they were sleeping. She must have seen him in Naomi's bed or heard their groans. He imagined her standing over them, sneering, plotting how to make them pay. That they were still alive was not surprising. She wanted him to know what was coming, to dread it.

His foot sprang out in an involuntary spasm, kicking Naomi.

'Ow!' she cried.

'Sorry.' He performed an awkward manoeuvre to extract himself from behind her and jumped onto the floor.

'Come back to bed,' Naomi said, her voice hoarse and groggy. 'Stay.'

Luke didn't reply. His tongue would have been tied even if he'd wanted to.

He dressed in a hurry, jumping to pull his jeans up. Distracted, he wore his T-shirt inside-out but had no will to right it. He hid the flower under his pillow. Then, with shaking fingers, he pulled the door material aside to form a tiny slit and peeked through it. A rising dawn shone tentacles of light along the damp forest clearing. A bird chirped. Something like a mouse scurried across their threshold, stopped, then rushed away. Grey smoke was rising from the chimney at the roundhouse. Someone was awake. He hoped they were safe.

He listened carefully – for what, he wasn't sure. Footsteps? Her cackling laughter?

He let go of the door and went to sit on his bed, his breathing laboured, his heart racing like an overworked engine. How could she have found him here? Did she follow him and Dorothy? But how? He'd seen no car behind them on their final stretch. Somehow, she must have kept her distance. Did she plant a tracker on their car when they had stopped for lunch? It wasn't beyond her. She had a knack for technology and stalking. *Nowhere is safe from me, you hear?*

There was no telling what Karla might do next. They were all in danger. He had seen her in action. His previous attempts to delude himself that Karla was a distant figment, a bad dream, were shattered. She was real, and she was here in the commune. She must have kept herself hidden, observing him settle into his new life, waiting for the ideal opportunity, and now he had given it to her.

The memory of the woman he had seen at the petrol station came back to haunt him, but rather than fear, he now felt anger, a seething rage that Karla had followed him to his new life. She should have left him well alone.

The bell sounded from the roundhouse, but it was not the usual short ring that signified a meal was ready. Instead, it rang and rang with the urgency of a fire alert. By the measure of the light outside, it was too early for breakfast. Something must have happened. Whatever it was, he could be certain of one thing: he had brought it upon them.

The faces in the roundhouse were creased and puffy from a combination of the previous night's drinking and not enough sleep. There were no clocks in the commune, but Luke thought it was probably about five a.m. or maybe six. Far too early, yet, for him, far too late.

'Sit down, everyone,' Stella said.

Slevin was shaking from the cold, yet still only in shorts and no shirt. 'What the fuck?' he said as he hugged himself.

'Sit down,' Stella repeated. 'This can't wait. I made coffee. We'll need it. No breakfast, I'm afraid. There's nothing to eat.'

'You're not our leader,' Joel said, then seemed to think better of it, pulled up a chair, and sat on the opposite side to where Stella stood. Unlike the rest of them, he was fully dressed and ready for the day in his combat ensemble, his trademark machete hanging from his belt.

Luke felt numb. He slumped into a chair, as did Naomi and Slevin.

'What's going on, Stell?' Slevin said.

Tight-lipped, Stella brought the pot of coffee and four mugs to the table. She poured the coffee and handed out mugs, to Slevin first, then Luke, then Joel. Then she poured one for herself.

Naomi smiled. 'You forgot me, Stella.'

'I didn't forget. You're not getting any.'

'What?'

'Not until you explain yourself.'

Naomi glanced at Luke, then turned to Stella. 'My private life is none of your business.'

Stella stared at her for a moment, looking puzzled, and then her eyes hardened. 'Oh no, Naomi. I have zero interest in whichever of these fine stallions you had for afters last night.'

'Wasn't me,' Joel said, placing so much weight on the statement, it sounded like an accusation. He looked from Luke to Slevin and then at Luke again.

'Come on, Stella,' Slevin said, tapping his fingers on his coffee mug. 'Come on.'

Stella turned around and walked over to the food preparation area. She returned with a note in one hand and the car keys in the other. She slapped both items on the table. The note was written in block letters, almost perfectly square, as if the author had tried their hardest to disguise their own penmanship:

> NAOMI HID THE KEYS IN HER CABIN SO YOU WON'T RESCUE MICHAEL. NAOMI KILLED FAYE.

Naomi flinched, then shook her head.

'Who wrote this?' Joel said.

'Not me,' Slevin said.

Luke knew with unwavering certainty who had written the note.

'That's not the question,' Stella said and turned to Naomi. 'Is it true? We could have saved Michael, taken him to a hospital. And if the keys were here all along...'

Slevin folded his arms over his chest, stared at the keys and shook his head.

'Have you lost your mind?' Naomi said. 'Michael and Faye were my friends, and I don't believe anything happened to Faye. She just bailed. Joel, you said it yourself, didn't you? She ran away. Couldn't cope.'

'Well, you did go with Slevin to look for the keys,' Joel said. 'You could have found them and put them in your pocket. Plus, someone took one of my blades when all this was happening. I can always tell if someone touched them.'

Naomi pressed her fist to her lips, then lowered her hand, seeking Luke's. He held back, frozen by the knowledge that

Karla was near. Everything in his planned new life was unravelling. Everything.

After a moment's silence, Naomi sat up and straightened her shoulders. 'No,' she said. 'I'm not arguing about these stupid accusations. Didn't do it. Whoever wrote the note has an agenda, can't you see? Why would someone do that? Whoever you are, come out with it.'

Stella sat down. With a resigned shrug, she said, 'I've done my bit.'

'Well, then…' Joel said. In an odd gesture, he knocked on the table three times, as if on a door.

Naomi narrowed her eyes. 'Well then, what?' She glared at him as if waiting for him to say something more before she pounced.

'Well then, we vote. I mean, the evidence is there: she had the opportunity to get the keys when she volunteered to search for them with Slevin.'

Naomi sprang to her feet to stand over them. She raised her voice, but only by a fraction, every word tinged with cold anger. 'Says who? An unsigned note? That's not evidence. If someone wants to accuse me, let them. But I'm not having this… this anonymous nonsense.'

'Joel says one of the knives was taken,' Stella said. 'You left us in the roundhouse to go to the loo after Faye went for help. You were gone a very long time.'

'I didn't do anything to Faye. Why would I? What reason could I possibly have? And I wasn't the only one away from the roundhouse. Where were Luke and Slevin? And you, Joel, where were you? Likely story, that, about a missing knife.'

'Sit down,' Joel said. 'I said sit!'

Naomi waited a moment, then sank back into her seat, looking dejected. 'Whatever,' she said. 'Think what you like. I don't care. If you believe this note, you're idiots.'

'Raise your hand if you think she did it,' Joel said, at the same time raising his own.

Slevin looked at Stella, sighed, then raised his fist.

Stella shook her head. 'It's a serious accusation,' she said, 'and Naomi does have a point. If someone wants to accuse her, they should speak up, not hide behind a piece of paper.'

'Lukas?' Joel said.

Luke hesitated. He knew who had written the note, and it wasn't any one of the five of them. He wondered if Karla was listening, just outside the roundhouse. If he ran out, would he find her there? Could he get his commune mates to capture her? But what would he say? By the time he explained and convinced them, she'd be long gone. Worse still, they had no idea what she was capable of, especially if she'd brought her brother along.

No, he decided. Brother or not, she'd probably be carrying weapons. She wouldn't have come empty-handed. He'd put all of them at risk. Just as he was considering his vote, Naomi, the danger they were in, another thought struck him, built on the foundations of his anger and new-found confidence. No one was invincible, not even Karla. What he needed was a plan, but this kind of plan also needed time and cunning. He wouldn't let her destroy the commune and make him hers again. His days spent in nature with these people had given him something new and entirely surprising: it had given him hope. Still, he had to vote now.

They were all looking at him. Naomi was scowling at his indecision.

'I don't think we have solid proof,' he said, swallowed, then swallowed again and raised his hand, 'but based on what we know...'

Naomi glared at him, and he looked away. *Just because Karla had planted the note didn't mean Naomi didn't hide the keys. Wasn't she a runaway killer?* If he defended her, he'd lose favour with the rest of them, and he wasn't sure he could later repair the damage from that kind of rift. And anyway, what could they possibly do to Naomi?

The answer came from Joel's mouth. 'Naomi,' he said in an officious tone, 'we won't jump to conclusions just now, especially when you're accused of causing the death of a commune member, maybe even two.'

'You sound like a toad,' Naomi said.

He ignored her. 'We need time to discuss and investigate and to wait and see if Faye maybe comes back. Tonight, we will let you know what we've decided.' He stood. 'Until then, we need to keep her secured. If she's dangerous—'

'Dangerous?' Naomi said.

'If she's dangerous,' Joel repeated, 'we don't want her free in our camp. Slevin, get me some cable ties, the thick ones we used for the roof tarps, and some rope.'

Naomi hissed at Joel. 'Never. Going. To happen. Matey.'

Joel reached down, drew the Parang Machete from its sheath and raised it. 'Don't test me. I'm warning you.'

'What will you do, stab me? Are you crazy?'

Joel spoke with steely calm. Luke had never seen this side of him before. 'Considering what you did,' he said, 'I wouldn't think twice. Stay where you are. I'm good with knives.'

'*I'm good with knives*,' Naomi said, mimicking his words. But she remained seated, seeming to have shrunk into herself, on her face a deep, sorrowful expression, as though she had lost the will to argue.

CHAPTER TWENTY-SIX

Naomi was going nowhere, even though she'd tried to free herself so vigorously that her wrists bled. The cable ties were thick and strong, beyond breaking. She should have stood up to Joel, should have resisted being bound, but for no reason she could fathom, she had just let them tie her up like a timid lamb. Maybe it was the dreadful hangover or the shock of the accusation in the note. *Who could have written it?* But she was not herself when they ganged up on her. Against their angry faces, her body felt listless and empty of rebellion. *What a stupid, demeaning outcome. I should never have let it happen.*

They had left her in Dorothy's cabin, her hands and shins bound with cable ties, a tight rope securing her midsection to the chair she sat on. With dogged zeal and more rope, Joel had also fixed the chair to one of the cabin's poles, its base buried and cemented in the ground.

Naomi had no sense of time. Two hours might have passed, or it might have been more. Who could have possibly noticed her pocketing the keys? Only Slevin, but his back was turned when she checked Dorothy's bag and found them there. Maybe someone saw her through the cabin's door, but weren't they all in the roundhouse at the time, looking after Michael and wondering what to do? The more likely explanation was that someone realised her little act of concealment when they searched her cabin. They would have found the keys inside her folded green jumper. Still, she hadn't killed Faye, even if that was her intention.

Her prospects looked grim. The suspicion about the knife she'd returned to Joel's cabin, coupled with the newly found keys, had put her in a precarious position. Worse still, if Faye was really dead, and they would find her body, what then? *They'd be so angry, there's no telling what they'd do.*

She heard footsteps outside and straightened her back. She was helpless and hated it. She thought of praying, but her lifelong Catholic vocabulary seemed inappropriate under the circumstances. Not even a merciful god would side with her after everything she'd done. *I have wandered too far into the realms of sin, oh Lord. I am beyond redemption. Why would you help me?*

Stella marched into the cabin, her hands behind her back, her head held high like Mother Superior walking the halls of a convent. Despite this pose, her eyes looked sunken, full of sorrow. When Stella brought her hands forwards, Naomi noted with alarm a Swiss army knife clenched in her fist.

Although Stella did not vote against her, there was no doubt she wasn't on her side. Naomi prepared for more abuse, or worse. What on earth could she say to Stella? The rigid ice queen had been outwardly indifferent to Michael and Faye during their time at the camp, but she clearly appreciated the couple, the uncomplicated double-act that was always doing things for the commune with doe-eyed enthusiasm as if they were out to earn gold stars. All Naomi wanted was to live a quiet life at Synner's Crag, do what's necessary and, for the rest of the time, enjoy the commune as a safe haven. She was not averse to work, only to expansion plans and grand schemes that were obviously not going to succeed, like the channel Joel wanted to dig from the stream to the camp through an impossible, rocky route and against gravity. He'd probably supervise the work but not partake. *All that doesn't matter now. They've turned against me. Why is Stella carrying a knife?*

Stella sat on Dorothy's bed, her knees too close to Naomi's. She placed the pocketknife on the pillow beside her and joined her palms as if in prayer, blew into them and looked at her with narrowed eyes.

'I'm hungry,' Naomi said.

'We're all hungry,' Stella said in a friendlier voice than Naomi had expected. 'The supreme leader declared the fields out of bounds, so the boys are out on an expedition to get some mushrooms. The plan is for nettle and mushroom soup tonight. If they don't find mushrooms, it'll be nettle soup. At least we still have salt, and there's an endless supply of nettles. I'll make it as thick as I can. Hope it doesn't give us the runs.'

'You've come for a chat?'

'I've come to make amends,' Stella said, 'and to get an explanation.'

'I've already explained.'

'I'm going to release you,' Stella said. 'Or not.'

'I'll go with option one.'

'I want the truth.'

Naomi eyed her suspiciously. Was Stella laying a trap to trick her into confessing? It was best to probe some more and lie some more. 'If I confess to these stupid accusations, why would you release me?'

Stella sighed. 'Look, I'm not sure I believe it. Not all of it, anyway.' She looked away. 'We... we all carry some guilt. All of us. Well, except for Luke and Faye.'

Naomi thought she heard footsteps outside the cabin. Then came a thud, as if someone had tripped on a rock.

'Anyone there?' Stella called out. 'Boys?'

No response came, but she thought she heard more movement, like someone running away.

'Must be some animal or something,' Naomi said. 'So, you feel guilty for provoking Adrian in the roundhouse? For stealing from his fields in the first place? Nobody complained when they were eating it, did they? Except for Joel Stalin.'

Stella said nothing and let her hands fall to her lap, her shoulders slouched. She gave Naomi a serious nod, followed by a shake of her head.

'Not just that,' Naomi said. Then, a realisation came to her. In a sympathetic tone, she asked, 'What really happened to Lilian?'

Stella's lip quivered, and her hand rose to tug on her ear. A flicker of pain crossed her face.

Bingo, Naomi thought, but held back from showing any outward satisfaction. She waited for more.

When Stella finally spoke, her voice was low and gruff. 'We told her to meet us at the cave.'

'We?'

'Joel, Slevin and I. We just wanted to talk to her about something, away from camp, in case it got heated.'

'And did it? Get heated, I mean?'

Stella nodded. 'Very. Especially when we told her she had to leave the commune.'

'What's she done?'

Stella shook her head. 'It's not important. Not any more. Maybe I was too harsh, and Joel with his stupid knife... He never knows when to stop, does he? He didn't want to hurt her, he told us a million times after, but he... he wasn't thinking.' She bit her lip. 'He never does.'

'He stabbed her?' Naomi whispered.

Stella shook her head again. 'When Lilian said she won't leave, he held his knife up in the air, threatening like, and walked towards her. She panicked, and then she... she walked backwards really fast to get away from him. He should have stopped then. She was scared enough. She was holding her hands up and shouting, "You're not doing this to me! I'm not going!" and Joel was relentless. and I... I should have stopped it. I didn't think it would...' Stella looked down and mumbled, 'She died.'

Naomi softened her face and leaned forward, as much as the rope allowed. 'So, he killed her?'

Stella drew a deep breath and hugged herself. 'You know the deep fall, the shaft at the entrance to the cave where you can barely see the bottom? One minute she was still screaming, and then she...' Stella's tears flowed freely now, from her hardened face that never cried. 'It happened so quickly. She didn't stand a chance, fell straight down. One moment she was walking backwards, and the next she tripped back and disappeared. We heard her hit the bottom, and then... no screams. It was so quiet, so quiet.'

'Are you sure she died? Even if you fall, you can still—'

'Joel checked. She... she died instantly, broke her neck. It was awful. We got back and pretended, to ourselves, to everyone, like it never happened. Didn't know what else to do.' She buried her face in her hands. 'It was so awful, Naomi.'

'So, you just left her there?' Naomi said.

'Slevin and Joel... Well, the three of us, we discussed it. We didn't kill her. It was an accident, just a horrible, horrible accident. What's the point in getting the authorities involved, and then there'll be police and suspicions and who knows what? We decided to leave her where she was, in peace.'

Noami lowered her head, stared at the ground and waited.

'I haven't slept properly since,' Stella said. 'My stomach hurts. I feel like I want to be sick a lot of the time.'

Three Hail Marys and sacrifice a goat, Naomi thought. She wasn't being callous about Lilian's death. She was angry. *The bastards killed her. For what?* Even so, Stella's contrition presented an opening, an opportunity.

Stella blew her nose on her sleeve. 'And then Dorothy dies and Michael and… This isn't normal. I've never seen anyone die before. And Lilian. Every time I think about it, I imagine… What if we were kinder, softer, whatever it takes? I wish we just…' She choked.

Naomi stopped herself from saying, *It was an accident. You couldn't have known she'd fall.* It was better for Stella to weep and stoke her guilty conscience, especially as the next part was going to be tricky. She'd read somewhere that people were more suggestible when they experienced mental pain.

'Maybe it was Luke,' Naomi said.

'What?'

'The keys. Luke was with Dorothy when she returned from London. He's the one who said he saw Dorothy put the keys in her coat pocket. Maybe she gave him the keys to carry. Maybe he just saw where she put them. I don't know. It wasn't me. Honestly, I had nothing to do with the keys. Maybe he wrote the note to throw off suspicion.'

Stella wiped her face with her fists. 'Why on earth would Luke hide the keys?'

'How much do we know about him, Stella? Like, really know? And think about the note that came with the keys. Can you imagine Joel or Slevin writing it? Joel writes like a child, and Slevin can't spell. I think he's dyslexic. That leaves you and me, so unless you wrote it, it had to be Luke. And no, I don't believe anything actually happened to Faye. The whole thing must have tripped a fuse in her brain. It was just too much. She probably lost it, unless Luke… Did he come back to the roundhouse after Faye left?'

Stella's puffy face was unreadable. Naomi waited with bated breath. Had she, with her weave of words, done enough to sow some doubts? If Stella released her, she would never again allow herself to be bound. Her sole goal was survival and to be free. If things turned against her again, she'd be ready. There was a small stash of money she had kept from her escape, hidden in one of the boxes under her mattress, just in case. Not a huge sum, but enough. She'd head north to Scotland, get a fake ID and then take a ferry to Belfast. From there, it shouldn't be difficult to get to Dublin, away from nosy UK police forces.

'This isn't easy, Naomi.'

'It's very easy. Use your knife. Cut me loose. Is there any coffee left?'

'Luke? You sure? I mean, we left him covering Dorothy's grave with Slevin, and then Joel went to tell them Faye was off to get help.' She thought about this for a moment. 'He didn't come back to join us until much later.'

'Well, it's not definite,' Naomi said. 'Slevin or Joel were also away at the same time. But then you have the note, and neither of those two could have written it, so you tell me, Stella. You tell me.'

CHAPTER TWENTY-SEVEN

Luke was assigned to carry the cotton tote bag that contained the scarce bounty of their foraging mission: a total of five mushrooms that Joel had inspected and deemed edible. Inside the bag, they looked laughably small and already shrivelled.

'A mushroom each,' Luke said when they gave up on the hunt.

Joel wiped his mouth with his sleeve. 'We can split Naomi's between us. She doesn't deserve to eat.'

'You decided she's guilty,' Luke said, 'based on an anonymous note?'

'She's guilty,' Joel said. 'Did you see how she denied it? I can tell, you know. I can sense lies on people like a foul smell.'

'The human polygraph,' Slevin said and chuckled. 'Really, Joel, you of all people. You might have superpowers, but this? Definitely not one of them.'

Joel's fat, sweaty cheeks burned red. He waited a few seconds, and only then, in an odd out-of-time response, barked at Slevin, 'Shut up!'

A ruckus of birds fled from the treetops in a chorus of wing flaps.

The three of them followed the trail in the woods, an uneasy silence between them. Luke tried for a lighter tone and spoke to Slevin, who was hitting random trees with a length of stick he had picked up on the way. 'You never wear a shirt. Aren't you cold? I mean, Northumberland isn't equatorial Africa, even in July.'

'Nah, dude. This ain't cold. Not compared to where I was before.'

'Oh, here we go,' Joel said. 'You wound up his key, and now he won't shut up about it until we get to camp.'

'Walk ahead, mate,' Slevin said to Joel, dismissing him with the back of his hand. 'You don't have to partake in human conversation.' He winked at Luke, waited for Joel to lead by a few steps, then stuck his tongue out at his back.

Luke was about to encourage Slevin to say more when he thought he spotted a silhouette, like a shadowy figure of a woman in the depths of the woods. He shivered and clenched his fists, his nails boring into the flesh of his palms. Yes, it was *her*. He had no doubt.

Slevin grinned at his discomfort. 'Even talking about the cold gives you the chills? Dude!'

Luke felt a veil of fear masking his vision. He hoped Joel, who was now a few steps forward, wouldn't walk too far ahead.

'I was with the British Antarctic Survey,' Slevin said. 'It was wild.'

Joel spoke out without looking back. 'It was so, so cold there, the chill here is nothing to Slevin. Nothing. So much nothing, it took us months to get him to shut up about it.'

'Don't mind him,' Slevin said to Luke. 'Living in the South Pole was amazing.'

'What did you do there?' Luke asked, trying not to look sideways, but straining the corners of his eyes. *I have to act like I haven't seen her, not let on she's lost the element of surprise. I'm ready for you, Karla. I'm...* His train of thought stopped mid-track. Over the last few days, something had definitely changed. *I'm ready for you, Karla.*

He pretended to wipe a speck from his shoulder and used the movement to steal a glance to his right. No sign of her. Maybe she had stayed behind, tracking them at a distance, or maybe she was rushing ahead to lie in wait. It was also possible she had let him see her. Torment was Karla's art form, and she was a consummate artist. The note accusing Naomi had her finger paint all over it.

'I was a field assistant at Rothera Research Station,' Slevin said.

'What?'

'In the Antarctic. You all right, mate?'

Luke did his best to focus and act normal. 'What was it like?'

'Surreal, dude. I was there over the Austral winter. Everyone leaves when summer is over, except for twenty-one of us that stayed at the station to maintain it. You're completely cut off from the world. If something happens, there isn't really a way to evacuate you for about seven months. No law as well, which is a good thing if there's erm… tensions that need sorting in more traditional ways.' He kicked a small rock off the trail.

Luke gave him a questioning look.

Slevin sighed. 'We had to deal with a few entitled tossers, and it went south, pun intended, but that's a story for another time. Other than that, I loved it there. You don't worry about material things. You get a place to live, food, everything you need, and you work to keep the place running and support the scientists. Hard work, lots of books and movies. The outside world might as well be on Mars. In the Antarctic winter, you're on your own.'

'I guess that explains why you joined a commune,' Luke said.

'The climate here is better,' Slevin said, 'but there's no supply ship, so food isn't a given, except for, you know, Adrian's fields.' He giggled and snorted, then seemed to compose himself.

'Were you close with Michael?' Luke said.

'Come on, dude,' Slevin said. 'Don't go there. We're having a good time, telling war stories. I'm sad. Of course, I'm sad, but he's gone. No one can bring him back.' He looked down at his shoes. 'Shit, man. Death follows me like a curse.'

Death follows me too, Luke wanted to say. Instead, he put a hand on Slevin's shoulder. 'Dorothy died in her sleep, and Adrian shot Michael. It's got nothing to do with you.'

'It's not just…' Slevin said, but stopped himself and shook his head.

Luke was keen to keep the conversation going, for appearances' sake. 'I guess you need a lot of patience to be stuck with such a small group for months with no way to leave.'

Slevin wiped his nose with the back of his hand. 'You get one week off, like a holiday in mid-winter, which is the darkest time there. No sun at all, no daylight. There's a lot of drinking and singing and games. Honestly, it's like being eighteen again. If I could do it again, I'd go back in a heartbeat, but I don't think they'd ever take me back.'

'Because of the—?' Luke started to say.

'Look, I can see smoke,' Slevin said. 'Stella's cooking. Well, she's boiling water, anyway.'

As they walked into the camp's clearing, Slevin raised his stick and spoke to it, 'Thanks, mate.' Then he threw it back into the forest. They followed Joel to the roundhouse, with Slevin calling out, 'Honey, we're home!'

As they stepped inside, the three of them stopped cold and stared.

'Coffee?' Stella said.

'What's *she* doing here?' Joel said and pointed at Naomi.

'It's rude to point,' Naomi said.

Joel crossed his arms, and Luke observed that this was Joel's default, crossed arms over his chest. It was like he was demanding something from everyone else that they could never provide, or maybe it was just his way of trying to hide himself.

'I let her go,' Stella said.

'Can I ask why?' Joel said.

'Because she didn't do it. Any of it. And I believe her. We're not animals, and we don't have the right to tie someone up.'

'You've changed your tune,' Slevin said.

'About this, I didn't have a tune,' Stella said.

'I didn't give you permission,' Joel said.

Stella shrugged and poured coffee into two cups. She handed one to Luke and the other to Slevin. She offered none to Joel. Luke dreaded the day when he was the one refused his coffee. He wondered what Naomi thought of him now, after his betrayal when he voted for her to be restrained, despite spending the night in her bed. She hadn't looked at him once since he'd entered the roundhouse.

'I'm taking her back,' Joel said. He grasped the hilt of his machete. 'Slevin, help me.'

Naomi reached down to the floor and raised her own bush knife. Joel looked at it with narrowed, angry eyes.

'I hope you don't mind,' Naomi said calmly. 'I borrowed it. Self-defence against impulsive prats. You come near me, I'll get you, so don't tempt me. I have form with knives. I've had training in a harsh environment. You won't know what hit you.'

Luke took a sip of his coffee and sat down. *I'm staying well out of this one.* Joel might be skilled with knives, but Naomi seemed hard and determined. If he had to place bets, he'd bet on her.

Slevin leaned his back against the door frame's pillar and

observed the confrontation with a wry smile, like a boy enjoying the sight of a fight in the playground.

Joel glared at Naomi but didn't move. For a moment, he looked confused, swallowing several times. Then his hand moved slowly away from his weapon's hilt.

Naomi gave Joel the finger. This threw him into a rage. 'How dare you!' he hissed, stomping his foot on the ground.

'How dare I, Mr Witchfinder General?' Naomi said. 'Let's see. *The commune wasn't for Lilian, so she left.* Isn't that what you told Dorothy?'

Slevin's eyes widened, and he turned to Stella. 'You told her?'

'You had no right,' Joel said to Stella. 'This was meant to stay between us. The commune takes precedence. If word got out...' he stopped himself and grunted.

Stella bunched her hair, then released it. 'Aww, Jojo,' she said to Joel. 'You upset about me telling, or about what happened? Honestly, I want to know.'

Joel's face froze as if holding back an expression too scary to share. Luke knew this mask well. He had practised it himself more than once: emotions reined in so tightly, the ends of your nerves became numb. He also knew from Lilian's diary that she had gone to the cave to meet Joel, Slevin and Stella. *What happened? Did they hurt her? Evict her? Kill her?* When he played Truth or Truth with Joel at the cave, Joel confessed to killing someone by accident. *Was it really an accident?* The possibility unnerved and comforted him in equal measures. If they had it in them to do something so extreme, maybe they all stood a chance against Karla.

Stella looked away from Joel. 'You find any food?' she said to Slevin.

Slevin motioned to the tote bag Luke had placed on the table and shrugged.

Stella took the bag without looking at Luke, almost

purposely ignoring him. He rewound his memory and realised she had done the same when she handed him his coffee. *What have I done wrong now? Apart from bringing a violent psycho to the commune, but they don't know that. Not yet.* Then his thoughts dredged up Karla again. He'd have to tell them, but this wasn't the time. On the other hand, if she was stalking them, eventually she'd strike. He shouldn't leave it too late. His fingers reached up, as if of their own accord, and pinched his throat. *Not tonight. There's too much going on. Tomorrow, somehow. I'll have to bring myself to do it, talk to them, explain. I owe it to them.*

Stella picked out a mushroom from the bag and brought it to her nose. 'Hmm,' she said, 'nutritious. I've got nettles and salt boiling in the pot already. I'll add these in. It'll be a step up from herbal tea, but not quite soup.'

'I'm not hungry,' Joel said. 'We'll have a commune meeting in the morning. Then we can discuss… everything.' He walked backwards until he was out of the roundhouse, as if someone might stab him in the back.

'Whoa, that was heavy,' Slevin said.

Naomi placed her knife back on the floor at the foot of her chair and said, 'Time for new elections?'

'Shh,' Stella said. 'What was that?'

'What's what?' Naomi said.

'Shh,' Stella repeated, then whispered. 'I heard something, like there's someone just outside the back of the roundhouse.'

'Probably just Joel eavesdropping,' Slevin said.

'Or Lilian's ghost,' Naomi said and inexplicably smiled.

She's dead then, Luke thought. *This confirms it. Three deaths. With Faye, maybe four.*

CHAPTER TWENTY-EIGHT

THE DAY BEFORE THE RECKONING

When morning came, the commune's members again seemed like they hadn't slept much, but this time not on account of late-night celebrations or booze. *Hunger,* Luke thought, *and whatever happened to Lilian.*

Everyone knew, except for him. He wanted to ask Naomi about it, but she had been distant and only spoke to him briefly, to say she was going to sleep in Dorothy's cabin. She threw her bedding and some clothes into a sheet that she used as a sack and left. Despite his worry for her safety, he couldn't object. The way she looked at him made it clear she wouldn't listen. And why would she, after he'd voted to have her restrained?

Luke had other reasons to be tired that morning. He had lain in bed, knowing that at any moment Karla might appear at his door. After a while, he got up, went outside and returned with a rock the size of two fists, which he laid by his side, ready to strike. He had considered borrowing the axe they used for chopping wood, which was planted in a tree trunk next to the boys' cabin, but decided against it. Someone might notice, and he'd have to explain. He kept his clothes on, just in case. *I'm ready for you, Karla.* There were moments when he wished she would come. *Do your worst. I'm not scared any more.* This was not entirely true, but he would repeat the lie until it wiped away any doubts and he believed it completely.

They ate the previous night's thin broth of nettles and mushrooms unheated, the many unspoken words hanging in the air between them.

Joel broke the silence. In a jovial voice, he said, 'Stella, listen, I accept your decision about Naomi.'

Stella put down her spoon and looked at him.

'I don't agree with it,' he said, 'but I accept it.'

'Not wanting to lose your position of power and become a pleb?' Naomi said.

'Don't poke the bear,' Slevin said.

'Bear?' Naomi said. 'More like a piglet.'

'That's enough,' Stella said. 'Thank you, Joel. I know it was a bit of a shock.'

Naomi chewed on her lip. 'We're doing diplomacy now?'

Stella curled her hands on the tabletop. 'Enough! I've heard a lot of accusations in the last twenty-four hours. We've been so stuck in our own heads that we forgot something important. Adrian will be back tomorrow, and we need to have a plan.'

'What accusations?' Slevin said.

'It's not important,' Stella said. 'I suggest we use the time to prepare, if that's all right with you, Joel? I know we're all hungry, so please, let's cut everyone some slack.'

'You're in line for a sainthood,' Naomi said. Then, she seemed to think about it, and added, 'It's not always the best thing to aspire to. To be a saint, you have to die first, don't you?'

Joel shrugged. 'We should kill Adrian,' he said.

'Dude, what?' Slevin said.

'It's the farmer or us. He's already murdered Michael. Or do you prefer he gets to shoot us instead?'

'Seriously?' Slevin said.

'For once,' Naomi said, 'I agree with Joel.'

'We're not killing anyone,' Stella said.

'See,' Naomi said, 'a fucking saint.'

'Saints don't fuck,' Slevin said.

'I rest my case,' Naomi said.

Joel planted his hands on his waist and pushed out his stomach. 'What's your idea, then, Stella? Bake him a cake?'

Stella scratched her wrist. 'Like you said at the bonfire, we need to be ready. Meet fire with fire.'

'Maybe we should dig a trap,' Luke said, 'or barricade ourselves in the roundhouse.' He shrugged. 'One thing I know for sure. We should be the ones surprising him.'

Luke still couldn't bring himself to tell them about Karla, but under the guise of preparing for the farmer, maybe they could ready themselves for both threats.

Naomi looked at him for the first time that morning. 'You obviously have a lot of practice dealing with murderers like Adrian. I'll defer to your vast experience.'

Luke met her raised eyebrow with his own. 'Intimate experience,' he said, 'as you well know.'

Slevin covered his eyes with his palms. 'It's sarcasm central here, today.'

'Hunger,' Stella said. 'It's just…' Her words trailed off, and her hand shot down to her stomach.

'What's going on?' Slevin said. 'Stella, you all right?'

Stella's eyes were closed now, her expression strained, looking like she was in pain. She put her hand to her mouth. 'I think I'm gonna be sick.' She rushed to her feet. 'Yes, it's coming.' She ran out of the roundhouse. They heard her retching outside, along with the sound of liquid vomit and expressive coughs.

Luke looked into his half-empty bowl of soup and counted fingers. Could Karla have laced it with something overnight? Rat poison, for example? He checked himself. His heartbeat had accelerated, and his stomach rumbled. Were these the result of his worry or the effects of poison? He looked around him. No one else looked ill.

'Are you sure the mushrooms were safe?' Slevin said to Joel.

'I'm an expert on mushrooms, you twat,' Joel said.

Slevin puffed out his bare chest. 'Who are you calling a *twat?*'

Luke decided to intervene. They couldn't afford macho arguments. Bickering would only distract them. They had no idea of the danger they were in. 'It's not the mushrooms,' he said. 'It can't be. We ate the soup last night, and the mushrooms were chopped into small pieces. If there's a bad one in there, we'd all know by now.'

'I'll go check on her,' Naomi said.

'No,' Slevin said. 'I'll go. Can't stand the company right now. We can make plans later.'

After a few long minutes, Luke was relieved to see no one else was sick, and he himself felt fine. Stella returned to the roundhouse, looking pale, but otherwise unharmed. He said a silent *thank you* to the universe and counted fingers for luck. Danger was ever-present now, but it had not been dished out in yesterday's soup. It was, however, a wake-up call. He'd have to keep a watchful eye on the food too, if there was going to be any. But how? He couldn't be in all places all the time. He took his cup of coffee and went outside to sit on a folding chair next to the clay oven. The hazy sun felt warm on his cheeks.

Joel marched out of the roundhouse and came to stand awkwardly beside him.

'All right, Joel?' he said, more out of politeness than interest.

'You ever experience love?' Joel said, looking down, not meeting his eyes. 'Like the real thing.'

'Context, please?'

Joel shook his head, looking bothered.

'Joel, what's brought this on in the middle of a famine and a world-ending crisis?'

Joel leaned over him, bringing his face close to his own. Luke could almost taste his stale breath. It smelled like a swamp.

'Answer the question, Lukas. Did you ever experience love?'

'Yeah. I think so.'

'If you *think so*, then it wasn't real.'

'All right.'

'When it happens,' Joel said, 'when it *really* happens, you can't sleep, you can't eat, your thoughts become confused. You lose control. It's like an illness takes over. And the world, it seems like it could be perfect, if only they loved you back.'

Luke couldn't think what to say in response.

Joel took a step back, and his face relaxed. 'Yeah, sorry, no. It doesn't matter. I don't know why I told you that. Hunger, probably. We're all a bit on edge. Forget I–'

'Is this about Lilian?' Luke said.

Joel grabbed him by the shoulders and squeezed with the force of a vice, sending daggers of pain down his sides. 'The commune has to come first. Before relationships, before love.'

Luke relished the pain. He'd known much worse. 'She didn't love you back, then?'

'Shut your mouth, Lukas. You've only been here five minutes. You have no say in anything. You're not even a member yet.' With that, Joel let go of him and lumbered away, wide sweat marks showing under the armpits of his khaki T-shirt.

Curiouser and curiouser, Luke thought. The clues were starting to add up, forming the outlines of what might have happened to Lilian. Love can be cruel. Crazed love can be deadly. There would be the story they'd tell, maybe even to themselves. Then, there'd be the truth, revealed in little unguarded statements like Joel's.

After the tense breakfast and the chat with Joel, Luke decided to give the smelly toilet a miss and find a suitable tree along the eastern forest path, away from the chance of unwelcome encounters and conversations. He took a roll of paper with him. Once he was far enough from the commune, he left the path and found a tree that was flanked by bushy growth. Behind it, he would not be seen, even if someone walked past. He concluded his business, meagre as it was for lack of food, and was about to head back when he heard voices. He crouched again to wait for them to pass.

The voices grew nearer. It was Stella and Slevin.

'I'm feeling better. Don't fuss,' Stella said.

'Was worried about you,' Slevin said. 'You sure we shouldn't be back there, start making plans for tomorrow? You leave them to it too long, and they'll come up with some silly hare-brained scheme, like, you know, killing the farmer.'

'I just need some time away,' she said, 'and also…' She hesitated. 'Listen, I want to talk to you about something.'

'You're thinking they suspect us,' he said. 'I can tell.'

'What? No. We were very careful. No one suspects.'

'What, then? Is it serious?' he said.

'Yeah. I found something out. But not here. I'll tell you when we get there.'

'C'mon!'

Their voices grew more distant, and Luke could no longer make out the words that followed. The world felt like it was closing in on him. The mortal threats from Karla and the farmer, Naomi the runaway murderer, Joel the crazed knife-wielding man and now Stella and Slevin, who were hiding something. He thought back to his conversation with Dorothy on their drive north. *Rising with the sun, simpler, nature,* promises that now seemed a world away from Synner's Crag.

CHAPTER TWENTY-NINE

At a distance from the tensions of the camp, Stella felt she could breathe again. There were things to do, plans to flesh out, but in the pressure cooker the commune had become, it was difficult to think straight. A hike with Slevin to their favourite spot was not only a pleasant distraction but also a necessary one. The hidden waterfall with its watery spray and shallow pool of clear, chilly water was a place where she could calm herself, talk to Slevin and decide on their next move, detached from everything and everyone else. They could also stop on the way and eat some berries. Maybe it would make the hunger pangs subside a little. No matter how many nettles she used, the resulting soup had not been in the least filling. The five mushrooms, finely chopped into the previous night's pot, had added nothing of substance.

She never had cause to think of death, but in the last few days, it seemed so close. When her mother died, shortly before Stella joined the commune, it felt like a timer had started to count down to her own end, an hourglass tipped, the remaining sand of her life draining. It was as if her mother's age at death was a magic number. This was nonsense, of course. There were other factors, for example, her father. *How long will he live?* She wondered what he was doing at that moment. Probably sitting in the conservatory of the widow's house in Penrhyndeudraeth – Stella still thought of her as *the widow* – with a cup of tea and a plate of Digestives, staring through his half-moon glasses, trying to figure out an especially challenging crossword clue on the phone app that had become his favourite pastime. Everyone else in the commune seemed to despise their parents, and this included Joel, but Stella had nothing but warmth for her own.

Slevin took off his shorts and jumped, stark naked, into the icy pool. He washed his head in the waterfall's splash, then squeezed the water out of his hair and climbed back onto the muddy verge to stand close to Stella, his skin a field of goosebumps.

'What's with the serious face, eh? You think too much, Stell.' As he said this, he pulled his shorts back on, not seeming to mind the damp patches that spread through their fabric.

She kicked off her trainers and let the soles of her feet absorb the pleasant coolness of the muddy ground. 'I saw Lilian's ghost in my dream last night. She didn't look happy.'

'That's an understandable position for her ghost to take. And if you're superstitious like me, bad things come in threes. Lilian started the cycle, then Dorothy and Michael. Mind you, I'm not including Faye. I'm sure she's fine.'

Stella looked at him, then down at the flaky skin patches on her bended knees. 'So, in a way, it's all our fault.'

'Or Lilian's. Hey, hey. Don't be like that. Look at me.' With a gentle hand on her cheek, he turned her head towards him and held her gaze in his. 'I'm here, all right? We're here for each other. We're Stella and Slevin. No one can touch us. We're a force to be reckoned with.'

She gave him a tender smile, and he kissed her on the lips.

She removed his hand from her cheek, kissed it, and then let it drop.

'Anyway,' he said, 'Someone's messing with us, and it's not Lilian's ghost.' He fished out the keys to the Peugeot from his pocket, plugged his finger into the key ring and rotated them in circles around it. 'I went to check on the car. Someone slashed the tyres proper deep.' He threw the keys high into the air. They flew in an arc, then plopped into the water at the far end of the pool.

Stella looked at him, wide-eyed. 'What the fuck?'

Slevin shrugged. 'If we called the AA, just towing it away would cost more than we have. It's practically useless.'

'Why would Adrian kill our car?' she said. 'Doesn't he want us to eff off?'

'Maybe Naomi–'

She interrupted him. 'It's not Naomi.'

'If you say so.'

'Listen, Slev, there's something we need to discuss. We're going to have to come clean about us. We have to tell them.'

'And start a Joel shitstorm?'

'Yes.'

'Why would you do that? Everything's fine the way it is.'

She hesitated, then made up her mind. 'I think Naomi already guessed. I saw the way she looked at me when I was sick this morning.'

It only took him a moment. 'Sick, in the morning. You mean…? What? Like morning sickness?'

Clever boy, she thought.

Slevin's face changed from incomprehension to marvel. A wide grin spread to the far edges of his cheeks. 'I'm going to be a daddy?'

She nodded.

He wrapped his arms around her and drew her into a bear

hug. Then, he released her, held her shoulders and gave them a little shake. 'Stella Crane! Dude! I'm going to be a daddy!'

'Dude?'

He regarded her thoughtfully. 'You sure you're pregnant? I mean, you were drinking like a trooper. How do you know?'

'Yeah. No more drinking. Didn't really clock it until I was sick today. I missed a couple of periods, and it felt like something in my body was changing, but you know me, I repress. But yeah, it all adds up. I've been peeing a lot, feeling tired. My breasts are sore. I'm silly for not putting two and seven together. It's just…'

He rubbed his hands and came to sit next to her. 'It's what happens when Mummy and Daddy have sexual relations.' He shook his head, joyfully spraying water in every direction like a dog after a bath.

She ran her hand through his wet hair, touched his nose with the tip of her finger, and leaned in to kiss him on the cheek. 'So we can tell them? About us, I mean? I don't want to keep it a secret any more.'

'I thought you liked them to think you're a sexless old maid. Of course, we can tell them, and Joel can do one. I'm going to be a daddy! We'll raise a kid in the commune. I'll teach our little girl to play the guitar!'

'What makes you think…'

'Seriously, dude, with your super genes? Not a chance in hell it's a boy.'

'We still have to get through the next few days. The Adrianmageddon is coming.'

'Nah. It'll blow over. No one's coming for us, Stell. Farmer boy will calm down, and things will go back to normal. We can rebuild, plant veg, maybe recruit some new members. We'll move into a cabin together, or the bell tent. I promise to wash at least once a week.' He hesitated. 'You're carrying our baby now. You should eat properly. I know what we said, but maybe I should go get you some food from the fields.'

She shook her head.

'No one needs to know. It'll just be for you and the little dudette and, of course, Daddy will need to taste it for quality control. You don't have to answer right now. Wait until you're proper hungry.'

'I'm already hungry. So hungry, I almost don't feel it any more. But you're right, the baby comes first. I just want you to be careful, all right? Don't know what I'd do without you.'

'Have no fear, Slevin's here. Slevin's not going anywhere. Now, m'lady, Daddy's going for a celebratory swim.'

'Again? It looks freezing.'

'Oh yeah, bracing. Makes me feel alive. Pretty please, Mummy, can I have a swim?'

'It's your funeral. Your orphan and I will say nice things. Well, go on then. I need to go for another pee anyway.' She reached for her shoes.

As she crouched in the bushes, she could hear him whooping with joy in the water. She smiled. *Everything will be okay*. His words warmed her heart. *We're Stella and Slevin. No one can touch us. We're a force to be reckoned with. I'm going to be a daddy!* She shook her head. *Dude!*

Then came a loud thud and a splash, like a rock hitting something with great force. Slevin was suddenly silent, no longer howling.

She hurried back to the pool, and her mouth gaped open in a silent scream. The water had turned a bloody red. Slevin's body was floating in it, inert, face down. The back of his head was a broken mess. She looked up to the top of the waterfall, then down again at her lifeless lover.

They had hidden their secret for over a year, always meeting away from the commune. They were so careful. Why? Because of Joel's stupid jealousies? No. Because it suited them both, keeping up appearances as if love didn't matter. Or maybe they thought common knowledge would break the spell. And now, their love had been crushed by a rock that someone must have heaved from above, from the top of the waterfall. It was too awful. She could barely feel her body. The scale of what had just happened was too big, *too big*. Her legs turned to jelly. She fell to the ground, her hands clasped over her chest.

No. Slevin. Please!

These thoughts crossed her mind in a split second, and before she knew it, she was in the icy pool, raising his head above the water, trying to revive him, all the while knowing it was hopeless. It must have been a huge rock. The cheerful, beautiful Slevin would have died the instant he was hit. One look at the gore on the back of his head told her so. But his face was still his. She kissed him on the lips and rocked him back and forth, holding his body in the freezing water. Then, in a moment of clarity, she looked up again. Whoever was up there could target her next. If it were just her, she wouldn't care, but now there was someone else to worry about, her unborn baby, *their* unborn baby.

With all the force she had in her, she dragged Slevin out of the water and away from the pool, laying his head softly on the muddy ground. Then she ran as fast as her legs could carry her, breathless and shivering, unsure if she was running to something or away from it.

CHAPTER THIRTY

SEVENTEEN DAYS POST DISCOVERY

'What have you got for me today, Mr Czerniak?' Sandra said. 'I expect the cheque has cleared, so you're working for me now, correct? You're *my* private investigator.'

He gave her one of his well-rehearsed, professional smiles. 'You're my client, yes.'

'Let's not play with each other. I expect you not to work for other people while you're on my case.'

Alex checked himself to stop his annoyance from showing. He rarely got riled by clients, but Sandra Saint-John was grating on him. There was something beyond her bitter nature that made him wary. He couldn't put his finger on it, like a nagging thought that gnawed at his sense of her. What was it?

'Your case will never suffer from lack of focus,' he said, preferring not to press the point that his contract made no promise of exclusivity. 'I've now seen a copy of the report about the death of Slevin Grimlow, as well as some interesting information about the survivor, Luke Bridestone.'

'Tell me about Luke first. Where did you say they're keeping him?'

'University College Hospital, still in the Critical Care Unit at UCH Tower. He's in a separate room under police guard, just in case.' He berated himself. *Why did I tell her that?* He brushed his palm over his stubble. 'Can I ask you a question first?' Without waiting for a response, he added, 'Have you ever been to see this commune?'

'Oh, I was never invited. I think Dorothy would rather drink bleach than have me visit. Why do you ask?'

'Just curious. Have you been to Northumberland, for any reason?'

'Ever?' She paused, then shrieked out a series of giggles that ended in a coughing fit. She touched his knee in that familiar way he disliked. 'Mr Czerniak, you devil. You're not implying I had anything to do with...' She showed him her palms and made a jazz hands gesture, 'all that.'

'Of course not,' he said, his denial coming out weaker than he intended. 'Hadn't even crossed my mind. Just interested to know if you've seen the place.'

She grinned and tapped the side of her forehead twice with two fingers. 'I'm not an idiot. You must know that by now. If it were me behind these tragic, *tragic*, deaths, I'd get someone competent and expensive to do it for me, you know, like I hired you. I certainly wouldn't travel hundreds of miles. To what? Smash Slevin whatsit on the head? I'm a very sick woman.'

He tried to look casual, to mask his surprise. 'Funny you should say that. Slevin Grimlow died from a crushing blow to the back of his head, possibly by a rock. He died instantly.'

A moment of silence passed between them. He thought he detected a guilty blush colouring Sandra's cheeks, though he was uncertain of his diagnosis. He made a mental note of the questions he'd later write in his notebook.

She jabbed a finger in his direction, at the same time shaking her head. She was more animated than in their previous meetings, all knee-jerks and hands and meaningful nods. Was it possible her sickly appearance before was an act?

He would have to dig deeper into his client's history and medical records, look for inconsistencies.

Through a reproachful smile, she said, 'The family liaison officer might have told me. Can't remember. Or it might have been a lucky guess. Oh, don't look at me like that. You work for me, remember?'

'Of course I work for you, and please don't misunderstand.'

He knew she understood him perfectly, and that in itself was of note. He drew in a breath for calm. He was getting ahead of himself. Maybe what he saw was just another glimpse into Sandra's stony heart, compounded by a lucky guess as she suggested.

'As I was saying, Slevin Grimlow was–'

'You have pictures?' she said.

'I wouldn't advise–'

'Let's see them.'

She set the three A4 colour prints he handed her on her lap and reviewed them one by one, unfazed, as if they were holiday snaps. When she reached the third, a close-up of the back of Slevin's shattered head, she pursed her lips. 'Someone must have wanted him very dead indeed.' She handed the pictures back to him. 'What else do the police know?'

'They said investigations are ongoing, which in this case is code for *we have no definite leads at this time*. But the way he died does throw a spanner in the works.'

'Oh?'

'Slevin was originally a suspect. Before he joined the commune, he spent a winter season on a British research base in the Antarctic.'

'The North Pole?'

'The other one. Six of the base's crew didn't make it back that year. The place is completely isolated in winter. For months, they're on their own, living in close quarters. The victims died under suspicious circumstances, but it was a difficult investigation. Antarctica isn't an easy crime scene to reach, and for some reason, the fifteen surviving crew kept shtum, wouldn't talk to the investigators. Slevin was a key suspect. He'd been wild and unruly.'

'Then it doesn't surprise me Dorothy recruited him. Murderers were exactly her type, if her ex-husband is anything to go by.'

'The police felt at the time that Slevin got away with it. Because of the remote location and the fact that the bodies were destroyed in a fire, they couldn't get evidence to a good enough standard for a prosecution. They couldn't charge him, so they had to let him go. Then he joined the commune.'

'Do they think he murdered at least some of the people at Synner's Crag?'

'For this case, he was originally pegged as *the understudy*. Now, they're not so sure. Someone might have come after Slevin exactly because of what happened in the South Pole station, because no justice was served.'

'What do you mean, *understudy*?'

'If they didn't find credible evidence anyone else played the leading role, they might have concluded he did it, at least some of it. That he was murdered so violently adds some... complexity. We don't have a definitive timeline for when each of the deaths happened, but if I'm honest, I–'

'I expect you to be honest with me. What is it?'

'In our last meeting, I mentioned the pathologist on the case and the mistake he made when he originally said that Michael's wound was from a gunshot. The police are now a little sceptical of his skills, which means they're also unsure if he's right about the exact sequence of deaths. And before you ask, no, they can't get a different pathologist. Police budgets. They'll have to make do.'

She leaned forward. 'So, one theory is that Slevin

murdered everyone, and then Luke Bridestone killed him in self-defence.'

'That's... a possibility. But my understanding is they were found in completely different locations. Luke fell from a cliff edge. Plus, there might be another suspect in the mix. I'll know more when the police confirm her identity.'

'Interesting,' she said. 'So, what if Slevin, this other person and Luke kill everyone. Then Luke kills the other two, feels remorse, and throws himself off a cliff. How's that for a theory?'

'In my experience,' he said, 'it's best not to jump to conclusions at such an early stage. We're still waiting on four autopsy reports, and those could change everything.'

'And if Luke killed a killer, what would happen then?'

Alex had expected this question. After all, what his client wanted to know, more than anything, was whether Luke might be guilty of a crime. 'From what I understand, it depends on the circumstances. For example, did Luke act proportionally to the threat? If someone breaks into your house, you can use reasonable force to defend yourself, but if you then chase them down the street and smash their bones with a bat, your chances of pleading self-defence are pretty slim.'

'Before you distracted me with those gory pictures, you said you had something on Luke? Was this it? Is there something more?'

He hesitated. 'It's nothing major. Not yet, anyway.' He saw the expectant look on her face and decided to fob her off with a crumb. 'All I know is that Luke's had dealings with the police in the past. They're keeping their cards close to their chests on this one.'

'What aren't you telling me?'

'You're my client. I tell you everything I find.' Alex didn't know why he'd lied to her, but at that moment, in the stuffy lounge of Sandra's house, he wasn't prepared to say more, at least not until he had reconciled himself with his own suspicions.

To his relief, Sandra took him at his word, or pretended to. She rubbed her hands and then rose to signal that their meeting was over. 'Brick by brick,' she said, 'we'll build the case against him. Mark my words, I'll get my inheritance.'

Once again, he noted that she seemed strong and healthy now, any trace of her illness gone. He left Sandra Saint-John's house with a heavy heart and a whirlwind of troubling thoughts. Then, he reminded himself of what he had said to her: best not jump to conclusions.

CHAPTER THIRTY-ONE

On the way to pick up the girls from school, Alex ran a red light, and his heart sank to his knees as a blue Mercedes nearly crashed into him, coming to a stop mere inches from his Renault Clio's passenger door. Through his closed window, he made signs of apology and contrition. The other driver, an elderly gentleman with a dandy's hair, who wore a pinstripe suit and crimson cravat, responded with a lude gesture and a stream of muted, expressive words which Alex was thankful he couldn't hear.

Back home, he served the girls freezer-to-oven pepperoni pizza, being careful to hide the packaging deep in the recycling bin. Mary wouldn't approve. He did his best not to show his girls how distracted he was and prayed for the bedtime ritual to go smoothly. The wrong gods must have heard his prayers, because Poppy decided that sleep was not for her, jumping and screaming blue murder while Rose watched her sister with patient delight, waiting for the tantrum to end so she could follow it with her own, grander performance, emptying the toy basket onto the floor and flinging her one-legged Barbie in the air whenever her father put it back in its place.

By the time Mary got home at ten p.m., the two girls had exhausted themselves to sleep, and the pandemonium was over. Alex was sitting at the kitchen table with a glass of Cabernet Shiraz, blessing the silence.

Mary kissed him and slumped into a chair. 'I smell pizza,' she said.

Alex poured her a glass of the red wine. 'You caught me, detective.'

She shook her head, then looked at him with her inquisitive eyes that saw everything. 'Rough day?'

'Can we sell them to the circus?'

'I'll make enquiries. You okay?'

'I met with Sandra Saint-John, again.'

'And?'

He didn't have secrets from Mary, nothing held back. That was the foundation for the success of their marriage. They were the kind of couple that felt entirely comfortable with each other and never locked their bathroom door. Still, it wasn't yet time to focus the police's attention on Sandra. Not yet. The bonus at the end of this assignment would guarantee their daughters' education. Poppy and Rose were the priority. *Lies of omission aren't lies*, he told himself without conviction.

'Alex?' Mary said.

'She's like a terrier shaking a dead otter.'

She smiled above the rim of her glass. 'You just made that up?' Then she seemed to notice his pained face. 'Is this about Luke Bridestone? Did you tell her about the business with the violent woman and the murders?'

He sighed and stared into his wine. 'Not yet. When it comes to Luke, she's got tunnel vision. She's so determined to find evidence that he's behind it all. Can't blame her, I suppose.'

'We've looked at her more closely, you know,' she said, then pronounced her name with elongated vowels, 'San-dra.'

He set down his glass. 'Oh?'

She took a sip of her wine. 'All we found was a garden-variety family scandal. Twenty-one years ago, Sandra Saint-John had a baby and then gave it up for adoption. She was forty-eight at the time, probably thought a pregnancy was beyond her, so the whole thing was a surprise, too late for a termination. We spoke to the social worker who handled the adoption. She wasn't as tight-lipped as you'd expect. Apparently, in a moment of weakness, Sandra confided in her. At the time, the social worker decided there was no benefit in telling anyone about it. She kept Sandra's secret to herself.'

'Why would that be a scandal?'

'The father.'

He looked at her, puzzled. 'Who?'

'Her nephew, Joel.'

'Joel, really?'

'He would have been twenty then.' Mary removed her hairband, shaking her head to let her curls loose. 'Before the birth, the social worker wanted to check if there was any chance of keeping the baby with either of its parents. She arranged a meeting with Sandra and Joel. Joel's mother, Dorothy, was also there. The social worker said that, over coffee and biscuits in Dorothy's kitchen, the two older women ganged up on Joel. He was still in shock. She remembered him as a bit of a man-child, looking much younger than his age, chubby and spotty. Apparently, his mother and aunt weren't close, didn't see each other much, so Joel only found out that week about his unexpected child. The two women were stone-cold determined, saying there was no choice but adoption. Joel didn't talk much, but the social worker thought he didn't look happy about it. After that meeting, they refused any contact with social services except to liaise about the adoption. It was a girl, apparently.'

'Isn't that a crime, an aunt with her nephew?'

'Incest, yes, technically. At twenty, Joel was legally an adult, so both of them would be guilty of an offence, and the existence of their child is proof enough. But, like I said, the social worker didn't report it. Now Joel's dead, and Sandra's sick. We'll need to go through bureaucracy hell to find the adopted offspring and get a DNA sample to match with theirs, if that's even possible. Not entirely sure, what with sealed adoption files and all that.'

'Not worth the trouble, then,' Alex said.

'If we manage to prove they're the parents, she's bang to rights, but she'll probably be dead by then. It could take years to get to trial.' She traced the rim of her wine glass with her finger. 'My officers are overstretched with all these murders, and you have to consider the effects on the poor adopted child, living her life in London somewhere with no idea about any of this. I mean, of course, crimes should be investigated, but I'm not sure I can even justify public interest in this case. The CPS barely has the budget for paper clips.'

'Do you know if Sandra kept in touch with Joel after he and Dorothy left London?'

'Not likely. Royal Mail doesn't reach the commune, and they didn't have phones. Unless she used a messenger or a carrier pigeon, there's no way.'

'A messenger,' he echoed, then swirled the remaining wine in his glass and downed it in one.

She set her wine on the table and took his hand in hers. 'What are you thinking?'

'Oh, nothing, just a hunch I'll have to follow up, but I'm shattered. Early night for me, I think.'

'One more thing,' Mary said. 'Faye Hindmarsh. We finally got her report.'

'About time.'

'Yeah. I'm struggling to find a pulse in this pathologist. Anyway, Faye was killed by several blows to the back of the head. Well, I could have told you that from the scene. We found the murder weapon. It wasn't hidden very far from her body: a bloody log.'

'Anything useful in the report?'

'If you remember the crime scene, she was found about twenty metres from the path they used to get to the commune. Our theory is she tried to get away and was stopped. There were DNA traces from two people on the murder weapon. One from someone we can't identify. No record in the database, except the DNA tells us it was a woman. The other was Naomi Abraham, the commune's friendly escaped murderer, understudy number two.'

CHAPTER THIRTY-TWO

THE DAY BEFORE THE RECKONING

Slevin's brutal death dazed Luke, numbing his senses, as if he had dissociated from his body. Everyone around him seemed like echoes of themselves. In the short time he had spent with Slevin, he'd come to know the scraggy, pockmarked man a little better, thought they could perhaps become friends. No doubt Karla saw this too, wherever she was, stalking him like a predator, exacting her retribution in slow, deliberate steps.

Barely able to speak, with wide, crazed eyes, Stella had led them all to the waterfall to retrieve Slevin's body. By the time they got there, a hurried, silent procession fuelled by urgency and disbelief, Slevin was gone.

'He was right there,' Stella said in a rasping, dead voice. 'There.' She pointed to a muddy patch, dark with blood.

'Why did you two have to come here in the first place?' Joel said to Stella.

'Shut up, Joel,' Naomi said.

'Just asking. It's an obvious question. Wouldn't have happened if they'd stayed at the camp.'

Stella turned to him, raised her hand and, without warning, smacked him on the face.

'Ow!' Joel cried. 'You hit me.'

Stella slapped him again, even harder this time. 'One more word. One!' She held up a shaking finger in warning and brought it close to Joel's face.

Luke's gaze darted to Joel's machete hand. *This could turn ugly.* But rather than angry, Joel appeared chastened, his shoulders slumped, his eyes cast down, like a small child on the verge of tears.

'Let's spread out,' Naomi said. 'Anyone find anything, shout.'

They looked for Slevin around the waterfall, above it, in the bushy thickets and surrounding woods. The wind rose to a gale, yet they continued their search, weather-beaten and hungry, scratched by branches and pricked by wild bramble thorns. When the wind was supplanted by rain and then hail, they gathered into a huddle and conceded defeat. Slevin was nowhere to be found. His body had vanished.

Back at the roundhouse, once again in dry clothes, Luke, Naomi and Joel sat at the communal table, drinking jug after jug of water to wet their ever-dry mouths and quench their dispirited souls. The storm outside intensified, announcing its violence with deafening thunder, hurling rain and gusts of wind at the structure as if seeking to tear it down. Stella had retreated to her single shed and rolled down the door's fabric.

'She shouldn't be alone,' Naomi said.

'I wouldn't bother her,' Joel said. 'It's bad enough with the three of us here. She'll only mope and bring the room down even more. Leave her.'

'I mean, it's not safe,' Naomi said. 'None of us should be alone. If the farmer got Slevin, he's definitely on a mission. His deadline was supposed to be tomorrow, so it looks like he moved things forward. He might come tonight. We need to be ready.'

'Do we know for sure it's the farmer?' Joel said.

'If you're looking to throw some more of your wild accusations,' Naomi said, 'we were all here when it happened. It wasn't any of us. Try again.'

Joel glared at her. 'I hear I wasn't the only one making wild accusations.'

Naomi took Luke's hand in hers under the table. 'I'm sorry, Luke,' she said. 'I was obviously wrong.'

Luke kept his face neutral. Naomi had acted distant recently and moved out of their cabin. Now it made sense. *What did she accuse me of? The keys? Faye's disappearance? Probably both.* He checked how he felt about this revelation. It didn't trouble him. It paled compared to the threat they now faced, because of him. He squeezed her hand, then gulped down more water.

'We should all stay together tonight,' Luke said. For a moment, he contemplated telling them about Karla, but then thought better of it. The time for his confession had passed. If they learned about her now, they would only blame him for not warning them earlier. If he had, Slevin might still be alive. He'd been such a coward, a shameful, spineless coward.

Naomi raised their joined hands onto the table. Luke held back a shudder, keeping his eyes away from Joel's. *Even now, I'm worried what he'd think?*

'Maybe it's time to leave,' Naomi said. 'There's only four of us left. This fight isn't worth it. Can't we find somewhere else? I mean, we have a little money. We can go first thing in the morning, catch a bus, have a decent meal, then hitchhike north, figure it out as we go along.'

Luke noticed Stella's figure at the door, staring at them through dark, haunted eyes. For a moment, a flash of lightning behind her made her figure look like a horrific apparition, a halo of light surrounding her red hair that was unbunched and wild, Medusa-like, dripping streams of rainwater. It was a relief to have her close. Safety in numbers. By herself, she'd make an easy target for Karla.

'And where would we go, eh?' Joel said to Naomi. 'It took Dorothy ages to find this land. You can't just settle in some forest and make a commune. Even us living here is probably illegal. Honestly, you have no idea about these things.'

Stella stepped into the room and stood over them. She planted her legs wide apart and curled her fingers into fists. Her expression transformed from the soft curves of heartbreak into rigid resolve. She wiped her face with her sleeve. In a gravelly, hardened voice, she said, 'We're staying. Adrian doesn't scare me. Let him come, the bastard. Let him come if he dares. Let him.'

They all looked at her. Even Joel had nothing to say, this time.

'Naomi,' Stella said, 'bring out the tequila.'

As Naomi rummaged in the wicker basket in the far corner for the glasses and a bottle, Stella came and sat with them, her back straight, her chin held high. 'All right. Joel,' she said. 'Call a meeting.'

'The Synner's Crag Commune meeting is hereby officially open,' Joel said, formal as ever.

They toasted Slevin, and Luke could see a single silent tear marking a trail over Stella's resolute face. She didn't touch her drink. He wished she would, to numb the pain a little.

'Before we discuss the serious stuff,' Naomi said, 'I'd like to propose a motion. We were meant to vote about Luke joining the commune. Now's as good a time as ever.' She turned to him. 'I've not been… as good a friend as I should have. I can see that now. I'm sorry.'

'It's all right,' he said. 'Really, there's no need. Not–'

She cut him off. 'Those in favour of making Luke officially a member of the Synner's Crag commune, please raise your hand.'

Naomi and Stella's hands rose, and they both said, 'Aye.'

Joel shook his head and kept his hands flat on his thighs.

Twat, Naomi mouthed. 'By a majority, Luke is confirmed a full member. Welcome, Luke. More tequila, please.'

Stella and Naomi toasted Luke, though again, Stella left her drink untouched. Joel drank his shot without raising it. *What he thinks doesn't matter*, Luke reassured himself. *Not any more.*

This small gesture, making him a member, gave Luke unexpected comfort and a pang of joy. *A toast at the gallows is still a toast.*

'Second order of business,' Stella said.

'You're not the leader,' Joel said.

'Shut up, Joel,' Naomi said. 'You want me to call a vote on that too?'

Joel shrank away from her and stared at his knuckles.

'Second order of business,' Stella repeated. 'Safety. We'll all sleep in the roundhouse tonight. That way, when he comes, he can't pick us off one by one.'

Good, Luke thought. Out of Stella's mouth, it sounded more convincing than when he'd suggested it.

'That's silly,' Joel said, his head still lowered. Then he looked up. 'If we're in one place, he can just shoot us all. It makes it easier for him, not harder.'

'The one thing I know for certain about violent men,' Naomi said, 'is they always talk before they hurt you. You saw what he was like last time, when he shot Michael. We can turn that to our advantage. We need to plan a distraction. If he comes in here, we can't all stand in the same place. He can only point a gun at one person at a time, and this time we'll be ready.'

'You plan to jump the man with the gun?' Joel said. 'You've seen the size of him, haven't you?'

'Trust me,' Naomi said, 'the bigger their size, the harder they fall.'

They spent a long time debating *plans of action*, as Naomi called them. Then Joel went to his cabin to fetch his collection of knives and a whetstone to sharpen them with.

When night fell, they laid mattresses in the roundhouse and used the communal table to barricade the door. A bucket behind a makeshift screen made of a hanging bedsheet served as a toilet. Each of them took a turn staying awake, in case Adrian showed up in the night, though apart from the occasional doze, none of them slept. The night became a silent vigil in anticipation of the fateful reckoning to come. The wind rose further, howling and smashing rain at their shelter. After a while, it eased, then died, to be replaced by utter silence into which they could project their guarded hopes and worst fears.

As the early morning birdsong announced the arrival of a new day, Stella made bitter coffee and added sugar straight into the pot. They drank it quickly, already alert with apprehension.

Luke realised his stomach was rumbling. They'd had nothing to eat since the previous day's lukewarm lunch of thin nettle soup. He'd never experienced real hunger. Now, his body was rebelling against the lack of food, though his mind was sharper. He almost felt high.

'Everyone ready?' Stella said.

'Aye aye, captain,' Joel said, sounding surprisingly cheerful.

'Yes,' Luke said, wondering what his commune mates would do if, instead of the burly farmer, the person waiting for them on the other side of the barricaded door would be Karla, an elegant woman with a friendly, lying smile. He would have to explain quickly, alert them to the danger. Once again, he considered telling them about her and, once again, he decided against it. When she came, he'd have to be the one to charge at her. *Don't hesitate. Don't let her speak. Stab first, explain later. I'm ready for you, Karla.* He hadn't counted his fingers even once that night.

Naomi stepped to the door and grabbed one side of the table that was blocking it. Stella took the other, and together they moved it aside. They all gathered at the entrance and stared with surprise at the wooden box on the ground.

'Jesus Christ,' Naomi said and crossed herself. 'What's he playing at?'

CHAPTER THIRTY-THREE

THE DAY OF RECKONING

The box that lay at the roundhouse's door was filled with food: fresh strawberries in punnets, tomatoes, cucumbers, bunched mint, two honeydew melons, three loaves of bread that looked home-made, jars of Marmite and blueberry conserve, a four-pint bottle of milk. Pinned to the box was a note:

Enjoy your last day. Eat. Then you're done. Goodbye.

Luke's mouth watered at the sight of the food and the heavenly smell of freshly baked bread. He didn't care about the note or the sentiment behind it. A quick glance at the others confirmed they felt the same. Their pangs of hunger had turned into violent stabs. For a brief moment, he considered advocating caution. What if the food had been poisoned? But then he reassured himself. The cucumbers and tomatoes were unevenly shaped, still covered in dirt. The produce must have come from the farm, maybe except for the melons, which he didn't think were grown locally, and the supermarket-bought Marmite, jam and milk. This was Adrian's doing, not Karla's. The farmer was warning them.

Joel carried the box into the roundhouse and laid it on the floor. Single-handedly, he set the communal table back in its place and laid the box of food on top of it. 'We'll need all the strength we can get,' he said.

Joel reached for the bread, but Naomi's voice stopped him. 'It stinks in here. We'll eat, but we're not animals. Let's be civilised and get rid of the toilet first.'

Joel hesitated, then pulled back his hand. 'Luke,' he said, 'newest member of the commune, go empty the toilet.'

'You didn't vote for him,' Naomi said, 'so you do it.'

'I've been here from day one,' Joel said. 'I'm the most senior member.'

Luke withdrew his hands from his pockets. 'It's all right.' He went across to the bucket and picked it up by its handle. His nose filled with the rank, sulphurous smell of the dark urine that sloshed inside it. At the door, he stopped and looked back at them. 'Don't let me stop you. Eat. Shouldn't take long.'

'Hurry, Lukas,' Joel said, 'or there won't be any left.'

'Don't worry,' Naomi said. 'I'll make sure fat-boy here doesn't eat it all.'

As soon as he stepped outside, he heard plates, cutlery and cups being set and the commotion of breakfast. Naomi's words, *Let's be civilised*, echoed in his mind, and he decided, despite his haste to return to the food, to do the decent thing and empty the bucket outside the camp's perimeter. There was a satisfying sense of virtue to disobeying his body's urgent demand to eat, feeling like he was above it, in control.

He walked quickly, as fast as he could without the smelly contents of the half-full bucket splashing out. The new day was bright, and the forest peaceful. The night's storm seemed like a distant memory. He contemplated what could have been, how things would have turned out without the farmer's threats, without Karla, without the terrible deaths. He imagined himself in the commune with Dorothy still alive, with Slevin and Faye and Michael. He had a vision of him and Naomi becoming a couple, a proper couple. *What if I had come here before, when I was younger, before Karla and the torment she'd put me through? My life could have been so different, an almost perfect existence.* And yet, his younger self did not understand the things that truly mattered: not in his early career choice to become a teacher, noble as it was, or the aspiration to a mortgage and a normal suburban family life with a wife and children. He remembered Dorothy's words to him on their drive north: *for our hard work, we get rewarded with something precious, something people out there can only dream of.* Now he understood. Was it too late?

At the foot of a tall tree, two paces from the start of the trail that led to the cave, he crouched down and emptied the bucket, careful not to get any of its contents on his hands. Then something occurred to him, like a realisation that had hidden just beneath the surface of his thoughts: the note that came with the food. *It couldn't be.*

It was. The handwriting was familiar. His heart sank to his stomach, and he stood upright. The box with their breakfast was not left by the farmer after all.

As he straightened his back and turned to face the camp, there she was, Karla, wearing a studded leather biker jacket and a black baseball cap. Despite the rugged outdoor environment, she stood tall over her sharp stiletto heels that could pierce his groin with a kick. Her skin was pale and clear, her eyes black and vicious, like a shark eyeing its victim. She bore her too-white teeth and exhaled a satisfied grunt. In her hand was a gun, pointed at his chest. At her belt hung a stun baton, her torture weapon of choice. He took a step back and dropped the bucket, nearly tripping over himself in a clumsy misplacement of feet. The barrel of her gun followed his every move, like a third eye. She gave him a coy, cheerful smile.

'What were you thinking, my lovely?' she said. 'That you'd run away from me?'

He wiped his brow with the back of his hand and looked at her, his shoulders slumped as low as they'd go.

She sighed, then tutted. 'Ah, sweetheart. You've been a naughty, naughty boy. Not to worry, I'm here now, to take care of you.' She must have noticed his concerned glance towards the camp, because she added, 'Yes. Them too. I'll take care of *them*, and you'll help me, like you always do. We have blood on our hands, together, as a team, so let's not pretend you're suddenly a holy man, lighting incense in that ashram with that collection of rejects.'

He felt sick, and yet his chest was hot with anger, an anger that rose within him against her threats, against *her*. He reached for the memory of the heresies he had whispered to himself ever since he'd caught a glimpse of her in the woods. *Do your worst. I'm not scared any more.* He squared his shoulders. 'It's called a roundhouse, not an ashram, and don't you dare touch them.'

'Ooh, this is new,' she said. She spoke in that taunting, girly voice, high-pitched and all-innocent, like a veil intended to reveal more than it hid. 'What? You suddenly got yourself a personality?' She licked her top lip with her unnaturally long tongue that reminded him of a snake's. 'And you know who we'll tackle first? Did you enjoy your night of passion? Was she worth it for the pain she'll suffer? I'll make it last for hours.'

'You won't,' he said, with so much force, he surprised himself.

She scratched her chin. 'Hmm. Not heard you use that phrase before. I guess we have some work to do first, just the two of us and my stun stick, together, like old times. Even broken-in bulldogs sometimes have lapses. Not to worry. I'm the Luke whisperer, me.'

'Are you going to kill me?' he said.

With the fingers of her free hand, she squeezed the visor of her baseball cap, pretending to think about it. Then she shrugged. 'Maybe. It depends on a few things. Your friends, for example, if they beg. Begging adds a certain something, don't you think? Might put me in a better mood when I decide about you.'

'Leave them out of it.'

'My darling Luke, don't fret. They're already as good as dead.'

'Take me, then. Let them live.'

'By Mary and Jospeh and the butcher's daughter, how very noble of you.' She gave him a tight smile. 'No deal. But… seems to me you need reminding what's what, my lovely. Then, if you behave, I might even keep you. Mum says I should find someone more like us, but look at you, oh so dreamy, so lovely.'

Karla motioned with her gun towards the path, then aimed it back at him. 'Now walk. And if this new gumption of yours tells you to try anything, don't. I'm a thousand steps ahead of you. You should know that by now.'

He looked down. The laces of his left boot had come undone. In his first act of defiance, he knelt down and tied them without asking for permission. Then he stood, turned to face the trail and started walking.

They hiked up the muddy, less-trodden path towards Synner's Crag Cave, Karla behind him while he looked straight ahead. Luke had known her long enough to understand his predicament. Neither flight nor fight were possible. She was lethal, cruel and perfectly efficient, and she knew him too well. He wasn't sure how she'd cope with the terrain in her high heels, but he dared not look back. He hoped she'd trip and fall, but her steps sounded even and determined.

As he marched on, putting one foot in front of the other, he withdrew into his thoughts. After a while, a new idea came to him. He mulled it over and dismissed it as an impossibility, but the thought was persistent. It simply wouldn't go away. He catalogued every interaction he'd ever had with Karla, every time she forced her will on him, and the times she went away for weeks, leaving him in a state of frightened anticipation for her return. Of Karla's powers, the mightiest was fear. *In my terror, I was blind to it. She relishes control. How would she react if I took it away?*

At a fork in the path, he turned right without asking. She seemed determined to simply walk a distance, further from the commune and any chance of discovery, making sure his screams wouldn't be heard. This suited him well. He now had a plan and one chance to attempt it. He thought of Naomi, Stella and Joel, his remaining commune mates. His dread was gone, leaving only seething anger. His footsteps grew wider, quicker, more determined. He forced himself to slow down, not give the game away.

The vegetation grew scarcer, replaced by soaked earth. His walking boots were ankle-deep in mud, but he dared not look back to check how her heels were faring or if she'd taken them off. Not yet. They were climbing now, the sodden path becoming a narrow tunnel between bluffs of hard stone. He nearly slipped on the mud once but still gazed ahead. What he did, when he did it, could easily fail. It had to happen at just the right moment.

'I can see you scheming,' Karla called out from behind. 'Don't be an idiot.'

He raised his right hand as if in admission and shook his head.

'Good boy.'

He focused on the rocky elevation they were heading to, his posture deliberately slouched like a cowering dog. *She can read me like an open book. I have to clear my thoughts, avoid any chance of discovery.*

They reached the edge of a cliff, a precipice above a sheer, lethal drop. He stopped and stared across at the lush green valley beyond it, taking care not to look down.

'You know this place?' she said.

Without looking back, he said, 'It's called Synner's Crag. The area's named after it.' He recalled what Dorothy had told him about the place and added, 'The locals used to throw criminals off this cliff as a kind of test. If they survived, they were innocent. If they didn't... well, I guess it was a quick death.'

'Turn around,' she said. 'Face me. No sudden moves. Remember, I know you like I know myself. Any missteps, and *boom*.'

He nodded for her to see that he did. In his mind, he mulled over her words: *I know you like I know myself*. She was right, but this truth cut both ways. He started whispering, like a madman, words from the last poem he'd taught as a teacher, repeating them over and over again. '*Beware the Jabberwock, my son! The jaws that bite, the claws that catch! Beware the Jubjub bird, and shun the frumious Bandersnatch!*'

'What are you doing?' she demanded. 'Be quiet!'

Still whispering, he turned to face her, his back to the cliff's edge, his arms raised, pretending to surrender. *She seems distracted by the poem. Good. Here goes.*

CHAPTER THIRTY-FOUR

NINETEEN DAYS POST DISCOVERY

'Shall I make us a cup of tea?' Alex said. His throat was dry. He wasn't looking forward to this meeting. If he was honest, any meeting with Sandra Saint-John made his skin crawl.

'I think the kettle's on the blink,' Sandra said, 'and everyone's always offering to make me cups of tea, like it treats cancer. Please sit.'

'I can have a look at the kettle if you like. Maybe it's something simple, like the cord getting loose.'

'Please sit,' she repeated. 'You wore a tie. Is it bad news?'

'I had an event just before this, police lunch gala.' He cleared his throat. 'One has to work the sources if you know what I mean.'

'Have these sources told you if we're any closer to establishing Luke Bridestone's guilt?'

He had learned nothing new at the gala. It was one of the tedious Met Police awards he attended for Mary's sake. But it was a good excuse to introduce Sandra to the information he had decided, reluctantly, it was finally time to share.

'They've learned a great deal about him. Quite an interesting backstory. We now know that Luke Bridestone has confessed to a murder. Three murders, in fact.'

Her face lit up. 'He has? Oh, dear me. He's woken up? What did he tell the police?'

'He's still in a coma, still at UCH. He's woken up a couple of times, which bodes well for his chances, but he wasn't coherent.'

'I thought you said he confessed.'

'I said he confessed to murders, previous murders, before all this started.'

'I don't understand.'

Alex opened his notepad and flicked through its pages, taking his time. At last, he spoke. 'For a long time, Luke was an upstanding citizen. Before he worked at the crematorium, he was an elementary school teacher, well-loved by his colleagues and the kids' parents. He passed Ofsted inspections with flying colours, dated one of the teachers. Was supposed to marry her. Everything was rosy. He was even earmarked to become assistant head.'

'And?'

'One day, it all changed. He called off his engagement to Miss Hanson and stopped socialising. Nobody understood how this friendly, bubbly guy, the chair of the social committee, suddenly turned into a recluse. He became distracted, didn't seem to care about work any more. One of the teachers I spoke to said he'd lost a lot of weight. His eyes looked haunted. He snapped for no reason, including at the kids.'

Sandra uncrossed her legs and angled her head, looking perplexed.

'Eventually, the head teacher called him in for a meeting and asked what was going on. Apparently, he clammed up and wouldn't talk about it. Then, he was offered a choice: improve or leave. Luke had used up all the goodwill he'd earned over the years.'

'Did they fire him?'

'No. He left that meeting and never came back to the school. A few weeks later, he applied for the job at the crematorium, and there, he kept himself to himself. According to his manager, Luke was deemed unfit for contact with any mourners, but he was reliable for the grunt work. You know, burning people.'

Sandra didn't seem amused by this quip. Maybe this was an off-limits topic in the house of an ill client. He shouldn't have said it. It was just that Sandra looked so healthy now, her cancer had slipped his mind.

Alex returned to his notepad, this time to check his facts. 'One day, he turned up at Lewisham Police Station and said he wished to confess to some terrible things he'd done. He gave them three dates on which he pushed his victims onto the tracks in front of oncoming trains. Two men and a woman, all dead. He gave them the exact locations of those crimes.'

'Had the victims done something to him?'

Alex shook his head. 'They were all complete strangers.'

'Why, then?'

'According to his statement, he'd been in an abusive relationship with a woman he refused to name, said she forced him to do it. He wouldn't give them any details about her, except that she was violent and controlling. Every time he displeased her in any way, talked to another woman, didn't answer her questions the way she wanted, she would hurt him and threaten to make his life a living hell. For the worst offences, she'd make him repent by sacrificing someone, a stranger on a train platform. He took care to do it in places with no CCTV, which is why he was never caught. He begged the duty sergeant to arrest him. He was terrified of going back home.'

'Awful,' Sandra said and licked her lips. Alex could see the cogs in her brain turning. She was spending her sister's money, planning exotic holidays, imagining a cocktail on a beach in Tuscany.

'Not that it matters now,' she said, 'but if he confessed, why didn't they arrest him? Why wasn't he sent to prison?'

'It does matter,' Alex said. 'The police took him seriously and escorted him to a cell. Then, they went to verify his story. First, they confirmed that the three victims did, in fact, die, exactly at the locations and on the dates he told them.'

Sandra's eyes grew brighter.

'But then,' Alex said, 'they went to check the CCTV footage.'

'You said he did it in places with no cameras.'

'That's what he thought, but Luke was no CCTV expert. He didn't realise the old one-directional cameras, which he thought he was evading, were obsolete and no longer used. They hadn't been removed, but new multi-directional models were installed too, covering the entire platform. You know, the ones that look like domes?'

'I don't understand.'

'The first *victim*,' he made quotation marks with his fingers, 'the woman, was distracted by a phone call and took a step too far. The two men jumped. Most importantly, Luke Bridestone was nowhere near the stations when any of these deaths happened. He only chose deaths in stations where he thought there was limited CCTV coverage, but his own involvement was pure fantasy.'

'Okay,' Sandra said. 'Just because he's a fantasist doesn't mean he didn't kill at the commune. Isn't fantasy often a first step before a crime?'

Alex imagined her watching hour after hour of detective and CSI programmes, the talking heads of psychologists against the backdrop of sinister music. He realised he was enjoying stringing Sandra along. He found the woman distasteful, and worse. Nothing in the PI manual said you couldn't enjoy the job, at least a little.

'The police briefly considered charging him with wasting police time,' he said, 'but in the end, a compassionate sergeant, who saw how terrified Luke was to go home, decided to lean on his contacts and get him referred for a psychiatric assessment. This resulted in him being sectioned in a secure unit for a while. The woman who tortured him turned out to be a hallucination.'

'Mental illness? I mean, really?'

Alex nodded. 'His browser history showed he'd researched train station deaths, but this was weeks after they happened. His final evaluation says,' he read out from his pad, *'Luke Bridestone is a gentle, caring individual fallen on especially frightening times because of his illness. We do not consider him a danger to himself or others. With the correct treatment and mental health support, he can live a full and fulfilling life.* After a period of hospitalisation, he got released into the community with a pillbox of antipsychotics and monthly follow-up meetings.'

'Okay, and?' Sandra said, sounding gruff and disapproving.

'In Luke's last session with his support worker, he said his pills no longer worked properly. They did stop the imaginary woman from coming to him – he still believed she was real, no matter what he was told – but he felt scared, petrified she'd come back. Somehow, he'd convinced himself that the pills helped keep her away, like some kind of ritual, but he couldn't accept she was the result of his illness. It didn't help that on a couple of occasions, the hallucinations briefly returned, so the logic just didn't register. He still believed she was real and suppressed whatever he was told.'

Sandra looked at her knees, avoiding Alex's eyes.

'I spoke to Dr Shah, the psychiatrist who took care of him originally. He told me that to achieve a therapeutic breakthrough in Luke's case, they'd have to get him to at least accept the hallucinations were happening inside his head, not in the real world. Anyway, the day he left London would have been the last day he still had any of his medication with him. He didn't collect another prescription. Then he disappeared and was only seen again when they found him half-dead on a rock shelf, a mile from the commune.'

'So, Luke Bridestone came off his meds,' Sandra said. 'Wouldn't it be possible, likely even, that he went on a rampage?'

Alex tapped his pen on the notepad, waited a moment, then said, 'The police have their doubts. It doesn't add up.'

Sandra bit her lip. 'Why doubts? It's open and shut, isn't it?'

'If you look at each of the commune murders in what we now think is the sequence, the picture becomes a little muddled.'

'Looks clear to me.'

'The psychiatrist doesn't think so. His assessment is that Luke's hallucinations were a form of self-harm, and he was unlikely to have been violent to anyone else.'

'Some shrink in an office?'

'Quite,' Alex said. 'Except, Naomi Abraham, victim number five, was a convicted murderer herself, on the run. She escaped prison and disappeared off the face of the earth until her body was found. Slevin Grimlow, victim number four, as we've already discussed, was suspected but never charged for at least some responsibility for deaths at a South Pole research station. I hate to say this, but your nephew, Joel, with his arsenal of big, sharp knives, is a suspect in at least one murder, that of Michael Bind. As you'll recall, someone stabbed him in the leg, and he bled to death.'

Alex noticed a tiny twitch of her facial muscles when he mentioned the knives, and then it was gone. He resisted the urge to ask her about the present she had made to her nephew, the set of lethal blades. Did she send a note with it? Was it possible the knives were part of a plan that went wrong? It was better not to raise the question just yet. She might even fire him, contract or not.

'That's all very well,' Sandra said, 'but the fact remains: Luke Bridestone is alive, and they're all dead.'

He noticed her eyes tighten and decided to throw her a bone. 'You're right, of course. It's never a good idea to pre-judge the outcome. The final post-mortems are complete, and the police are reviewing them alongside their findings from the crime scene. The good news is that you won't have to wait much longer. The final report will take some time, but my source tells me they should have a definitive conclusion about Luke and his involvement in the next few days.'

'They had better,' she said.

Alex nodded. 'I'll be here as soon as I know.' Then he thought of his bonus and decided to bolster her confidence a little. 'In the meantime, don't lose faith. It ain't over until all the evidence sings. There's one Met detective who's convinced Luke can be tied to some of the murders, and if I'm honest, the police will look better if there's a live person to blame.'

CHAPTER THIRTY-FIVE

THE DAY OF RECKONING

'Beware the Jabberwock, my son! The jaws that bite, the claws that catch! Beware the Jubjub bird, and shun The frumious Bandersnatch!'

'What are you doing?' Karla demanded. 'Be quiet!'

Still whispering, he turned to face her, his back to the cliff's edge, his arms raised, pretending to surrender. *She seems distracted by the poem. Good. Here goes.*

He saw Karla follow his gaze to her stilettos. Then, too late, she finally understood.

Her smile faded, and her face dulled to a flat, soulless grey. Luke had never seen her like this. How could she not know what he had planned? Maybe he'd succeeded in distracting her, or maybe he'd made it so she wouldn't notice. Did he have this power over her all along, or had he developed it in the past few days?

She raised her gun and loaded the chamber with a click, looking practised, like a hit woman in a movie. *Just like in a movie*, he thought.

'You think you're so clever,' she said. 'You deliberately walked me through the mud.'

He smiled and relaxed his shoulders. 'Yes,' he said. 'And

your shoes are pristine, like you just tried them on in the store. High heels in this terrain? I don't think so. It's time, Karla. You can go back to wherever the fuck you came from.'

'Language, Luke. I won't tolerate—'

'No, you won't. Of course you won't. So, I was the one who left the flower on my pillow when I went out for a piss that night. I remember now. You made me pack it in my bag before I left London. Then you made me forget. You're not really here, are you?'

'I can still shoot you.'

'Go on, then, shoot. Go on. I haven't got all day.'

'We're in this together. You murdered those people in London.'

'You made me,' he said. 'One of your stupid punishments, remember? Anyway, the police weren't interested, said I didn't do it. I do wonder—'

She interrupted him, for the first time sounding an ounce less sure of herself. 'I smoothed things over for you. I... I...' She regained her composure. 'You're the one who came over to talk to me at the bar, remember? You're the one who wanted to be together.'

'But did I? Did I, really? A chemical imbalance in my brain, that's all you are. Nothing, just nothing. I imagined you into existence, so I can imagine you out. If only I'd listened to Dr Shah. It's so comforting to know, to finally know, what you really are. You're just...' he blew a raspberry at her, 'air.'

'So what if my shoes have no mud on them?' Her voice cracked. 'It doesn't mean—'

'Oh, Karla, my lovely,' Luke said in a tone he hadn't used in years. 'It means *everything*.'

Karla holstered her gun and took three determined steps to reach him, her face dogged, her posture majestic, like a queen standing before a traitorous subject.

Luke wasn't buying it, yet there was a part of him, like a

small quivering child, warning him of terrible consequences, of punishment and revenge. He had feared her for so long, dreaded what she'd say, what she would do next, cowering before her every angry demand, that even now, at the point of their final confrontation, he still felt a tremor rise in him.

Karla placed her hands on his chest and tried to push him backwards, into the deadly drop from the sheer cliff, from Synner's Crag. She seemed to use all of her force, but the shove was empty, lifeless, as if she was already gone from him, a ghost.

At the sight of her so close to him, Luke took a step back. The soles of his boots were almost on the edge of the precipice. The remnants of Karla's cloying scent were faint, barely there, yet their homoeopathic memory was still imprinted on his nostrils. He felt light-headed, and then, with a slip of his muddy shoes on the rocky surface, it seemed like he might lose his balance. *I'm going to fall. I'm going to die here. She'll win.*

He grabbed Karla by the shoulders and held on tight. She felt real, the leather of her jacket, her cruel eyes, the crimson lipstick, the pores on her face – yet her body provided no counterbalance, no support. Despite his lost footing, he managed an awkward turn, like a pirouette, all the while holding her tightly, turning her until her back was to the void. Then, with an angry shove, he pushed her off the cliff with all his might, taking in her final facial expression: defeat, regret, a vicious accusation. He was lost to her, and she to him.

Luke's relief was short-lived. After the effort of hurling Karla into the void, he was no longer grounded. His balance was gone. *I'm going to slip. I'm going to follow her.* Still, with morbid satisfaction, as he leaned back and forth like an inflatable air puppet, trying without hope to right himself, he saw her body dive through the air until it hit the rocky ground below, shattering like a porcelain doll into a thousand pieces. Then the pieces of her, of what he called Karla, evaporated like steam into the ether.

With his arms windmilling, hands grasping at vacant air, Luke felt himself fall as if in slow motion, not all the way like his demon, but onto a ledge a quarter of the way down. In the split second before he landed and his head hit a rock, a startling realisation came to him. Karla was gone and will never return. He had recognised her for what she was and vanquished her to nothing, a nothing she had been all along, a delirious invention that his thoughts had sprung on him, like a parasite sucking on his mind. It therefore followed that Slevin's death was not Karla's doing. It might have been the farmer or, the more likely explanation, someone else who held a grudge against the cheerful bare-chested man, someone whose handwriting he had recognised on the note that came with the box of food left at the roundhouse that morning. He knew who it was. He had seen Lilian's scribbles in her diary. Lilian was not dead. She had written that note.

PART FOUR

LILIAN

CHAPTER THIRTY-SIX

THE DAY BEFORE THE RECKONING

It had been a long day in the fields, and Adrian wondered if the duff tractor would start again the next day. He decided not to wait until the morning to find out. His hands were greasy and smelled of oil, the result of an hour's tinkering with the engine, replacing spark plugs, cleaning the oil filter, unclogging the carburettor and, in an act of frustration, pounding the engine with a ten-inch spanner, which may have been the reason it relented and coughed itself to a reluctant start.

He looked towards the house. The kitchen's windows glowed with warm light. Megs was making dinner. He salivated at the thought of her curried casserole, slow-cooked with tender melt-in-the-mouth beef cuts. Although she was originally a city girl from Gateshead, Megs had adapted well to being a farmer's wife. The unpredictability of his long days meant she would usually have to cook some sort of stew, ready for whenever he'd finished for the day or, during lambing season, when he could afford to take a break before going out again to tend to the expectant ewes in the herd. Unfortunately, she hadn't become accustomed to him in quite the same way she took to farmhouse-wifing. She had soured on him, complained incessantly, and coped with her isolation by overindulging in barbecue-flavoured crisps, tubs of salted caramel ice cream and boxes of assorted Quality Street and Lindt chocolates. The result of those indulgences accumulated over time to a heft that weighed on their relationship and made them both resent each other. In the early days, he had tried to suggest she join him in some farm work, move a little, but she was having none of it. *That's not what I signed up for*, she told him every time he asked. Out of kindness, he held his tongue, not saying what he thought. *That's not what I signed up for either*. Still, she was a good mother and an excellent cook, even if the shelves in their love department remained conspicuously empty. *Two out of three isn't bad*.

Adrian stubbed out his cigarette on a fence post and wiped his hands on the trousers of his stained overalls. He stole a glance at the house to ensure Megs wasn't looking out of a window and, just in case, walked casually until he was safely behind the hay barn. From there, he continued to the old staff accommodation caravan. He knocked and entered, not waiting for an answer, and quickly shut the door behind him.

'I waited for ages,' Lilian said in her seductive American accent that made his loins stir.

He didn't apologise, but took in her petite stature, the sleeveless top, the colourful tattoo of a monarch butterfly on her shoulder, the small lips and small tits, the bright eyes sparkling at the sight of him. He deserved her. She was his treat at the end of a wretched day. She made him feel young, or at least younger. Older men were her thing, she had told him. *Can't argue with that. Look at her*. Even the scrapes and injuries from her fall had not diminished her appeal in the slightest.

'Gonna take a shower,' he said.

After they made love, if love was the word for it, he sat up in bed, shuffled up so his back was supported by the heavily stained plywood wall and lit up, blowing out smoke in contented breaths. He wondered what his wife would say if she walked in on them like that. Would she throw things at him? Scream? Divorce him? Leave him to cook his own dinners? Or might she just say something like 'dinner's ready' and never mention it again? She must have felt about him the same way he felt about her. He never asked. What good would it do? It was better to leave things as they were, especially as he'd prefer to keep their boys on the farm. If she left, he was pretty sure they'd go with her. As a farmer, he had fields and orchards and so many chickens and sheep to parent. There was certainly no spare time for his own bairns.

Lilian rested her head on his thigh. *Those lovely, thick farmer's thighs*, an old girlfriend had once called them. He absent-mindedly patted Lilian's hair, which was soft to the touch and smelled of coconut shampoo. With his index finger, he traced her lips.

'Have you heard anything about *them*?' she said. 'Any news?'

'If the numpties have any sense, they'll leave, but I'm not going to push it just now. I think I gave them enough of a fright to stay out of my fields. I'll wait another couple of weeks and maybe go out there again. Takes a lot for me to play the tough guy.'

'Honestly, I don't think they'll bother you any more,' she said.

He kissed the crown of her head. 'You know what annoys me in all this? Dorothy. I expected her to be civil. If she came to see me, we could have reached some sort of agreement. She left me a note saying she'd come with a peace offering. Never showed.'

'Dorothy's dead.'

'Why would you say that?'

'I don't hide in this tiny caravan all day, Adrian. I keep an eye on the enemy, go on little reconnaissance missions.' She pointed at a pair of binoculars. 'Sometimes, when they're all in the roundhouse, I sneak into the camp and listen in.'

'That's a stupid thing to do. What if they saw you?'

'They won't.'

'I know you weren't happy when they told you to leave. If you really don't want them here, I can ask them again.'

'Is that guilt because you won't leave your wife?'

'Jury's still out on that one.'

'I'm not a stupid little girl. I know how this goes. You have children, and I'm not the house-cleaning type. You'd choose the steady milking cow over me every time.'

He wanted to say something soothing, but didn't get the chance.

'Why did you shoot Michael?' she said.

'You were there?'

'I came after. They were in a panic.'

'What? No. I didn't plan on it, I swear. I only wanted to frighten them, buzz a bullet at close range, you know? Show them how angry I was at the stealing. My aim's not that good any more, but don't worry, it's fine. I'm sure they got him to a hospital and fixed him up. I let my brother know, so if the police get word of it, he'll smooth things over for me.'

'They lost the car keys,' Lilian said.

'What?'

'He bled out, and they couldn't get him to a hospital. He died.'

She smiled at him. What an odd thing to smile about.

Adrian stubbed his cigarette on the wall, leaving a signature spot next to all the others that had come before it. He jammed his fingers into his armpits. 'Then I'm well and truly fooked. A murder investigation? Even my brother won't be able to save me.'

'It's fine,' Lilian said. 'I took care of it. Faye wanted to get help, but she never made it. She had an accident on the way.'

'An accident?' he said. 'Is she all right?'

'Don't worry about it.'

CHAPTER THIRTY-SEVEN

Lilian took her time in the shower after Adrian left, setting the water to a punishing, hot temperature. She stood under the steaming spray until her skin flared red and traced each of her many scars with careful, soapy fingertips. The outer lesions were healing nicely. The visceral inner wounds, those carved into her by *their* betrayals, still bled.

Adrian was such a soft touch. Even the threats he'd made at the commune were hot air with no substance. Of course he didn't have it in him to evict them. Now, he wouldn't have to. By the next day, they'd disappear, forever, all of them. Dorothy and Michael were already gone, and Faye, well… Lilian had nothing against her. Quite the opposite. She'd liked her pleasant, undemanding friend. But if Faye had called for help, Adrian would have been on the hook for murder, *well and truly fooked*. There was no choice but to put a stop to her delusional mission. Help could never get to Michael in time.

A swing of the log to the back of the head, and Faye fell to the ground, out cold, with not so much as a whimper. A brief hesitation, followed by two more strikes, and the awful business was done. There was more blood than Lilian had expected, spattered over her, so she had to remove Faye's hoodie and wipe herself with it. Then, she dragged the body away from the trail and left it in the woods behind a fallen tree. No one would find her there. There were miles and miles of forest. *I'm sorry, Faye. It's their fault, not yours.* Killing her friend was a sad, necessary burden. The trains of love and hatred had no time to stop and avoid collateral damage. As for the rest of them, they deserved everything they got. She was one-hundred-million-trillion per cent justified.

She hadn't been like this before. Quite the opposite. She'd enrolled in nursing school because she wanted to care for people. But Joel – even thinking his name made her livid – was the one, the trigger, that had set her off. Something in her brain clicked awake that day in the cave, a rage the likes of which she had never experienced. Then her mind performed a strange and surprising trick. The hatred constricted into a ball of blackness, like a tiny pulsating orb just behind her left temple. Her revenge would be meted out, but not through impulse. Instead, she'd be calculated and careful, like Naomi. And, she decided, she must confront Joel. It was not a choice. To put it all behind her, if that were even possible, things would have to be laid bare: a terse conversation had about what he'd done to her.

They had told her to meet them at the cave's entrance, then circled her like hyenas. Joel was waving his knife, and Stella was speaking to her like she was dirt, like her feelings for Adrian were a crime. And Slevin just stood there and said nothing, his hands in his pockets, looking like the Neanderthal he was.

'You can't be a commune member and fraternise with the enemy,' Stella had said.

'I don't see how it's any of your business who I *fraternise* with.'

'So, you admit it. You slept with him,' Joel said, then made a face like a confused mastiff's.

She looked him in the eye and steadied her voice. 'Well, technically, what we had was sweaty, outdoors sex, so we didn't *sleep* together if you know what I mean. Do you know what I mean, Joel? No, probably not.'

She wondered how he would react if she told him the truth, that she was in love with Adrian. Despite the temptation, she decided against it. 'He's not the enemy. You should stop raiding his crops.'

'I don't care who you shag,' Stella said, 'and what position you're in when you do it. It's the fact that you told him about us going into the fields.'

'We're not stupid,' Joel said. 'I'm also against these thefts, but we deal with things inside the commune, not by telling outsiders. Don't deny it, Lilian. How else would he know to come around exactly when we had his produce in the roundhouse?'

'Whatever,' Lilian said and gave them a sorority shrug. It wasn't actually true. Adrian had figured out the thefts all on his own, but she didn't feel the need to explain this to their bitter, righteous faces.

'Didn't stop you eating it though, did it?' Joel said. 'You wanted to throw us off the scent? Well, now, because of you, he's angry and making threats. Because of you, the whole commune is at risk. We took years to build this place. Not been here five minutes, and you try to ruin everything. Shame on you!'

'Because of me?' Lilian said. 'Stella and Slevin were the thieves. Get your facts straight, dumbass.'

And then everything happened too quickly. They told her she was banished from the commune like some Amish elders, and she was fuming, and she screamed at the top of her lungs, 'You're not doing this to me! I'm not going. You can't make me.' Then, Stella told her not to be hysterical, and Joel waved his knife again, and she walked backwards, still arguing with them, crying, holding her hands up, and Joel kept coming, and she lost her shoe but kept retreating, and she didn't look where she was going, and suddenly there was no ground under her feet, just empty air.

As she felt herself falling, falling into that deep shaft at the cave's entrance, the only thing that registered within her panic was that final look on Joel's face. There was neither worry in it nor shock, just a blank stare as if to say, *Oh, okay, this happened.* It was a bizarre reaction for someone who was supposedly obsessed with her and who, from the day she'd arrived at the commune, had given her those disturbing, lustful looks. It seemed like her fall had solved a problem for him. A neat solution. If only he had known the half of it.

She was lucky that day. There were cardboard boxes and old sleeping bags that were dumped into the shaft and lay at its bottom, cushioning her fall. She was bruised and out for a time, and when she regained consciousness, she was all alone with no way up. She shouted and cried for what seemed like forever, feeling sick to her stomach, probably concussed.

Nobody came.

At first, she thought they had gone to call for help. Wasn't that what decent folks did? Alert Mountain Rescue, or Cave Rescue, or whatever it was called in England. Any minute now, emergency personnel in high-visibility jackets will rappel down to her, cover her in a silvery blanket and take her to a waiting ambulance. She conjured up the face of a friendly cop at her bedside, asking her what happened. She imagined saying that she didn't see where she was going and fell, an accident, but as the hours passed, her story changed: *Joel threatened me with a knife and then pushed me down. Stella and Slevin helped him.*

But no rescuers came. She was utterly alone. They had left her for dead.

She tried to climb, but it was no good. The shaft's walls were too far apart to plant her feet on both sides and push herself up. Through repeated attempts, she realised their surface was also too slippery, providing no purchase for any kind of climb. Still, she tried and tried until her nails cracked and her hands bled.

In despair, she looked up through the circular chimney of her prison, breathing in the smell of bat dung and dampness. Her head hurt. Her right leg was swollen and painful from the fall. Her arms were smeared with smelly dirt, and her hair was covered in filth. She was thirsty, so thirsty.

Eventually, she gave up and curled into a ball on the ground on top of a musty sleeping bag that smelled like old piss. She would die of hunger and thirst. They had abandoned her like a nuisance that was well rid of. She replayed the look on Joel's face. *Oh, okay, this happened.*

Hours passed, and the bare light from the distant mouth of the shaft gave way to utter darkness. Bats fluttered above. Several times, she thought she felt something crawl over her. Was it rats? She kicked at the source of a scuttling sound, and her foot hit a rock, sending excruciating stabs of pain through her toes.

She was so scared. The fear drove away any chance of sleep, and she lay there, her hand over her mouth, all the while planning what she would do to them if somehow, some way, she managed to get out alive, if walkers or someone visited the cave and heard her and called for help. First and foremost, she imagined what she would do to Joel. A million times, she imagined his face: shocked, then frightened, then dead.

Morning came in a trickle of cold, bleak light. Still, no one came for her. The taste in her mouth was like chewed-up dirt. She'd die in the cave alone, left to rot. In the clammy grime of her clothes and everything around her, it already felt like she had started to decompose.

In a moment of unreasoned madness, she decided to crawl, head first, through the small diagonal opening that led downwards from the base of her prison, probably to nowhere. It was a tight, suffocating passage with sharp edges that might have her stuck in darkness forever.

She removed her remaining shoe and inched in, her arms in front of her – there was no room for them at her sides – pushing herself forwards with her toes and the tips of her fingers. The air felt thin, the darkness absolute. All that was left was the sounds of her breath and heartbeat, the pain of her compressed body and a terrifying fear. *This will become my grave. Maybe one day someone will find me, a year from now, or in many decades. They'll have no record of me, an American thousands of miles from home.* She imagined a headline in an obscure local news website, *Mystery Human Remains Found in Cave*.

The passage narrowed into an even tighter squeeze. As she tried to push further, a dagger of protruding rock tore into her shoulder, forcing her to stop. She grimaced in pain and could feel the warmth of blood on her shoulder. *It's no use. I need to go back.* At that moment, she would have given anything to see even the limited light at the shaft's mouth again, to breathe more freely, to escape a suffocating death in miserable, frightening blackness. *What was I thinking? What a stupid idea it was to crawl in here. Should've stayed where I was. Barely any hope is better than none.* She tried to crawl backwards, pressing her hands to the ground and curving the stubs of her toes, but only managed a tiny fraction of retreat. It almost felt like the passage behind her had narrowed and closed.

There was no going forward. There was no going back.

I'm stuck. I'll die here, alone in the darkness. It'll probably take days.

Tears ran down her cheeks, carrying the taste of salty filth to her mouth, yet she could not reach with her hands to wipe them.

She closed her eyes and invoked an image of Joel's puffy

face. Boiling anger coursed through her like lava and, like a miracle, wiped away her fear. *I am rage, flowing through the tunnels.* She no longer dreaded pain, but now welcomed it, pushed through it. She was moving forwards again, the razor-sharpness slicing through her shoulders, then more cutting edges, more wounds, more blessed pain. The warmth of oozing blood was a relief. She was moving again, one cleave to her skin at a time. *Give me more! More! More!* A thousand cuts until I live or die.

And then she blinked. *Is that light? Oh my God, light!*

The passage expanded, and she found herself in a sizeable cavern with rays that shone through an opening at its far end. She raised herself to a hunch, and then stood on shaky legs, rubbing her bleeding shoulders and the cuts on her chest and stomach, her arms and her thighs. With marvel and disbelief, she limped to the opening, then stepped out into the sunny morning.

As her eyes adjusted, and her lungs filled with deep, greedy breaths of fresh air, she felt alive, reborn. With the entire capacity of her lungs, she cried a roar of victory, then laughed and laughed like she had lost her mind. She'd won the bloody battle. Now, come hell or high water, she'd win the bloody war.

Adrian took her in, nursed her wounds, and didn't ask too many questions. All she had told him was that they asked her to leave the commune, and then she'd had a nasty tumble down a hillside. He seemed pleased to have her all to himself and had settled her in the old staff caravan. After a while, she gave up on fanning the flames of his anger. It was obvious that Adrian wouldn't follow through on his threats to evict the commune's members. If she was honest, she didn't consider it punishment enough anyway.

Revenge became her new obsession. She'd stalk the commune from a distance and sometimes make stealthy visits to the camp, listening in on their conversations, hiding behind cabins and the roundhouse. One time, when they were all drunk at the bonfire, she went into her old cabin to look for her baby blanket and to collect her passport, which was hidden on top of a roof beam. When she couldn't find the blanket on her side of the cabin, she searched Naomi's things and found both it and the car keys they'd been so frenzied about. *You naughty girl, Naomi!* She delivered the keys to the roundhouse with a note. *Sow division, confuse them, make them tender and ready for the plan's final course.*

And then she left them a parting gift. A box of vegetables, mint, bread she had baked while Megs was away, spreads, strawberries, melons and milk. The strawberries were ripe red, and the melons just perfect. She hoped they would enjoy them. She hoped they'd have their fill before she came to them to have that final talk, the one to end the commune once and for all.

CHAPTER THIRTY-EIGHT

THE DAY OF RECKONING

Naomi was sleepy after the excesses of the meal, so sleepy that her limbs felt like they'd been cast in cement. The strawberries and melons, consumed in tandem with greedy bites into an oversized hunk of bread she had smothered in Marmite, had settled in her stomach like a solid orb of food. *It is what it is*, she thought. Eating after hunger does away with self-control. She washed it all down with fresh milk from the farmer's box of parting goodies. *If I died now, I'd die happy*. She noted, without surprise, that no one had touched the cucumbers, tomatoes or mint. Salad was too much trouble to bother with, especially when the dirty vegetables needed washing.

Joel and Stella were likewise slumped in their chairs, appearing relaxed.

Naomi looked at them, at the state of them. Now she had eaten, priorities rearranged themselves in her head. *Adrian could show up at any minute with his gun and threats. He's dangerous. We should get ourselves ready.*

As if he heard her thinking, Joel stirred. 'Stella,' he said, 'you want to make a pot of coffee? We should have some coffee to wake up.'

'Make it yourself,' Stella said. 'I'm half asleep, can barely move.'

'By now, none of you should be able to move,' said a familiar voice from the door. 'Not a lot, anyway.'

Naomi struggled to keep her eyes in focus. Was she imagining things? 'Lilian?' she said to the figure standing at the door. 'Aren't you dead?'

'Well well, isn't that the very definition of a rhetorical question?' She creased her face. 'Actually, maybe not the definition. I'd check Wikipedia, but there's no reception here. Yes, I have a cell phone. Breaking commune rules again, silly me.' She shrugged and rounded her lips into a toddler's pout. 'So, so sorry, Joel.' She waved at him. 'Hi Joel!'

Joel tried to get up, but his legs would not support him. He slumped back into his chair.

Naomi checked herself, her brain fog, the heaviness all over, like she was weighed down by layers and layers of chain mail. 'You drugged us?' she said.

'I learned from the best,' Lilian said. 'Thank you. And you really were my bestie, really, top friend, until you let them ambush me, until Joel here left me in a hole to die, literally.' She seemed to consider this for a moment. 'My teacher in junior high always gave me a hard time for using *literally* wrong. He'd be proud of me now. You guys literally left me to die. Perfect grammar this time, gold star.'

'I thought you checked,' Stella said to Joel. 'I thought you said she broke her neck.'

'I... Well... I...' Joel said and stared at Lilian, wide-eyed.

Naomi tested her muscles again, trying to order her limbs to move. They were limp, beyond obedience. Another try. Nothing.

Lilian pulled up a chair and sat to face them.

For some reason, Naomi noticed her clothes. Lilian was wearing light-green jeans and an oversized chequered shirt she had never seen before. Then she thought of how she had confided in Lilian, told her how she had drugged her husband before stabbing him. Was Lilian's plan the same, stabbing included? Lilian didn't seem angry. Quite the opposite. There was a cool, casual tone to her words, like she was playing a game. *Could I talk her out of it?* She was thinking like a project manager again. *What words could I use to change the outcome here? There must be something, a middle way, maybe a quid pro quo?*

'I didn't know,' Naomi said. 'I had no idea what they'd planned for you. I only found out a couple of days ago.'

'She knew,' Stella said.

'I didn't!'

'Uh-huh,' Lilian muttered. She spun her chair around and sat with the backrest between her legs, her arms crossed over it.

Naomi turned her head to Stella. 'Why would you say that? Why lie?'

'Whatever,' Lilian said. Her eyes darted to the door and then back to them. She adjusted her chair so she could see both the entrance and the three of them. 'Where's the new guy, the one who just joined?'

Nobody answered.

Lilian shrugged. 'Never mind. I don't have any beef with him, as long as he doesn't storm in here. Never got a good look at him, even when I was watching you. He keeps his eyes on his shoes a lot. Did you guys notice? What's with that? Stockholm syndrome?'

'What do you want, Lilian?' Stella said. 'Honestly, we thought you were dead, that there was nothing we could do. Clearly, Joel didn't check like he–'

'You know what *I* thought?' Lilian said, interrupting her. 'I thought you were one of those people no one ever loved. Your face, it's like nobody cared about you, a good and proper fridge-freezer. How wrong was I? What a surprise it was to see you two kissing, and...' She made a crass imitation of Slevin's voice, 'Stella Crane! Dude! I'm going to be a daddy.'

Stella's eyes widened. 'You were there? And you're the one who...'

'I was there,' Lilian said calmly, 'and yeah, I'm the one who. He was quite heavy to move, but walkers sometimes visit that waterfall. I didn't want to traumatise them. Had to use a wheelbarrow. I'm considerate like that.'

With a push that seemed to take her every ounce of effort, Stella forced herself up. She stood on buckling knees and bared her teeth. Her arms shook, and she used the edge of the communal table for support, fighting against gravity. She grunted with the effort. 'Argh!'

Breezy and unworried, Lilian got up and came to face her. 'Don't exert yourself, Stell. You need to be angry for two now, or three, if we count secret lover boy. Honestly, Joel should be grateful. Didn't I just enforce one of his precious laws: *thou shalt not consummate your love, how dare you?* Last time I checked, breaking the rules was punishable by death.'

Well, Naomi thought. *Stella and Slevin, together? What an unlikely pairing. And a baby?* There was so much going on.

With an effortless shove, Lilian pushed Stella back into her chair. Stella slumped, looking winded, but she was still shaking, her eyes wild with anger.

'No one's going anywhere,' Lilian said. 'If you're too stupid to realise it yet, I've injected the strawberries and melons and laced the Marmite, the jam and the milk. It was important you all ate it, so I tried to be thorough. Couldn't bake it into the bread. Thought about it, but they taught us at nursing school that heat can do unexpected things to medicine. Won't bore you with my specific formulation. This ain't a true crime documentary. All you need to know is that your muscles won't work, and you'll feel *very* relaxed. I hope you didn't overdose, and you can at least listen and hopefully speak when spoken to. Really, I mostly need Joel to stay awake. He's a fat fuck, as they say here, big body mass, so my bet is we'll be okay with the dosage.'

Back in her chair, Lilian looked at each of them in turn, then clapped twice. 'All right, folks, let's get to it while we can. I wanted us to have a little chat before I make my final decision about, you know, what happens next.'

Joel, who hadn't spoken since Lilian arrived, looked her in the eye. 'I was…' he hesitated, then continued, a tremor in his voice. 'I would never have left you there if I thought you survived that fall. I looked down to check. I was sure that…' He paused. 'I was in love with you. I would have done anything to save you if I'd known. I care about you. Please, Lilian. Can't you see that?' Two snail trails of snot rolled down from his nose to his chin. 'I told you to leave because the commune has to come first. I have a responsibility. People look up to me. But it was an accident. I'd never hurt you. You know that, Lilian. You know it's true.'

Naomi blinked, surprised at Joel's confession and his remorseful tone. Were the drugs making him speak so freely? He never talked about emotions. Maybe his pathetic speech would help? Didn't Lilian say she hadn't decided yet what she'd do to them?

Lilian placed the tip of her finger in front of her open mouth, gave it a lick, used it to draw a cross on her forehead and then addressed Joel in her broadest Minnesotan accent. 'Oh ya. You betcha, I know how you felt.' Then she burst into an unexpected cackle of laughter, which she seemed unable to contain. Tears streamed from her eyes. She drew a tissue from her pocket, wiped her face and blew her nose.

'You had a funny way of showing it,' she said to Joel. 'You think I didn't hear how you talked about me when you thought I couldn't hear? *That silly American girl from a hillbilly family.* Wasn't that what you called me, despite looking at my tits all the time? *Yes, we should keep her in the commune. No, I won't admit I want to make her my silly American girl.* Is that how you show your fucked up love? How about threatening me with a knife, eh? Them's the rules of the commune which must be obeyed. *I love you so much, but I will stab, stab, stab you if you don't leave, okay?* Honestly, what kind of person does that?'

As she spoke, Lilian's cheeks blushed a livid red. Her previous composure seemed to have fled from her. *She's angry now,* Naomi thought, *and, unfortunately, she has a point.*

'Let me tell you about my family, Joel,' Lilian said, 'since you never asked. My mom's name was Martha. My dad's was Richard. They did their best for me, but if I'm honest, their best wasn't close to good enough. I think at some point, early on, they regretted this child they'd got themselves.'

'We all have our sob stories,' Stella said, the syllables heavy on her tongue. 'You're not special, just a disturbed child. There's no excuse for what you did to Slevin. None,' she hissed. 'You're an unhinged, murderous bitch! And now you've drugged my baby.'

'Oh, sweetheart,' Lilian said, calm again. 'I have many excuses. You ain't yet heard the most impressive one. My parents weren't only inadequate, much worse, they were British. They moved to Minnesota after they adopted me in London. It took me a long time to track down my biological parents. My search led me to this room.' She turned to Joel. 'Hello, creepy dad. I see incest is still your thing.'

Naomi's drug-laced thoughts sped up for a moment. 'You're making this up,' she said.

'Am I, Joel?' Lilian said. 'Am I, *Dad?* Do you want to tell them about you and my mother? It's a miracle I don't have deformities, what with the family sex and all.'

Joel appeared unable to respond, his eyes wide, his lips agape, making him look like a giant, astonished baby.

'You and Dorothy?' Naomi said to Joel.

'Not Dorothy,' Lilian answered for him. 'The Wicked

Witch of the West, her sister, Sandra.' She turned to Joel and squinted at his still-dropped jaw. 'So... if you're my dad and Sandra's my great-aunt, that also makes you my what? First cousin once removed? Not sure. Our family is *very* confusing. Maybe I'll draw a diagram and figure it out. Good thing I didn't have this information when we did our family tree in eighth grade. Just think what *that* would have looked like.'

Joel blinked several times. He was trembling all over like a duckling shivering in the cold. He wheezed out a succession of hyperventilated breaths, then caught himself and stopped, staring incredulously at Lilian. Naomi reasoned that, but for the narcotic paralysis that had locked him in his seat, he would have fled the room.

It's true then, Naomi thought. The revelation had changed her assessment of their situation. A child's anger at her parents. Well, that was an entirely more serious and dangerous thing.

'When you abandoned me there in the cave, it was like you left me all over again. Not that you'd make outstanding father of the year or anything. You're a repulsive person. But at least I found my grandma, and that's something, isn't it? A little balance against your betrayals.'

'She didn't want you. She's the one who told me to give you up.'

'Joel, stop,' Naomi said. 'This isn't helping.'

'I don't care about your lies,' Lilian said, then turned to Naomi. 'He was jealous of my relationship with Adrian. My own father, he—'

Joel interrupted, his words barely intelligible through his sobs. He looked even more pathetic now. 'I didn't know I was your father.'

'And then you left me there to die, alone and scared, in the dark. None of this would have happened if... None of it – Michael, Slevin, Faye.'

'Faye?' Naomi said.

'I had to stop her. If she'd gotten help, they'd come after Adrian, and I couldn't let that happen. Not to him. I liked Faye. It wasn't her fault. Just had to be done.'

'So, you killed her?' Naomi said, forgetting herself, her predicament. There was so much going on, too much.

'Oh, don't pretend, Naomi. I saw you chase her with a knife. Should have left her to you, but I didn't know until after. I'm sure you would have done a better job, what with the whole escaped murderer thing. One less corpse on my hands.' She shrugged. 'But who's counting? I guess by the end of today, there could be more.' She raised her hand and counted on her fingers to the number five, 'Faye, Slevin, Joel, Stella, Naomi. Oh, I'm not counting Michael. That one's on Adrian. He's a crappy shot. It was a lovely funeral, by the way. Yes, of course I was there, and at Dorothy's. I've become damn good at sneaking around.'

'You... killed Dorothy?' Naomi said.

'What? No! My own grandmother? Are you crazy? No.' Lilian turned to Joel. 'Well, Dad, you got anything to say to me? Could you have handled things a little better, maybe? A little less homicidally?'

It all rests on this, Naomi thought. *Our lives or deaths, how all this turns out, everything. Everything hangs on the words of a giant baby.*

CHAPTER THIRTY-NINE

Despite the sedating effects of the drugs, Joel experienced a personal awakening. *Lilian is my daughter. I can see it now: Sandra's nose, Dorothy's holier-than-thou attitude. There's no doubt. She's my child, my DNA mix, my continuation after I'm gone. Am I going? Am I going now?*

Something nagged at him. Lilian was looking his way, waiting for him to speak, but he simply observed her, trying to sieve out the emotions of his attachment to this young woman who had turned into someone else entirely in the space of only a few words. Did the revelation about Lilian being his daughter swap his previous obsession with her with something parental? He searched his attraction for her and found nothing new. The change would need some time and work and reflection. If he had time, that is. His situation was at once absurd and confusing. He imagined a bewigged computer-generated barrister standing in front of a judge in an Xbox game court. *M'lord, we have fresh evidence that casts a rather different light on this case. The defendant is not, in fact, a witch who has entrapped her victim with magic, but an upstanding daughter with a father who, by any measure, displays most rancid characteristics, most rancid. I put it to you, it is he, not she, who should stand in the dock. It is he who bears the burden of a guilty mind and should be judged for it in the harshest terms.*

At last, Joel spoke. 'Have you gone to Sandra? Have you talked to… your mother?'

'No, Dad, I came to see you first.'

Dad. The word was like a bee sting in his ear.

'I hoped we'd get to know each other and then go speak to Mom together. Didn't count on the whole leaving me to die thing. So, you still haven't answered my question. Could you have handled things better, maybe?'

He would have liked to handle his whole life better. For the two years after learning about Sandra's pregnancy and the awful days until the adoption, he barely left his room, often replaying in his mind the meeting with the social worker where the baby's fate, Lilian's, was decided.

'I'm not going to keep it,' a heavily pregnant Aunt Sandra had said. 'And neither will Joel.'

Dorothy twiddled her thumbs and glanced with fright at the social worker, then at her sister.

'It's all right,' Sandra said. 'She knows.'

Dorothy coughed. 'You told her?'

'Tracey's fine.'

'What happens here stays between us,' the social worker said in the low, ever-so-calm voice of officialdom. 'My only concern is the baby's welfare. I'm not here to judge. I understand that Joel is the father. I'd like to hear what he has to say. It would be better for the child if it could stay with its biological parents.'

'Joel lives with me,' Dorothy said, 'and I'm certainly not going to take care of my sister's mistake. And what would we tell people about where the baby came from? It's an awful stain on us.' She shook her head. 'I can't even begin to imagine… Can't bear it, the shame of it.' She spoke to Sandra and Joel. 'Shame on you both!'

'We can figure out together how you'll present the new baby,' the social worker said. 'Joel, what do *you* think?'

'You've got your answer,' Dorothy said. 'There's nothing to discuss.'

Joel picked up his Obi-Wan Kenobi mug and hurled it at the kitchen wall. It shattered to pieces that swam in a pool of milky tea on the floor. Splashes of the liquid trickled like tears down the floral lilac and cream wallpaper.

'Thank you for coming to speak to us, Tracey,' Dorothy said, 'but you've upset Joel, and he's a sensitive boy. Please leave.'

'But I–'

'I'll have a chat with my son when he's calmed down. If there's any change, my sister will let you know.'

Joel got up, walked to the kitchen's corner and cowered on the floor, his back to the condiment cupboard. He covered his head with his hands and rocked back and forth. He didn't remember how he got back to his room. Later that day, when his mother came to speak to him, her hands on the door frame, he had his decision ready.

'I want to keep the baby,' he said.

'That feeling will pass,' Dorothy said. 'It's like that Labrador puppy you wanted. You were so fixated on the idea that you didn't think through what it meant to walk it every day, feed it, take it to the vet. Two computer games later, you forgot all about it. Can't you see this baby's a disgrace? What you did with your aunt was repulsive.'

'What *I* did?'

She took a step back. 'Yes, it takes two, and I don't want to hear another word about it.'

He never raised his voice to her, but this time he did. 'Of course you don't. You...' he grunted. 'You...' His head spun with anger. He pounded his bed with both fists.

'I'll bring up a sandwich for you shortly. Remember what I

said. This feeling will pass. There's no need to dwell. It's over and done with.'

He didn't touch his food that day. It took a full week for him to return to playing on his Xbox, but when he did, it was a relief. Shoot-em-ups kept his thoughts from spiralling. He sometimes played through the night and into the next day, eating packet after packet of crisps, until he was so exhausted, he started missing crucial shots at the enemy.

This was also when his obsession with knives began. Weapons from his gaming world being made real brought him some comfort. He kept the two Japanese knives he had bought with his savings hidden from his mother and practised their use in front of YouTube tutorials, making sure his door was locked. It never occurred to him to hurt anyone in real life. No. Not like his father, who had stabbed his second wife. Cathy was a beautiful, petite woman who wore pearl necklaces and elegant dresses. If Joel had married someone like her, he'd be so grateful, he wouldn't dare hurt her.

Joel didn't show his anger about the stolen baby again, but in an act of quiet defiance, he vowed to never call Dorothy *Mother*.

The baby girl was born six weeks later and given up for adoption. In the years that followed, Joel continued to live in his attic room in the eaves of Dorothy's house, eventually finding a job at a stationery store, where he became an expert on pens, rulers and the thickness of printer paper. He'd often get Dorothy to leave his meals on a tray outside his door, only coming out to collect them after he heard her footsteps tread back down the creaking stairs.

And so, time passed, each year draining down the sinkhole of his life more quickly. Before Joel knew it, he was thirty-six, a man of routines and solitude and nights online, slashing and shooting and hoping to reach one more level, and another, and another, powering through the inevitable GAME OVER deaths.

Then, one chilly spring evening, Dorothy asked him downstairs to the kitchen table for 'a little chat'. The fake fire heater was set to high, but did nothing to melt the chill of Joel's apprehension. He knew by her tone that something momentous was about to happen.

Without so much as a reassuring word, she told him of her decision, speaking to him as if he were a halfwit. 'You can't waste your life in your room. We need to leave here. It makes us both miserable. I think I've found a way. We're going to start a commune. Do you know what a commune is? I got you some books on the topic, and I found just the right land. It may not seem like it now, but you'll love, love, love it.'

Rather than love, it was hatred that Joel felt towards the idea of leaving his familiar environment, his Xbox and computer, the routine at the stationery store, his accumulated knowledge of the thickness of lead in sketching pencils. He barely spoke to Dorothy for the four months it took for the purchase of the land to go through. He said almost nothing as they drove to Northumberland and pitched their two tents on the land Dorothy had acquired. Yet he read the books she had given him and helped clear the earth of their new encampment. It was something to do.

When Stella and Slevin joined a month later, Synner's Crag commune inaugurated its first communal bonfire. Joel got drunk for the first time and let himself speak to the new strangers like they were friends. People, chatting, singing – it was a novel experience, his road-to-Damascus moment. Suddenly, he wasn't an awkward, discarded dreg of a person. He could engage in real conversations with people. Slevin patted him on the back like no one had done before.

The commune turned out to be the answer to a question Joel never knew to ask. His conversion was complete overnight, and like many a convert, he sought purity and was proud of it. The commune had to be run right. There would be no property that's entirely private, other than, he reluctantly conceded, clothes and a few small personal items. Meals were to be taken together, and work shared out. They were real communists in the purest of forms, except, of course, for a little hierarchy. After all, he and Dorothy were the founders. It was only natural that they should be treated with respect and deference. Some chores were better suited to newer members, which was only right, considering.

It's so weird, he thought. *After all these years she's found me. And she's Lilian, and… and… She's asking for something. What is it? What does she want me to say?*

CHAPTER FORTY

'I'm sorry, Lilian,' Joel said at last, though the apology sounded hollow and forced.

'I know,' Lilian said. 'You're so sorry. Devastated, even. It's too much for you to bear. C'mon, Dad, is that the best you can do?'

Naomi wished he would weep, look contrite, give Lilian the show she needed, but at the same time she understood. Despite his initial shocked words, Joel didn't know how to do the things his daughter longed for.

Naomi hoped for Luke to come through the door, overpower Lilian, and guard them while they recovered from the effects of the drugs. He was supposed to empty the toilet bucket and then come back. He must be desperate with hunger by now. She said a prayer for him to return, at the same time, somehow, knowing that he wouldn't. Too much time had passed. *Where is he? What happened to him?*

Lilian stood up from her chair. Her face was tense while her shoulders looked strangely relaxed, like a mix of doubt and determination. She came to stand before Joel, placed her hand under his chin and raised his head, forcing him to look her in the eye. He blinked incessantly.

'Three little sinners, sitting in the roundhouse,' she said. 'One stabbed himself, and then there were two.'

'What?' Joel said. His legs shook, and he seemed to be making an effort to move, though his muscles wouldn't obey him. His fingers twitched.

Lilian took a tissue out of her pocket, wiped the snot from his face with gentle strokes, then discarded the tissue on the floor. She brought her face close to his and looked at him as if trying to discover something hidden. 'Oh, Dad,' she said and gave him a tender kiss on the forehead.

'I'm sorry, Lilian,' Joel said.

'Yes, you are,' Lilian said. With a firm hand, she drew his Parang machete from the sheath on his belt and showed it to him.

Joel looked at the knife, at his incapacitated hands, his eyes filled with incomprehension and fright.

With slow, tender movements, Lilian wrapped the fingers of both of Joel's hands around the blade's handle and cupped them in hers. Then, she guided his hands up until the tip of the blade touched his chest. 'It's a real tragedy,' she said. 'All of it. You were so overcome by remorse for what you did to your daughter that you killed yourself.' Her voice was now monotone, drained of feelings. 'I appreciate you finally coming around to accept responsibility. Goodbye, Dad.'

Joel's expression was weirdly relaxed, like a stunned lamb waiting for its execution. 'Goodbye, Lilian,' he said, resigned. 'I really am sorry. I hope you know that.'

'You betcha,' Lilian said. With a nurse's careful precision, she pushed the blade straight into his heart. Then she twisted it, once to the right and once to the left, and held it there, her hands over Joel's, over the knife's handle, staring into his eyes as they glazed over.

Naomi dared not speak. In desperation, she tried again to regain control of her limbs. They would not budge. If only she could escape this place, she would run and run and never look back.

As if awakened from a reverie, Lilian let go. Joel's hands remained fixed in their rigid, dead grasp of the knife. Blood oozed from his wound.

'Lilian,' Stella said, her voice barely audible.

Lilian ignored her. It was as if her business was done now, and she was oblivious to the world around her. She walked out of the roundhouse. The beaded strings that covered the door swayed until they settled.

Naomi dared to breathe again. Was it over? How long would it take for the drugs to wear off? To her relief, the fog inside her mind was starting to lift. Her limbs were still limp, though. The rest of her body was taking its time. As soon as she could move again, she'd head to the stream. The cold water should help.

With effort, she turned her head. Stella looked in worse shape than she was in, mumbling incoherently. She stared at Joel's stiff body, the knife in his heart. The look in his eyes appeared different now, as if the horror had changed post mortem into something else, a sadness, a deep sort of sorrow. Despite herself, she felt for him, for the man who was stabbed by his daughter only moments after finding out who she really was.

Her thoughts turned to the future. Who was left now? She and Stella, and Luke – if he was still around. Not much of a commune. They couldn't stay at Synner's Crag, not after the awful train of deaths. Her previous plans of escape had always been about a solitary journey to a new life, but now she thought it might be better to keep the company of those who had shared her ordeal. What if... What if the three of them went to the Scottish Highlands, moving from campsite to campsite and using Michael and Faye's bell tent for shelter? Maybe they'd find seasonal work and a Scottish farmer who'd let them stay on his land. Would Luke come with her? Would Stella?

She realised she was always making plans for an escape, always thinking of her next flight to safety: the life of a murderer on the run, the life she unknowingly chose when she married Des. What if something had come up, and she'd never showed up to their first date? What if she'd then met someone else, or decided relationships simply weren't worth the trouble? Des was her curse. Her whole life could have been different without him. He wasn't inevitable. He just happened to her, the way things do. She caught him like you catch the flu, like you trip on a crack in the pavement and fall.

Stella stopped mumbling and seemed to regain control of her voice. 'Is she gone?' she said.

'I hope so,' Naomi said. 'Can you move?'

'My nose itches. I can't scratch it.'

'It should wear off soon. Then, we need to get out of here.'

'I'll rip her throat out. She'll pay for Slevin. I'll stab her until there's nothing left except for holes and blood. If she thinks she's getting away with it—'

'All great choices, but don't you think it's better to just leave? We can start again somewhere, forget about all this. I have some ideas for how we can—'

'I'm pregnant. My child will never have a father.'

'I know. Why put your baby at risk? Let's just—'

'What did she mean when she said you're an escaped murderer, that you came after Faye?'

Naomi would have shaken her head if she could. Stella clearly had no concept of priorities. 'The words of a crazy person.'

'I think I can move my fingers.'

Naomi could see Stella's middle finger twitch. *Good. It's a start*. How long would it take for the paralysis to subside? How long would they be forced to sit there with Joel's dead gaze upon them? *It could have been worse*, she reminded herself. Lilian could have killed them, too. She must have decided they'd tell no one what happened, which was fair enough when it came to Naomi, the criminal on the run, but Stella had no such baggage to hold her back. Instead, she had scores to settle and a furious anger. *Why would Lilian take the risk and let her live?*

As soon as the thought crossed Naomi's mind, the answer came in the form of footsteps, followed by a shadow, and then a figure at the door.

'Sorry for the wait,' Lilian said. In her hand, she carried a jerrycan. She unscrewed its lid and doused the roundhouse, moving from the communal table to the storage boxes, the wooden beams, the floor and walls.

The smell of petrol filled Naomi's nostrils. Panic took over. Her bladder emptied just as Lilian poured the liquid over her hair and body. Then, Lilian did the same to Stella, who coughed and spat out the smelly liquid.

Naomi's eyes stung, and she blinked, helpless and terrified. 'Lilian, please,' she begged, struggling against the hold of the drugs. 'I did nothing to you.'

'You were supposed to be my friend,' Lilian said.

'I was. I still am. They came back from the cave and said you decided to leave. Please!'

There was a pause. 'Maybe you're right,' Lilian said. 'But you kept going on and on about how a good project manager makes sure there are no loose ends. I learned from your wisdom. You're an excellent teacher, and I say this with kindness.'

'I'll never tell. I'm wanted for murder, for God's sake.'

Lilian placed the jerrycan on the floor and seemed to consider this. 'You mean I should only burn Stella?'

Naomi managed a nod.

Stella's face twisted, and she grunted something like an expletive, but her words were only part-formed.

Lilian sighed, then picked up the jerrycan. 'I'm real sorry. You know me. This isn't the person I am, at least not before... before all this.'

'You're not. Let me go.'

Lilian waited a moment, seeming deep in thought. Then she sighed but said nothing.

Naomi thought of fire, of pain, of regret. She imagined a string of *what ifs:* what if she had run away after Michael died, after Faye, after they accused her of hiding the keys? She clung to a tiny strand of hope that Lilian might change her mind. What else was left to her but an unreasoned belief that she could leave the roundhouse alive?

'I'll disappear,' Naomi said. 'No one will ever hear from me. I won't speak a word about it. I'm your friend. Untie me.'

'I'm pregnant,' Stella said suddenly. 'You'll be murdering my baby.'

Lilian looked at Stella, stony-faced, and rubbed the back of her neck.

'Let me go. All I care about is my baby.'

Lilian hesitated, then shook her head. 'I just want this over now. Please stop talking. You're only making this more difficult.'

'You don't have to release her,' Naomi said. 'She'll tell the authorities, but I won't. I can't.'

Stella spat out her response. 'Naomi knew about our meeting at the cave, that we were planning to send you away. Now she's playing all innocent. If you kill me, she has to go too.'

Naomi felt her shoulders shudder, but the rest of her was still paralysed. *Whatever I say now, even if I deny it, will sound hollow. It's my word against Stella's.* Arguments were useless. 'You're obviously going to do this,' she said, overcoming the nasty taste of petrol in her mouth, 'so I wanted to tell you that I'm sorry: for Joel abandoning you, for how you were treated here, for everything that happened to you. We all carry our crosses. We all have to suffer the shit life throws at us. How we deal with it is what matters. You can walk away and let us live, or be an entitled, crybaby cunt.'

'Oh, wow, well,' Lilian said. 'I'm so glad we've had this little chat. Say nothing else. It'll be poetic. My mother says a person's last word, if it's bad, is like a curse that follows them to hell.' She stepped to the door and stood there for a moment, surveying the room. Then she lit a match and threw it on the floor. It didn't take and landed, extinguished, on the ground.

'Lilian!' Naomi cried against the fog of her senses, all composure gone from her. Now was the time to beg, or die. She opened her mouth but found nothing to say. She was entirely and fatally empty of words.

Lilian looked at her, and their eyes locked. At the same time, the next match, more successful than the first, ignited the roundhouse into an almost instant furnace of flames.

CHAPTER FORTY-ONE

TWENTY-THREE DAYS POST DISCOVERY

Alex took a moment to stand in front of Sandra Saint-John's door, observing the Victorian windows with their rotting wooden frames, the cherry tree and overflowing council bins, the ginger cat that pawed its way on patrol along the paving slabs. If everything went to plan, this would be his last visit. He wouldn't miss her.

He straightened his back, took a deep breath, wrapped his fingers around the door-knocker's brass ring and announced his presence.

'First of all, Ms Saint-John, I'd like to thank you for hiring me for this job,' he said from his now familiar seat before her.

Sandra was wearing a brash purple caftan, clasping her hands and looking imperiously at him. 'I don't need niceties,' she said. 'You should know that by now.'

'Okay.' He gave her a curt smile. 'The police investigation into the commune has reached some definitive conclusions, at least as far as your question about Luke Bridestone is concerned, enough for you to decide what to do next. There are a few open questions about other people, but...' He shrugged.

'Is he guilty?' she said.

'This will be our last meeting, so I'll need you to settle your account first. No offence. That's how these things are done.'

Sandra removed a stray strand of hair that had wandered over her eye. She crossed her legs. 'I don't like your tone. I told you I'm good for the money.'

'I'm sorry, but our contract is clear. Full funds before I share the outcome of the investigation and the answer to your question: is Luke Bridestone a viable suspect for murdering any commune members, and can he therefore, potentially, be excluded from inheriting your sister's house?' He tapped his black notepad with his pen.

'I prefer to pay once I've heard the results, and that's final. I don't have the funds available anyway. Don't worry, Mr Czerniak, you'll be compensated fairly for your... efforts. And you must admit, you haven't done much detecting for me, have you? All I got was updates about the police investigation, and also, the whole thing didn't take long.'

Alex thought of his daughters to calm himself: Poppy dancing around their lounge to her favourite tune from *Frozen*, waving her hands in the air; Rose's drawing of their little family as stick figures beside a green blob she said was a tree. A client's resentments were perilous. Things could quickly get heated, decisions taken out of spite. He'd given up a lucrative client to work for Sandra. If things soured now, it would have been for nothing. He kept his tone neutral. 'Each case is different. An infidelity might need a stakeout. Money laundering is all about forensic accounting. For this case, the thing that matters, the only thing that matters for your purpose, is what the investigation decides: did Luke Bridestone commit a crime in the eyes of the law, and will the CPS be likely to prosecute? I have the kind of access others can only dream of, and I have the answers with me today. All I need from you is what we agreed, nothing more.' He cringed inwardly for saying these words, but his mother would be proud.

'I'm a sick woman,' Sandra said.

Alex nodded. 'I'm not sure how long it will take the police to release their official findings. For such a large-scale investigation, it could take months, probably longer. With so many victims, the bureaucracy is mind-boggling: departmental approval, oversight. Still, I've been told the results, as far as they concern Luke, will stay the same.' He leaned forward and spoke in what Mary called *his earnest voice*. 'What I have to share with you today are the conclusions from the final autopsies and the case overall.' He settled back into the seat and waited a beat. 'Any judgment on your claim for the house will depend on these conclusions. If Luke never wakes from his coma, there won't be a trial, but you might be able to use them to apply for the will to be set aside if – and only if – they're what you want them to be. I've done what you hired me for.'

'That's a lot of words,' she said. 'Maybe I'll just wait to see what the police say. Shouldn't take long now, should it?'

'By the look of things, the latter end of next year, and I've heard your latest hospital scans weren't…' He noticed her bite her lip. 'I'm so sorry.' He pointed the tip of his pen at his notepad. 'If he's guilty, a little tip-off to the press could light a fire under The Powers that Be and speed things up. Otherwise, the evidence files will take their normal slow train.'

Alex checked himself. He felt uncomfortable in his pitch and the kind of pressure he was exerting. He had never held a client over a barrel like this, but with Sandra Saint-John, it was a necessary evil. No doubt she would refuse to pay for his services, given half a chance. It was true the job had not been as difficult as he'd expected, and once or twice he'd considered giving Sandra a steep discount, but her difficult behaviour had dissuaded him, not to mention his suspicions that Sandra was somehow involved in what happened at the commune.

'I could have hired someone else,' she said, 'at a much lower price.'

'I'd prefer a bank transfer.' He placed a printed invoice with the amount and his bank details highlighted in yellow marker on the stained teak side table next to her, then flattened it with his hand.

She looked incensed, but Alex recognised her act for what it was.

'What would you have me do?' she said, her hand on her heart. 'I can't just magic half a million pounds out of thin air.'

'With the utmost respect,' Alex said, 'you've released the equity on this house. It needs a bit of a facelift, but the equity-release company liked your circumstances. You currently have £550,000 in your Halifax account.'

Her face reddened. 'You're a little shit, aren't you?'

They sat in silence. Sandra wanted to make him wait as punishment for her wounded pride, but would she risk the payoff she'd been so dogged about? It was a finely balanced decision.

'May I use your toilet?' he said, already getting up.

'You may,' she answered through gritted teeth. Then he noticed her looking longingly at his notepad, which was perched on the chair's armrest. He picked it up and left her alone for five long minutes. When he returned, she had her ancient laptop open and was on the phone answering security questions from her bank.

It didn't take long for his phone to ping with a message from his own bank. £500,000 deposited.

He nodded to her. 'I'm grateful.'

'Go on, then. You got your money, now give me Luke Bridestone.'

'Before I do, can I ask you a question?'

'Be quick about it. I haven't got all day.'

'Since your nephew joined the commune, were you ever in touch with him? Did you send him any messages, or did he communicate with you?'

'Why ever would I?' she said.

'So, you didn't.'

She shook her head, a little too vigorously. 'No.'

He opened his notebook. 'All right, then.' He drew a silent, deep breath. 'The police are confident the final three victims were also the last to die. They are Naomi Abraham, Stella Crane and, I'm sorry, your nephew Joel. Their bodies were found inside the round communal building at the centre of their camp. They were so badly burned and battered that their autopsies were a challenge. The structure was built from heavy poles and beams, some of which collapsed on top of the deceased when it burned down. The pathologist couldn't say which injuries were sustained before the fire and which during, or exactly how the victims died. Well, except for Joel, which I'll get to. That said, the working theory is that the fire came after they were murdered.'

Sandra fidgeted, looking impatient. 'You said they've reached a conclusion.'

'Even without complete proof, what was found at the scene paints a picture. I'm sorry to have to tell you, but...' He hesitated.

'But what?'

'The police believe your nephew battered the two women to death, probably with a blunt object that later burned in the fire. Mind you, it's not conclusive. Like I said, their injuries could have happened if they were hit by falling beams. When we get to your nephew's cause of death, you'll understand why he's the likely suspect.'

'What about the others?' Sandra said, and Alex noted that she hadn't asked how Joel could be suspected of murdering

Naomi and Stella if he, too, died in the same place. Her focus was on Luke. Always on Luke. He suppressed a shudder.

'When it comes to your sister, the investigation's best guess, based on profiling your nephew, is that Joel confronted Dorothy in some sort of argument. This brought about her heart attack. They suspect he threatened her or even meant to harm her, but she died before he got his chance. In his anger, he even hurt her body post mortem and broke her spine. He must have been very angry about something. Would you have any idea what?'

'I haven't seen Joel in years. How would I know what went through his mind?'

'Her death seems to have been the start of something, almost like a plan. He was set on a trail of destruction. Michael Bind was stabbed in the thigh with a large knife. The use of that particular weapon also points to Joel.'

One of the knives you sent him, he wanted to add, but didn't. 'Michael died of blood loss, and no one was allowed to call for help or escape to alert the authorities. Hence, Faye Hindmarsh's death, likely the work of Naomi Abraham. Naomi was already a convicted killer. She had good reason to stop the police from descending on the commune. Her DNA was found on the murder weapon used on Faye.'

'So, it wasn't all Joel,' she said, seeming anxious for the story to change.

'The commune still buried Dorothy and Michael, but then things took a turn for the worse. There's no clear evidence about who attacked Slevin Grimlow, but your nephew and Naomi are considered the most likely suspects.' He met her furious eyes. 'There's a lot of detail we'll probably never know, except that Naomi Abraham is suspected of one or more of the killings, and your nephew is potentially involved in the rest. I know it's not what you wanted to hear. A family member… It's difficult.'

'You still haven't told me how Joel died. If he and Naomi were the only suspects, and Joel killed Naomi, doesn't it mean another person was involved?'

'Your nephew killed himself, maybe out of remorse. After attacking Stella and Naomi, he poured petrol over the two women and all around the structure, but not over himself, which is telling. Then, he set it on fire. Before the flames could take hold, he stuck a knife into his own chest. He would have had seconds to do it. Petrol ignites very quickly.'

'I can't see how they'd know this. Luke was the last one alive, wasn't he?'

'Joel's burnt body was found with his fingers still tight around the knife's handle and no petrol residue. That's why the police considered him the prime suspect for the deaths of Naomi and Stella. Crime followed by remorse.'

'Everything you told me,' Sandra said, 'is conjecture and speculation. Is that all they have? I mean, someone might have done *this*, and someone else might have done *that*. What kind of incompetent police force is happy with half-maybes?'

'You're right,' Alex said, 'but a lot of crimes never get solved. In this case, the police can only follow the evidence they found. I know it's hard to hear.'

Alex didn't want to tell her that there were still unanswered questions: about the additional, unknown, DNA found on the log used to hit Faye Hindmarsh, about Joel's motivation, about the knives Sandra had sent him, possibly with a message, about the timeline. He himself wasn't entirely convinced by the narrative the police had settled on, at least for now. His intuition told him there was more to the story. His wife agreed, unofficially asking her officers to keep an open mind for any new theories. Still, none of the gaps in the investigation would point to Luke Bridestone, and Luke was the only person his client was interested in. Alex was employed to find an answer to one question only. He felt confident that he had: Luke had nothing to do with any of the deaths. The police, for their part, had decided to keep the case open a while longer. Without new leads, it would eventually be closed and declared solved.

Sandra sat rigid in her chair, her eyes wandering as if tracking an unseen fly. Then, she ignited like a match set to fuel. 'Damn the truth! You knew what I wanted.' She paused and, with apparent effort, softened her face. 'You've robbed me of all my money. Is there nothing you can do?'

Alex shut his notebook, placed it in his briefcase, closed the lid and clicked its clasps shut. 'Shall I make us a cup of tea?' He expected her usual refusal or an excuse about the kettle not working.

Sandra swallowed, took a moment to recover, then nodded. 'Black, no sugar. Leave the bag in.' Her voice was hoarse, like a heavy smoker's.

She drank her bitter tea quietly, raising the cup from its saucer for tiny sips, occasionally looking up at him, seeming to expect him to say something, to offer a solution.

'Is there anything else you'd like to ask, Ms Saint-John?'

She looked at him, probing, beseeching. 'And if Luke Bridestone wakes up and tells them he's the one who did it, at least some of it?'

'Even if he does recover and admits guilt, it's not likely anyone would believe him. The evidence doesn't support it. And Luke has form. You'll recall he's already admitted to crimes he didn't commit. I don't think it'll wash.'

She stared ahead, her shape appearing crumpled, her usual stiff manner gone, like a deflated doll. Alex hoped she wouldn't ask for some of her money back. Looking at her sorry state, he'd be hard-pressed not to help her.

'I have an oncology appointment in Greenwich,' she said. 'Do you think, on your way, you could drive me there, at least?'

The plea in her eyes was desperate, as if despite everything she'd said to him that day, she didn't want them to part ways.

For a moment, Alex considered affording her this one last favour, but then he remembered the school run. 'I'd have liked to,' he said, 'but I have to pick up my daughters. Let me call you an Uber. I'll pay.'

CHAPTER FORTY-TWO

THIRTY DAYS POST DISCOVERY

Sandra hugged the branded canvas sports bag that lay over her knees in the back of the black cab. She looked out of the window at the passing London traffic, willing herself not to check for the hundredth time that the bag's zip was fully fastened. The driver was not chatty, and she was thankful for small mercies, yet every time he looked in his rear-view mirror, she felt self-conscious. Never, since the age of seventeen, had she worn a tracksuit. The white stripes over the cheap blue polyester fabric she had bought for the occasion at a sports apparel shop with loud music and spotty teenagers made her feel like someone else, someone unlike her at all. Maybe this was a good thing. Separate yourself from the events until they become a little story you tell yourself. She was a spectator of this other person's actions, a person in itchy, manufactured fabric. The dark sunglasses helped complete the illusion.

When the driver dropped her off in front of University College Hospital, she reminded herself that the procedure would be quick. In and out in a matter of minutes, if she was lucky and nothing delayed her, and if Luke was no longer guarded, fingers crossed.

Face forward, she walked confidently past reception into the bowels of UCH tower, breathing in the familiar scents of tangy disinfectant and floor cleaning fluids. In the two years since her cancer diagnosis, she had come to know hospitals, their harsh lighting, their long soulless corridors, efficiently adorned with confusing signs and inoffensive posters, meant to cheer you up but, in her case, always dragging her soul into the dreary depths of desolation.

Much as she hated the buildings and their systems and procedures, she loved the nurses and doctors, all of whom had been kind to her beyond what she deserved. She often repaid them with grumpy ingratitude. That's just how she was. When you're young and healthy, it's easy to change. Come ailment and the advancement of years, it felt like too much effort.

In a disabled toilet with a stained Formica floor, Sandra changed into the patient gown and comfortable slippers she had brought with her. She rummaged in the bag for the black wallet pouch and wore it with its string around her neck, adjusting it to the side of her waist.

She stored her tracksuit and white trainers in the bag and looked at herself in the mirror. She sighed and thought of her sister's last visit. Why did Dorothy have to be so stubborn? And this business with the will. *Now look what you made me do.* At least the private investigator, *the useless oaf*, was good for one thing. He had told her where to find Luke Bridestone.

She walked slowly, bag in hand, looking just like any other patient. *God knows I've had plenty of practice. An Oscar-winning performance. If you hadn't been so selfish, Dorothy, I would never have to do this.*

At the end of a row of plastic seats that were screwed to the floor, like someone might walk off with them, she found an abandoned three-legged walker. She added it to her ensemble before boarding the elevator to the third floor. She needed to look frail, but not so frail that the ward's staff would tag her as confused and start asking questions. Her main concern, however, was that regular patients were not expected to wander into the Critical Care Unit. If he was previously guarded, Luke may still be in a separate room, hopefully not at the centre of things, so she could reach him unnoticed.

Sandra needn't have worried. There was too much commotion and activity for anyone to stop her. Her hospital garb had made her invisible. Nurses and doctors were rushing like busy ants, their steps urgent and determined. She was like a ghost amongst them, staying close to the walls.

Luke Bridestone's room was easy to find, at the very end of the corridor, near an emergency exit. A uniformed policeman stood by the door, looking bored. *Shit!* Then, with relief, she noticed the officer was drinking coffee from an extra-large paper cup. *Good. That coffee will have to come out the other end.* She took a seat and waited, the walker by her side. As long as no one asked her questions, all she had to do was wait.

A pale skeletal man came to sit beside her. He was attached to a wheeled drip, and his lips moved in a continuous tremor.

'Waiting long?' he said. His voice was deep and clear, a young man's voice, emanating from a decrepit mouth.

She didn't answer.

'I'm Henry,' he said.

She turned her head only slightly, not wishing to face him, not wishing to engage.

'It's all right,' he said. 'I'm a long time past my flirting days.' He chuckled. 'And anyway, look at you. You're way out of my league.'

Vanity overtook caution. 'Oh, I'm sure that's not true.'

'You're kind,' he said. 'I can tell you're a kind person. What are you in for, if you don't mind me asking?'

She shook her head. He must be confused. There were no walk-in treatments on this ward. You had to be wheeled in to qualify.

'Me,' he said, 'I'm just here so they can prolong the agony. If they pointed to a room and said, *there, go in there, and we'll put you to sleep with no pain, just sleep, you know…* I would go in a heartbeat.'

Sandra took a second look at him, the skin that hung on his frame like creased parchment, the Rorschach of age spots on his cheeks and forehead. She noticed, too, his smell: wet cardboard and urine. A man on his final stretch. She had seen a few of his kind on the cancer ward.

'Unfortunately for you,' she said, 'the NHS does not provide that particular service just yet.'

'I'm Henry,' he said again.

Surprising even herself, Sandra took his veiny hands in hers, her thumbs gently patting the thin ridges of his knuckles.

'I'm Dorothy,' she lied. 'We should all make the most of the time we have. Think of Christmas. Think of all the things that…'

The policeman stretched, looked right and left, then walked off quickly towards a set of double doors.

'Be well, Henry,' she said. 'I have to go. Will you look after my bag for me?'

'Don't you need your walker?' he called after her, but she ignored him.

It was an effort to walk slowly, to look natural, but Sandra made it to the door of what she hoped was Luke's room without being challenged. No one noticed as she entered and closed the door behind her. The wall on the left had a large window, revealing an adjacent room, but the bed within it was unoccupied. Another stroke of luck. She checked the whiteboard next to the bed and exhaled in relief. *Luke Bridestone*.

The sleeping man looked so peaceful, so innocent. Even the oxygen mask, the tubes, the colourful lines and cables did not diminish his youth. *Young compared to me*, she thought, *but you're in a coma. You might never wake up properly. I'm doing you a favour.* She thought of Henry, the sickly man outside, and what he'd said. *If they pointed to a room and said, there, go in there and we'll put you to sleep with no pain, just sleep, you know… I would go in a heartbeat.*

Well, this was the room.

She reached into her pouch and brought out the 50ml syringe she had ordered on Amazon. She was no great criminal mastermind, but her plan was solid and logical. She had purchased high-strength rat poison and mixed it with bleach. Once she injected it into the comatose man, she would inject him again for good measure, this time with air. A nurse once told her that air in the bloodstream can kill. Then she would leave. They wouldn't do a post-mortem on a man in a coma who simply let go and died. It was the natural way of things, entirely expected.

Must hurry, she reminded herself. *Can't be caught.* All business now, she traced the surface of Luke's wrist. There were needles stuck into it already. Good. They won't notice another prick to his skin. Now she needed to find a vein. She was good at finding veins. There had been plenty of tutoring at the University of Cancer.

She aimed the needle at her target and cursed. She had left her reading glasses in the bag outside. Could she risk going out to get them? No. The whole thing could fall apart. The policeman won't be gone for long. She considered injecting the fluid into the man's drip, but thought better of it. It would cloud the clear liquid, and anyway, it had to be a vein in the arm, the only sure way to get it done without raising suspicion. Luke had to meet his fate unobserved, so she could get her inheritance. *Almost there!*

With one hand, she identified the location for the injection, and with the other, she edged the needle towards it. Yes, that's it. The needle pricked his skin and went in.

And then Sandra had a premonition of the man awakening from the pain of the needle. It was as if she herself felt the needle piercing her own wrist. *Don't be silly. Push the plunger. Do it. People don't just wake from a coma.*

It only took a split second. To her utter horror, her premonition came true. The man opened his eyes. He was groggy, looking at her with incomprehension, taking in her patient's gown, the hand that held the syringe, her determined face. He tried to speak, but all that came from his mouth was a weak grunt.

I should have worn a nurse's outfit, she thought, *but it's not my fault. He wasn't supposed to wake up. Go on, do it!*

With his far hand, the man reached across, grabbed the syringe and threw it away, heaving from the effort. He gasped for air and then threw a punch directly at Sandra's face. She fell back, taking the drip stand down with her. There was an almighty clang.

The policeman rushed into the room and looked from Luke to Sandra.

Time for Plan B.

'I'm sorry,' she said, trying her best to sound confused. 'I must have gone into the wrong room. This man attacked me. I'm just an old lady. Why did he attack me?'

The policeman followed Luke's gaze to the syringe that lay on the floor, filled with the murky brown liquid.

CHAPTER FORTY-THREE

Sandra had never had a black eye before, had never been in handcuffs, had never sat in a police station interview room. It was going to be a day of firsts. They had let her change from her patient gown into the scratchy blue tracksuit, which was only marginally better.

'Good afternoon, madam. I'll be the detective handling your case. Could you tell me your name, please?'

'I... I don't remember. My memory. I... I get confused. Where am I?' She looked at the woman before her and feigned a sudden insight. 'Police? What am I doing with the police? Did I get lost?' She made a point of touching her bruised face. It must look awful. *Good.* 'Was I attacked? I... I have trouble remembering. Dementia, you see.' She made her hand shake, unsure if this was the right symptom for the occasion.

'Do you remember where you live?' the detective said.

She tried for anger. 'Of course, dear. I'm not stupid. I live... My address is... My mind, you see, it's been... For years now. It creeps up on you. What was I saying?'

The detective sighed. It was working. They had no idea who she was. The challenge would be to convince them to release her. But how would they let her walk out of the station if they thought she wasn't entirely there? They might just keep her here until they knew what to do. An idea occurred to her. She was three steps ahead of the fools.

'I do remember something, dear,' she said. 'I got up in the morning, and I had some breakfast, oats with milk and cinnamon. You see, the cinnamon adds a bit of a kick, and you don't need sugar. And then,' she tapped her finger on her forehead, 'and then I had an appointment. Yes, that's it. The hospital in Greenwich, Oncology. If you can take me there, they'll know what to do.'

The detective nodded to her colleague, a fresh-faced policeman who sat beside her. He got up and left the room. The plan was working. They'd take her to Greenwich Hospital, and then she'd disappear in the maze of corridors, find a back door and get a taxi. They'd never find her, never identify her.

'I apologise,' the detective said.

'No need to apologise, dear. One day, you might be like me, and someone will be kind to you, the same way you've been. We all need to take care of each other. Ach, the sense of community is all but lost. No one knows their neighbours any more. It's nice to see—'

'No,' the detective interrupted. 'I apologise for not telling you my name at the start of the interview. It's protocol. I'm Detective Chief Inspector Mary Czerniak.'

'Nice to meet you, detective.' Her throat tightened. *Mary Czerniak? Could it be?*

There was a knock on the door, and the young officer returned. Sandra looked up at the man who stood next to him. The man looked at the detective and nodded.

'I believe you've met my husband, Alex,' the police detective said. 'There's no record of you suffering from dementia. It's time to drop the act, Mrs Saint-John.'

'*Ms* Saint-John,' Sandra said angrily, shock cutting short

any pretence she might have hoped to sustain. Her world was disintegrating into swirls of regret and self-pity. She felt genuinely light-headed. In her thoughts, Dorothy was laughing at her, mocking her, telling her in that condescending tone, like she had done years before: *If you had made the effort to be just a little nicer, someone might have married you.*

Alex remained in the room. Despite herself, Sandra was now grateful for his presence. Perhaps not a friendly face, but a familiar one in this unusual, frightening setting.

'Here's what we have,' Mary Czerniak said, no longer putting on the airs of a caring young person addressing an elderly, confused woman. 'You were found in Luke Bridestone's hospital room, attempting to inject him with a substance. While you were waiting to be examined by the medic here at the station, we got a warrant to search your property. You know what we found in your kitchen?'

'How dare you search my house!'

Mary Czerniak ignored her outburst. 'In a pot on the stove, we found a brown substance, similar in colour to the one in the syringe you used. On the worktop was a bottle of bleach and a box of rat poison granules next to a pestle that was used to grind them. Do you deny it? The liquid in the pot and the syringe smelled of both of these substances. This will be confirmed, I am certain, by a chemical analysis, which has already been ordered.'

'Nonsense.'

'I put it to you that you tried to murder Mr Bridestone, the beneficiary of your sister's estate. Do you deny it?'

'I deny it. I would like a lawyer now. Aren't I entitled to a lawyer?'

'You are, and we can call the duty solicitor or anyone you appoint, but just so you know exactly where we stand, I also have recorded evidence that you said to my husband, Alex Czerniak, and I quote,' she looked at her folder, '*Every death is tragic and all that. Still, there's one member remaining, that Luke Bridestone, and he might just pull through. If he does, he gets to have it: a house worth millions from people he didn't even know. Just a random stranger taking away my inheritance, and that, Mr Czerniak, will be an absolute travesty. Something needs to be done.* Then you added, *If he survives*. Listening to the recording, there was more than a suggestion in that statement. Of course, on its own, it won't implicate you, but added to your actual attempt on the victim's life, I'd say it provides additional colour for the jury to consider, and the callousness may well affect the length of your sentence.'

Sandra hissed at Alex. 'You recorded me?'

Detective Czerniak placed the folder on the table. 'Do you have anything to say, *Ms* Saint-John?' She emphasised the word *Ms* like it was a stick to beat her with.

'No comment,' Sandra said.

Mary Czerniak shrugged, clasped her hands and leaned forward. 'Sandra Saint-John, I am arresting you on suspicion of the attempted murder of Luke Bridestone and for procuring or conspiring with your nephew Joel Saint-John and others unknown to murder the following persons: Dorothy Saint-John, Michael Bind, Slevin Grimlow–'

'Wait! What are you talking about?'

The police detective ignored her protest. 'Naomi Abraham and Stella Crane. We're going to leave out Faye Hindmarsh. There's compelling evidence she was killed by someone else.'

'How on earth did you… What? I did none of these things. These people, these names, I…'

'You do not have to say anything…' She completed the familiar refrain that Sandra had heard so many times on daytime television.

'You're an excellent actor,' the police detective said. 'I'll give you that, but all the evidence leads to you. We may not find the person you hired or your communications with your nephew, but you did also say to my husband,' she again looked down at her folder, *'You would have thought the problem is nearly solved, what with most of them dead. The only slight snag is… they didn't all go then and there.* This, combined with the fact that you wanted my husband to procure a hitman, not really contradicted by your weak denial at the time… I guess, when it came to Luke Bridestone, you had to do the dirty work yourself, or maybe your funds dried up, so you couldn't afford a proper hitman.'

'Hitmen don't charge that much,' Sandra said and then immediately added, 'is my guess. I'm not some mafia boss.'

'Can you explain the deadly knives you sent to your nephew as a present? At least he was clever enough to destroy any note that came with them, but I think we both know that's how you started the plot. You worked with him, and he may have recruited others. The flaw in your plan was Luke Bridestone's survival.'

'Has he said anything?' Sandra said. 'Is that what he told you? That Joel did it?'

For the first time, the police detective looked unsure.

'Detective?'

'He doesn't remember anything. Not yet, anyway. His memory might return.'

Sandra looked at Detective Czerniak's smooth complexion. *Expensive facials,* she thought, *bought with the money I used to have. Instead of hiring her husband, I should have procured someone to see to Luke Bridestone. That would have been a much better plan. Must remember that for next time. Next time?*

'Our investigation might be missing some details, but your attempted murder charge for Luke Bridestone is solid, bang to rights.'

Sandra covered her eyes and took a deep breath. Her face hurt from Luke's punch. They were waiting for her to say something. Eventually, she forced her hands to the table and looked at Alex.

'What should I do?' she said to him, sounding softer and more vulnerable than she intended.

'I'm not a lawyer,' he said, 'but if I were you, I'd admit it, tell them everything. As Mary says, they already have enough evidence for your attempt on Luke.' He turned to his wife. 'Attempted murder, that's what?'

'If done for financial gain,' Mary said to Sandra, 'the starting point in a case like yours would be twenty-five years in prison.'

'Considering your... health situation,' Alex said, 'you won't get out in time to enjoy life, even if you were only convicted for the attempt on Luke. Might as well die with a clear conscience and give the victims' families the answers they deserve. You'll be doing the right thing by them. You'll be giving them something no one else can.'

'Give me your hand, Alex,' Sandra said.

He hesitated.

'Come on, Alex. We're in a police station. Even a prolific serial killer like me won't murder you here.'

Alex stepped forward and reluctantly offered her his hand. She took it between her palms, held it for a long moment, felt its warmth, and thought of her interaction with Henry, the old man at the hospital. Human touch. The simple act of holding hands. She wished she'd had more of it in her life. And love. And friendships. So much more. Could she have done things differently? Her life was full of bitterness and anger, but she felt certain these were hard-wired into her personality. Even if she'd tried, she didn't think she could have behaved differently. She endured the miserable lot she was born with, a sad and lonely life. She stared down at her knuckles, spotted and wrinkled, and thought of her predicament. Death would claim her earlier than any chance of freedom. Of that, there was no doubt. The length of her sentence was immaterial. Then she thought of Alex's words about the victims' families: *You'll be doing the right thing by them. You'll be giving them something no one else can.*

'I did it,' she said with great conviction, relief washing over her. 'I confess. Joel and I killed them all. They had it coming, with their stupid commune and stupid lives, thinking they were better than everyone else. I did it because of the money. There, I confess.'

But Detective Czerniak wasn't finished. 'Can I ask about your nephew? Why would he kill himself?'

Tears welled up in Sandra's eyes. It was a strange, unfamiliar sensation, crying. Was it for Joel? For herself? For the child she'd given up for adoption and never allowed herself to grieve? Perhaps the crushing knowledge of her ruined life had freed her a little. *Oh bollocks!* She took the tissue handed to her by the detective. 'I don't know why Joel did it,' she said, truthfully. 'That was not part of… our plan.'

'Thank you for your admission,' the police detective said. 'We'll need to take all the details from you.'

'No,' Sandra said. 'You've got your confession. Now leave me be. I'm dying, detective. Cancer is a fickle thing. In my last oncology appointment, I was told the cancer's back with a vengeance. I have a year left, if I'm lucky.'

Mary looked at her husband and, thankfully, he nodded confirmation. Still, he had betrayed her identity, *the Judas*. Despite this, Sandra could not dislike him. She had spent more time with him over their meetings than she had with anyone else in the last few decades, even more than her casual visiting carers, who were replaced as frequently as underwear, also her fault. Beneath his focus on money, Alex had a certain warmth and generosity of spirit. She liked him, she decided, and now she even got to meet his wife. He was the only good memory she'd take with her to prison, and then to her death. It was gratifying that she could do him this one last service, her first and final noble act. *He said it would help the families. Well, fuck it. Sure. I'll do it.*

'I will sign a statement confirming everything I've just said, but beyond that, no comment, and that's final. Don't waste my time, or yours. Do they have Netflix in prison?'

EPILOGUE

NINE MONTHS LATER

Lilian arrived for her date at the bistro in Canary Wharf twenty minutes late. She hadn't planned to be late, but her feet slowed her pace, the weight of reluctance making each step smaller than the one before. Since getting to London, she had forced herself to go on dates, flicking through endless profiles on dating apps, having mundane, predictable messaging chats with men who had soft hands and hardened hearts and a penchant for playing the kind of games she had no patience for. Without exception, they bored her senseless. Not one came close to lighting anything like the fire that had raged in her for Adrian, a fire that had once consumed her every waking moment and her every longing dream. She thought he was a known quantity, someone she could capture in her silk-thin web. A brief word here, a minor threat there, an imperceptible series of steps that would sow in him the seeds of devotion that were destined to grow into loving shackles. It took time and love, using her mask of sweet vulnerability, a tool she trusted to work wonders. Maybe she trusted it too much, at least in Adrian's case. She kept telling him she didn't expect him to leave his wife. Well, that was a lie.

Her intentions were not evil or cruel. There were certain men who wished for that kind of devotion, their miseries fuelled by the happy moments that followed. She could identify them on sight. Something about their expressions, their ever-so-slightly slouched gait, the way they spoke, even if they looked tough on the outside. Most of all, if she found them instantly attractive, it was as good a diagnosis as ever there could be. They were like magnets, pulling her to them, their internal chaos clear to her, crying out for order, craving the soothing control she could offer. Her adoptive mother was like that, marshalling her husband as if he were a pet.

One of Lilian's defining childhood memories was a family trip to Lake Superior. On the way, along the endless Route 53, her parents argued, or rather her mother pontificated, and her father tried a hundred forms of acquiescence. Then, as they approached Duluth, for once he dared to talk back. At the parking lot of a cement mixing company, she told him to get out of the car and just left him there, driving away with her daughter in the back seat. The two of them went for lunch in some burger joint with her mother's phone switched off. When they came back for him, two hours later, he was sitting on the sidewalk, his head held in his hands. Instead of complaining, he apologised. For the rest of the trip, he cowered like a trampled puppy. When they checked in at the local Motel 6, he offered to sleep on the floor.

During her school years in Falcon Heights and later in Winona, Lilian was a shy, timid girl with a target on her back, the subject of pranks and ridicule, stolen lunch boxes, tears and hidden anxieties. By the time of her graduation, she had learned to stand up for herself, applying the lessons she'd learned from her adoptive mother, though she considered herself more subtle and self-aware. Lilian could be just as effective without all the drama.

After leaving the commune, Lilian had come to understand

her complicated inheritance. Her mother had taught her manipulation and how to handle those around her, especially men. And then there was Joel, her birth father, who had abandoned her to die in a cave: *oh, okay, this happened*. Her meted revenge, driving a knife through his heart, did nothing to quell the dark orb that continued to pulse with cold, seething anger inside her.

Be more like Dorothy, she sometimes told herself, *more like your grandmother, who showed you so much warmth*. She didn't believe for a minute what Joel had said about his mother's part in her adoption. Dorothy would never have given her away. Dorothy was a model, an example to follow. But Joel's legacy was undeniable. She wondered if she had inherited some of her anger from Joel's killer dad, a darkness passed through the generations. At first, this frightened her, but fear was replaced with acceptance. There were no consequences to her actions at Synner's Crag. She got away with murder, and no one had tried to find her. They didn't even know she'd been at the commune, and Adrian's stray shot at Michael had guaranteed his silence.

Which part of my inheritance is on shift with me today? Dorothy or Joel? she would think during her nursing shifts, every time she considered injecting a difficult patient with something that would make them shut up already. Sometimes she held back. Other times she didn't.

It was painful, but in the end, Adrian chose his wife. Lilian briefly considered the possibility of the wretched woman having an unfortunate accident. After all, the farm with its tractors and power tools was a dangerous place. Yet, the woman had done nothing to deserve such a death. She had never hurt Lilian, not like Joel or Stella and Slevin. They deserved what happened to them. The farmer's wife was a victim herself, and hurting her would also crush Adrian, the man Lilian loved more than anyone she'd met before. She could not inflict this fate on either of them. Knowing this was comforting. *Be more like Dorothy.*

When Adrian drove her to the station, she smiled kindly, thanked him, and kissed him on the lips, a sweet final kiss. She hid her tears from him, reserving them for the long train journey to London.

Lilian entered the bistro and immediately recognised the man she'd been exchanging messages with for the last fortnight. Before him was a still-full glass of white wine, sweating in the heat. In real life, his shoulders appeared wider, his floppy hair conditioned like a model's, his beard neat and trimmed. He was older than her, just the way she liked it. For a moment, she thought she had seen him before somewhere, but then she dismissed this notion as the usual result of seeing his pictures so many times on the app, and bearded men were ten-a-penny in London.

He saw her and grinned, instantly warming her heart. And she could tell, there and then, without hesitation, that he was one of those men, the men she sought out. A thin veneer of confidence, under which there was a yearning need, a thirst.

She made to shake his hand, at the same time as he went for a friendly kiss on her cheek. They laughed at the awkward exchange.

'I'm Luke,' he said.

She wondered if it was his real name. She never used hers. Not on a first date.

'Lily,' she said and giggled. 'Well, we both knew each other's names, didn't we? Does Luke have a nickname? I always wonder about nicknames.'

Don't be awkward, she told herself. *Make normal conversation.* His smile made her stomach flutter. *Maybe this one, please!*

'Someone used to call me Lukas,' he said.

'Who called you that?' she said, unsure if her cutesy grin gave the right impression.

'A person, erm...' He hesitated. 'A friend.'

An efficient waiter arrived, left them food menus and took her order of a Prosecco. Nondescript jazz played from hidden speakers, mashed in with the sounds of diners working cutlery over crockery and glasses being laid to dry over the bar.

When Lilian's drink arrived, they clinked glasses. Conversation flowed naturally between them. They shared a love for old black-and-white movies from a gentler era. They both hated horror films. His favourite colour was blue. His favourite food was Chinese, especially beef with oyster sauce on noodles. Lilian also liked blue and was a fan of tacos and salsa, but also Chinese.

'Who doesn't like a good Chinese?' she said with delight. 'So, looks like we covered the standard stuff. Still, tell me, what do you do for work?'

For the first time, he seemed uncomfortable. He took a slow sip of his wine. 'I came into some money recently, so I'm taking a break, you know, to think what to do next. Before that... I've had a bit of a rough time. I don't like to talk about the past.'

Her intuition was right. *And look at him, those beautiful, tormented eyes. And he has money. He's perfect.* She'd have to play this just right.

She angled her head ever so slightly and gave him her most compassionate frown, then she reached for his hand on the table and covered it with hers.

'Someone hurt you?' she said. 'A woman?'

'Something like that.'

'Then she wasn't worth it.'

He pulled his hand back, almost in fright, and she retracted hers slowly, using it to straighten her hair as if nothing had happened. She gave him her sweetest smile.

'She's gone,' he said. 'Never coming back. It took some effort, and there were times I thought I'd never be free of her, but then I found out...' He shook his head. 'Never mind. I don't like to talk about it. Suffice to say, never again.'

My darling Luke, it's so happening again. The emotional bruises she recognised in him were perfectly formed. She could pick his lock in an instant, then lock it from the inside. *Happily ever after. Children, maybe? They'd be beautiful children.*

Luke gulped down the rest of his wine, caught the waiter's eye and pointed at his glass to signal he wanted another. Lilian had barely started on her own drink.

'You haven't told me what *you* do,' he said.

He looked so serious. She needed to lighten the tone.

'Guess,' she said. 'Here's a clue: I stab people. Sometimes I watch them die.'

'Serial killer?'

She giggled like a schoolgirl and hid her mouth with her fist. 'Not for my day job. I'm a nurse in an acute ward. I stab them with syringes. I'm a lifesaver. Not all the time, though. Can't be helped.'

'And you've been dating long?' he said.

She looked down at her drink, hoping to send the right message. 'I was with someone. It didn't work out. After we, you know, ended, I thought I'd go back to the States, but I like it here. My parents were originally from London. I know I don't sound it, but deep down, I'm actually British. There's something about this city that feels like home, like I've gone back to my roots and these are my people.'

The waiter returned and, with a flourish, replaced Luke's empty glass with a full one. Then he was gone.

'Relationships are hard,' Luke said. 'Especially intense ones, when you lose yourself to someone else.'

'But doesn't that fire, that burning fire when you find it, doesn't it make it all worthwhile? And trust. Trust is really important.'

He seemed lost in thought, his eyes staring at an invisible

spot in the distance. He raised his glass to his mouth, nearly missing his lips, then corrected the drink's trajectory and drank almost half of the wine in one go.

Lilian thought, with satisfaction, that she noticed a slight tremor in his shoulders.

He placed the glass gently on the table, held onto its stem for a moment, released it and placed his hand flat on the table, showing her a kind, borrowed smile. His mask was firmly back on, but she had seen beneath it.

She grinned back at him and gave him a nod as if to say, *the bad is always followed by the good. You're doing so well.*

'Shall we order some food?' she said. 'I'm starving. I fancy a nice bloody steak and some chips.'

'You're lovely, Lily. It's so nice to meet you.' He cleared his throat. 'My past, it's been... I mean... I have to be honest. I promised myself I'd be honest. You remind me of someone.'

'That doesn't have to be a bad thing,' she said. 'Please, stay for dinner.'

He raised his hand to placate her. 'You're nothing like her. You're great, really.' He stood and picked up his bomber jacket, which was folded neatly on the spare chair next to their table. 'I'm really sorry, but I have to go.'

He dropped some money on the table and walked out without looking back.

She took a tiny sip of her drink and wondered if she should go after him. No. It was no use. The perfect man was spoiled for her by the woman who got there first. And then the niggling thought returned and was quickly dismissed. *Haven't I seen him somewhere before?*

By the time she boarded the DLR train to Bank station, Luke, if that was even his real name, had blocked her on all the dating apps.

WHERE ARE THEY NOW?

Luke Bridestone used the funds he received from Dorothy's estate to pursue degrees in psychology and criminology. His PhD thesis investigated criminal and pseudo-criminal behaviour in people suffering from personality disorders. At the time of writing, he is a consultant at Broadmoor Psychiatric Hospital. He lives in Berkshire with his wife Anna and their two daughters, Naomi and Faye.

Sandra Saint-John pleaded guilty to a charge of attempted murder against Luke Bridestone. The other conspiracy charges in relation to the murders at Synner's Crag were dropped due to a lack of evidence. Before sentencing could be handed down for her attempt on Luke, Sandra died in her sleep while in detention. She was cremated at Honor Oak Crematorium.

Lilian Gracey was charged with cruelty and abuse against patients in her care as a nurse. She was found not guilty of all charges and later married her defending barrister, a successful KC who went on to become a Member of Parliament for the Conservative Party. Her husband currently holds the lowest attendance record of any MP in the House of Commons. His party's members often joke that his wife doesn't allow him out.

James Clipper, the pathologist who performed the autopsies on the Synner's Crag victims and who had made the crucial mistake of concluding Michael Bind's injury was caused by a gunshot, was dismissed from his job, triggering multiple case reviews. For reasons of efficiency and lack of staffing, the Synner's Crag case was never reopened. In the eyes of the police, the culprit had already been caught, even if they could not get the charges against her to stick.

Mary Czerniak received the King's Police Medal and was awarded an OBE by His Majesty, in great part due to her leadership in solving the Synner's Crag murders case, one of the most notorious crimes in the country's history. She is seen as a safe pair of hands for high-profile cases.

AUTHOR'S NOTE

Since she was a young girl, my grandmother Judith wrote in her diary almost every day. We never knew about this habit until, after her death at the age of ninety, we cleared her house. In her spare room, we found boxes upon boxes filled with many decades' worth of diary notebooks, scrawled in a girl's handwriting at first, then changing as she grew up, got married, had her four children, became a widow and then settled into old age.

Her final diary entry was made on the day she died. She wasn't feeling well, but had never been to a hospital and wasn't keen to go. Eventually, she relented. The last words she'd ever written, before being driven away, were the ones I used in Chapter Three. In that chapter, Dorothy berates herself for worrying about excruciating pains that would eventually turn out to be a fatal heart attack. She then reassures herself with my grandmother's words, 'There's no need to panic. I still have time.'

My grandmother devoured thrillers. I'm certain she'd have been delighted for her final written words to be quoted in my book.

Danny Dagan, November 2025

☞ Please leave a review to support this author.

ABOUT THE AUTHOR

Danny Dagan is a law school graduate and web expert who always preferred writing fiction. After a corporate career in London, he moved to Northumberland, where he finally found his perfect writing spot: a garden shed with views of the sea and a castle.

Danny's Debut, *The Game*, was published by Bloodhound Books in 2025, with the audiobook rights sold to Dreamscape Media. He then set up his own imprint, Guffy Pen Press, publishing *The Commune* in 2026.

Danny's books have been sold worldwide, but he is most grateful to the local shops on Holy Island, especially the Post Office and the Lindisfarne Heritage Centre, for selling hundreds of copies to locals and visitors.

ALSO BY DANNY DAGAN

THE GAME

When the adult children of five billionaires are abducted by a shadowy group, their parents face an unthinkable ultimatum: pay the highest price or lose their loved ones forever.

The name *Guffy Pen Press* originated from a local superstition on the Holy Island of Lindisfarne.

There's an old island tale of a fisherman and his crew who perished after encountering a hog before setting out to sea (in another version, the animal was taken aboard their fishing boat). Since then, *the three-letter word for a swine that starts with the letter 'p'* is never uttered or even written on the island. To speak it is considered a most egregious sin. Instead, locals use the word *guffy*. You'll see it on menus in local eateries, and there's even an excellent local dark rum, *The Guffy Curse*, produced and aged on the island by *793 Spirits*.

A guffy's pen can therefore mean the animal's pen or, in this case, an instrument used for writing. Hence: *Guffy Pen Press* with the guffy's snout as its symbol.

THE COMMUNE

Printed in Dunstable, United Kingdom